PRA
The Girls at th

"Valentine's dreamlike narrativ... ... .v..i...s Grimm tale alive with intrigue and gritty descriptions of the Roaring Twenties."

—*The Washington Post*

"Even more than the characters, their voices, or the sharp, quiet slicing of the understated prose, what I loved about this book was its own tense dance with its source materials. . . . There is so much more I want to say: about the ways in which women protect and support each other; about the way they feel like antidotes to *The Great Gatsby*'s brittle ciphers; about the pitch-perfect dialogue; about the dancing."

—NPR

"Dressed up in the thrill and sparkle of the Roaring Twenties, the classic fairy tale of *The Twelve Dancing Princesses* has never been more engrossing or delightful."

—*Library Journal* (starred review)

"Will make you want to strap on dancing shoes and find an all-night speakeasy to call your own."

—*Pittsburgh Post-Gazette*

"So evocative, well drawn, well cast, and well played that readers will be enthralled. This is a story of sisterhood, a passion for freedom and love that will resonate with many women."

—*RT Book Reviews*

"Valentine's novel has glamour in spades, evocative of the Jazz Age's fashions and dance crazes and the dark side of prohibition."

—*Historical Novels Review*

"A cinematic sweep . . . [and] lush period detail."

—*Publishers Weekly*

"Intoxicating. . . . Stands apart thanks to dynamic characters and a resoundingly well-rendered setting."

—Tor.com

"This unexpected fairy tale, deftly shifted into the age of prohibition, becomes a gorgeous and bewitching novel."

—Scott Westerfeld, #1 *New York Times* bestselling author of *Uglies*

"Delightful and suspenseful by turns, this story of tyranny, pluck, fierce love, and even fiercer responsibility is set in a New York of spangles and speakeasies, fox-trots and Charlestons. Valentine retains the shimmer and shadows of the fairy tale that underlies her novel, even as she transforms it."

—Christina Schwarz, #1 *New York Times* bestselling author of *Drowning Ruth*

"Genevieve Valentine has turned out an extraordinary and marvelous new thing from very old clothes. *The Girls at the Kingfisher Club* is a sumptuous rendering of one of my favorite fairy tales."

—Kelly Link, author of *Pretty Monsters*

"As fast-tempoed and intoxicating as a night at a Jazz Age speakeasy, and as enchanting as a good old-fashioned fairy tale. Genevieve Valentine gives us a dozen dazzling sisters it's impossible not to root for."

—Lois Leveen,
author of *Juliet's Nurse*

"I couldn't turn the pages fast enough and stayed up late to reach the end. Genevieve Valentine resurrects 1920s New York to bring an inventive tale of shifting social mores, family bonds, and heart-wrenching choices."

—Ronlyn Domingue,
author of *The Mercy of Thin Air*

ALSO BY GENEVIEVE VALENTINE

Persona
Mechanique: A Tale of the Circus Tresaulti

The Girls at the KINGFISHER CLUB

a novel

GENEVIEVE VALENTINE

WASHINGTON SQUARE PRESS

New York   London   Toronto   Sydney   New Delhi

WASHINGTON SQUARE PRESS
An Imprint of Simon & Schuster, Inc.
1230 Avenue of the Americas
New York, NY 10020

First Washington Square Press trade paperback edition June 2015

WASHINGTON SQUARE PRESS and colophon are registered trademarks of
Simon & Schuster, Inc.

For information about special discounts for bulk purchases,
please contact Simon & Schuster Special Sales at 1-866-506-1949
or business@simonandschuster.com.

The Simon & Schuster Speakers Bureau can bring authors
to your live event. For more information, or to book an event,
contact the Simon & Schuster Speakers Bureau at 1-866-248-3049
or visit our website at www.simonspeakers.com.

Interior design by Esther Paradelo

Manufactured in the United States of America

10 9 8 7 6 5 4 3 2

The Library of Congress has cataloged the hardcover edition as follows:

Valentine, Genevieve.
   The Girls at the Kingfisher Club : a novel / by Genevieve Valentine. — First
Atria Books hardcover edition.
     pages   cm
  1. Nineteen twenties—Fiction. 2. Young women—New York (State) —New
York—Fiction. I. Title.
  PS3622.A436G57   2014
  813'.6—dc23   2013023870

ISBN 978-1-4767-3908-3
ISBN 978-1-4767-3909-0 (pbk)
ISBN 978-1-4767-3910-6 (ebook)

For my sister, and the friends who have become sisters

one

NO SIR, THAT'S NOT MY GAL

By 1927 there were twelve girls who danced all night and never gave names, but by then the men had given up asking and called them all Princess.

"Hey, Princess, dust off your shoes? It's the Charleston!"

The men would have called them anything they wanted to be called, Dollface or Queenie or Beloved, just to get one girl on the dance floor for a song. But in that flurry of short dresses and spangles and ribbon-tied shoes, Princess was the name that suited; it seemed magical enough, like maybe it was true.

Wild things, these girls; wild for dancing. They could go all night without sitting, grabbing at champagne between songs, running to the throng at the table and saying something that made them all laugh, light and low together like the parts of a chorus.

It wasn't right, all those women sticking together so close. Something about the wall of bob-haired girls scared the men, though they hardly knew it. They just knew they'd better dance their best with a Princess, and no mistake.

No need to worry, though, as long as a man could dance. The nights were long and drink was cheap, and sometimes the Princesses' smiles were red-lipped and happy and not sharp white flashing teeth, and there were so many that if one of them turned down a dance, it was easy to wait and try again with another one.

"Princess, pass me a waltz?"

Some men never noticed their full numbers. (It was hardly fair to even ask a man to count; there were two pairs of twins—or three, hard to say—and it was easy to get confused.) They moved in little packs, two and three at a time, and it was tough to keep track. Some men thought there were only ten, or nine. The younger ones, boys just out from under their mothers' noses, saw only the one they loved in the crowd.

The older men understood how that mistake could happen— one had golden hair, one had bright green eyes, one had a swan's neck; together they were intoxicating—but there was no point. The girls were wild for dancing, and nothing else. No hearts beat underneath those thin, bright dresses. They laughed like glass.

The coldest one looked like someone had dragged a statue out for the night, as if she would scratch out your eyes if you so much as looked at her sideways.

No man was fool enough to ask her to dance. No reason to die young when there were eleven others.

There were willing sisters who smelled like 4711, or Shalimar, or smoke; always some sweet ones who closed their eyes and revealed dark pencil along their lashes, who laughed when a part- ner swung them around, who grinned and touched a man's shoe with her own when they tapped back and forth.

No need to worry about battleaxes when a man had a girl who could light up the floor. No need to worry about loving one when all of them would be back tomorrow night. No need for names at all, so long as when a fellow called her "Princess," she said, "Yes."

Turned out it was just as well, not knowing, once the newspa- permen came asking.

two
THAT'S MY WEAKNESS NOW

When Jo's father summoned her to his office, it was the first time she'd heard from him in almost a year.

She was in the upstairs library. It had been the schoolroom, but after the last governess was dismissed and lessons fell slowly by the wayside, only the bookish girls crossed the threshold for pleasure: Doris, Rebecca, Araminta, and Jo.

("What is there to even look at?" asked Lou, who read plumbing manuals and fashion papers and little else.

Jo said, "The atlas.")

"Miss Hamilton," a maid said from the doorway to the library. "Your father's asking for you."

Walters always sent a maid up to the girls' floors rather than go himself; Jo guessed he kept to the old ways of doing these things. This one was a stranger—there were always new maids, it seemed—and couldn't have been older than Sophie.

A little behind her, Araminta's and Rebecca's worried faces appeared in the hall.

Jo stood and smoothed her skirt.

As Jo passed, Rebecca whispered, "Good luck, General."

Walters was waiting for her on the second-floor landing, and he led the way, as though Jo might not know where the study was.

She might not have. Their father moved his study, sometimes, as rooms took his fancy. He summoned Jo every so often, and she'd sometimes find him in a refurbished parlor or the library downstairs, if he had grown tired of his proper study. The rooms lined the right-hand side of the house, and the girls who lived above those rooms walked on glass even more than the rest. For a year, when Rose and Lily were first learning to dance, Jo had found that his makeshift office was on the second floor just under their room, and they'd had to practice in Jo and Lou's room to be sure he wouldn't hear.

Their room was over the high ceilings of the ballroom, which would only have been used for parties; they were always safe.

As they approached the office (his proper office—he must be content with himself these days, to go back to old habits), Walters vanished with a doleful warning look, and Jo was alone.

She wasn't as frightened as Walters seemed to think she should be. The first time she'd been alone with her father, years ago, she'd realized what he thought of her. After that, the worst was over.

It had been easy enough, after that, for Jo to come downstairs and listen to her father talk about how he was dismissing the governess, how the girls shouldn't look out the windows so much, as people might ask questions.

She'd come down half a dozen times, carrying an armful of worn-out shoes, to argue for a larger catalog allowance.

Jo knew that her job, after he had spoken, was to be efficient, obedient, and grateful.

(She had tried once, when she was fourteen, to argue with him over something. Her face had stung for three hours.)

It was just as well that her father wanted to see her as rarely as she wanted to be seen.

Mr. van de Maar, her father's business associate, was on his way out; he carried the briefcase that always made him look as though he was smuggling cash out the front door. Jo wouldn't have been entirely surprised.

When he saw her, his face went a little pinched at the edges, like he was in an advertisement for starched collars.

That her father allowed him to know about Josephine worried her; it always looked as though it worried him, too.

He nodded without really looking at her and made his exit.

Walters cut ahead of her to open the door for him, and Josephine watched the busy street slice into sight and vanish again, a flash of full loud daylight.

When she paused on the threshold of the office, he was sitting as she always thought of him—behind his desk, upright, glancing disdainfully at a newspaper.

He was a handsome man; even before she'd really seen other men in the world, she'd known he was handsome. (He must have been handsome, for people to excuse her mother marrying him.) When he was lost in concentration he had the air of a head of state, and she dared not interrupt him even to knock. She folded her hands, waited.

At last he looked up.

"Ah," he said, "Josephine. Come in."

He had a way of saying her name, a tiny pause between the second and third syllables, as if she needed the reminder that she'd been expected to be a boy.

She stopped well on the far side of his desk. "You called for me, sir."

"Yes." He leaned back in his chair and picked up the newspaper. "Something this morning came to my attention. 'The lawless, repellent gin fever that sweeps our once-fair city has affected not only the low and easily tempted, but the high and well-meaning. The daylight banker spends his nights intoxicated, and the daughters of our storied families are lured in numbers, by immodest music and the demon drink, like princesses into that dark underground which leaves no innocent unsullied.' "

Jo's heart thudded once against her ribs. She tried to keep her face blank, her breathing even.

He folded the newspaper over his hands and looked at her. "What do you think of this, Josephine?"

"Too many adjectives."

He raised an eyebrow. "I meant, what do you think of this group of girls going out dancing at night?"

She waited just long enough before she said, "It sounds like a lot of trouble, sir."

"Do you think," he asked carefully, as if he'd only just now thought of it, "any of your sisters would know something about this?"

"None of them would go out without my knowing, sir."

He set the newspaper on the table and sighed. "Sit down, Josephine."

The desk between them seemed fifty feet wide. That suited her fine. She crossed her legs like Miss May, their first governess, had taught her, laced her hands in her lap.

"I've been thinking, lately, about how you and your sisters are growing up."

Jo thought it best not to reply.

"You can't spend the rest of your days in this house. It's not the right life for sweet girls. I've done my best to keep you away from the worst of the world, as your mother would have wanted, but I see now it can't go on like this."

The pause pressed against Jo's ears. She wondered if the day had come when she and her sisters could walk out.

The first thing she'd do would be to take them to the Metropolitan Museum, and then walk through the park to the opera, and they'd go out to eat at a restaurant that didn't have a basement door in the alley with a man waiting for a secret knock if you wanted to get in on the dancing.

"And so I believe it's time you all married," their father said.

Jo froze.

Married. Said like it was a prize for them, like it was a choice.

She thought about her mother, what situation she must have been in that marrying their father would have been the way out. It wasn't a compelling case.

He frowned. "Josephine?"

"I see," she managed.

She had, in the years they'd spent in the upper rooms, imagined what would become of them on the day that, one way or another, their father couldn't hold them any more. It had never stuck; she could get through one day, or two, with all of them in tow, but with twelve of them to care for and no money, no plan had any staying power.

But in all the dreadful things she'd worried over, she'd never imagined this.

(That their father was willing to let them go had never occurred to her at all.)

And now, marriage.

They'd be passed from one house to another, without ever seeing the city in daylight, moved into place like any other heirloom.

The girls could hope that these husbands, wherever her father planned to find them, would be kinder and more liberal men than he was. But the sort of man who wanted a girl who'd never been out in the world was the sort whose wife would stay at home in bed and try to produce heirs until she died from it.

Jo knew that much.

"I thought about having some parties here, but it might worry your sisters to meet strangers. And of course I wouldn't want to introduce you all suddenly into society—I imagine it would be overwhelming."

Jo said nothing.

"I thought perhaps I could inquire if there are families with suitable sons, and have a few of them come calling. It's quieter that way—more civilized."

He meant that this way, no one would bear witness to the twelve failed heirs of Joseph Hamilton.

She wondered if he planned to marry them off a few at a time, so society might never know how many of them there were—a dozen young men whose wives were unconnected, invisible except for a wedding portrait on the mantel and a ladies' maid upstairs.

"What would make a man suitable?" she asked, as calmly as she could.

He glanced up at her. "That's my concern."

She felt as if the floor was buckling under her. She made fists in her lap.

(If she struck him, they'd all suffer.)

"Naturally," he said, "I'd like to speak to the girls myself on the matter, as it becomes necessary, and I'll be asking you for insight about them. You're the eldest, and know them best, so if they're too shy to tell me something, you'd know."

He half-smiled, tapped the paper with his fingertips. "I wish my daughters to be happy."

"Of course," said Jo.

The third floor was silent as Jo climbed the stairs.

The three girls' rooms on this floor had their doors closed just as Jo had taught them, but no one was behind them, and the library was empty.

The fourth floor was a different hush—the quiet of a waiting crowd.

As she reached the landing, Jo saw Mattie's dark head disappear from the doorway to Jo and Lou's room.

Everyone was inside, then, and waiting.

Mattie hissed, "She's coming!" and before Mattie had finished Ella was already asking, "What's happened?" like Jo might have another red palm print on her face.

Her bedroom looked like a holding cell. Nine of them were crammed on the beds, a patchwork of blond and brown. Mattie was standing lookout, and Lou was silhouetted in the window, her red hair catching the light, her empty cigarette holder clamped in her teeth.

Against the far wall, twelve pairs of worn-out dance shoes stood in a wobbly line, sleeping and waiting for night.

"What's happened?" Ella asked, looking straight at Jo.

Jo took a breath. "There's a line in the paper about groups of girls going out dancing at night."

Rose and Lily clasped hands.

Rebecca pushed her hair back. "Is it us, for sure?"

"No. But Father's worried enough about the rumor."

"Does he suspect us?" asked Doris.

Jo wished there had been more stairs between the office and this room, so she could have planned a better speech. "He might."

Violet leaned forward. She was young and still worried sometimes about their father, the way one worries about angering the bartender. "What's he going to do?"

"Father wants us to marry," Jo said.

There was silence for a moment. Lou let out a whistling breath through her cigarette holder.

"He wants to meet with each of you," Jo said, "to get to know you, so he can speak to his acquaintances and see which young man he likes best to suit each of you. There will be some dinner parties, to get to know the boys he's chosen."

None of the girls laughed—not even Araminta, who had a habit of being romantic and absurd. They had all been sneaking out into the world long enough to know what sort of man wanted a captive bride, a girl that a father was handing out select. Men their father was choosing from among that sort, for reasons of his own.

"Oh God," Ella said finally, "what will we do?"

Jo had been calculating since the moment her father had spoken the word "married"; all the way across the foyer, up the sets of winding stairs, she had been thinking what was to be done.

Unfortunately, the house wasn't tall enough, and the cigar box with her savings in it wasn't full enough, and the world wasn't welcoming enough.

She had eleven sisters looking to her, and no good news to tell them.

Maybe one or two of the men their father picked would be better men than their father. It was all she could hope at the moment. She could hope that Rose and Lily, who were only sixteen, and Violet, only fourteen, would be allowed to wait a few years. Maybe Ella could stay and look after them, if they were careful about asking permission.

As for the rest, what could be done?

"I'll think of something," Jo said.

All of them looked relieved except Lou, who was gnawing on her cigarette holder.

"Let's go out," Ella said.

"Too soon," said Doris. "They put out that article. They'll be looking for us."

"Let them," said Hattie.

"We'll give them an earful," finished Mattie.

Rebecca frowned. "And if we end up in jail?"

"Better that than married off," said Lou.

Rose and Lily turned identical faces to Jo. "General?"

Jo looked at them all, piled like birds on the beds: eleven girls in New York's most refined prison.

She said, "Cabs leave at midnight."

three
CHARLESTON BABY OF MINE

The Hamiltons were a family who passed "wealthy" and fell short of "storied," in that twilight between the *Social Register,* in which they did not appear, and business interests that made them valuable.

If their son could have married into society, they might have been something; Mr. Hamilton's marriage had been too obvious to vault him over the line, but it had edged him closer, and were one son, one canny marriage, one step from being officially known.

Joseph Hamilton's business affairs were handled by a solicitor, their mail by an outside clerk, and their domestic affairs by a valet. These moneyed gestures caused no jealousy in the upper circles; since Joseph Hamilton didn't come among them to flaunt his discretion, they forgave him his wealth.

"Poor soul," they said. "Hamilton's all business, you know. Hasn't been to a party in years. Practically a recluse. They never were very grand."

This good grace served the Hamiltons well; society matrons never mentioned the fallen family who'd negotiated capital in exchange for the future Mrs. Hamilton.

(Mr. Hamilton had for once caught the wind, and when he bothered to go out, he kept his wife at home.)

The Hamiltons were so discreet that people were only sure of one child, Josephine, whose birth was announced in the *Times.* More slipped into the world unannounced—once in a while, someone's nanny saw two girls coming from the Hamilton house—but it was impossible to tell how many there were, and after long enough, people stopped wondering.

There were so many—he was trying so hard for a son—and eventually it seemed gauche, tenement crowding in a respectable house. It would be an embarrassment to keep dragging them out into society like a magician with scarves.

(Mr. Hamilton could not have made use of his daughters as much as he could have of sons, but that was a subtler game that required savvy positioning on the field of play: more experience than he had, more tricks than his unlucky wife would have known.

He was a man of the old age, where daughers were meant to be retiring; he simply retired them.)

It was a shame, thought some of the sons who spent more than they should and could use some Hamilton money; it was wise, thought some of the fathers whose daughters had taken to smoking. Mothers were happiest. The girls would be married or not, mothers thought, and there was no need to ask questions and stir up extra young ladies; plenty of daughters needed marrying off without some Hamiltons dragging their dowries into it.

No one ever told Jo about her family. All they told her was she must behave without question, because it was expected of her.

She heard some things. She knew they had money; she knew her mother was sad, and had been better off than this, once; she knew no one wanted to hear a word out of girls who were nothing but trouble.

She only saw her mother if her mother was well enough to come up to the fourth floor and smile and touch the tops of their heads as they stood, marveling.

She rarely was. (She was always sick, or made sick, or too sad to be well.) And on those visits she was pale, with dark circles around her eyes and lines drawn tight around her mouth, as if she'd been forbidden even to smile.

Jo believed it of her. Jo felt sorry for her. But Jo never ran for her like Lou and Ella did.

Jo guessed even then that Mother's purpose was to have a son, and she was kept from all other causes.

Them included.

The impression spread. At last, even Ella gave up running when she came, as if their mother was a bad penny. (Jo regretted it—their mother's face in that long moment before Ella broke down and went to embrace her.)

If only she'd have a boy already, Jo thought when she was feeling cruel. One son would be the end of all this trouble.

One son, and perhaps their father would be pleased enough to let her smile, or speak, or speak for them.

Every time her mother was confined, Jo thought, This will free her; this time, for sure, it will be a boy.

But beds kept filling their bedrooms, so it never was.

Soon there were four. Then six. The rooms on the upper floors filled and filled.

Jo was almost ten and felt years older, surrounded by her mother's children.

Lou, nearly eight, was a little flame, from her copper hair to her bloodcurdling shrieks. Six-year-old Ella was as placid as their mother, the same golden hair and water-pale eyes. Doris, hardly old enough to have a mind (five years old—a baby), followed Lou with a frown, playing at the edges of Lou's puzzles, screaming when Lou screamed.

"You must take care of your sisters," the nannies said, and Jo always said, "All right," without knowing what they meant.

They needed no care. They were always at home. The governess came for lessons, and their clothes came by catalog, and they had the attic if they wanted to leave their rooms. There was nothing for Jo to do but watch them coming and going, and worry.

They went out in pairs with a nanny for walks and air, past a museum they never went into, but there was no call for them to play outside, or meet other girls, or go in a crowd, or see the city.

"If you misbehave outside, would you like to tell your father why you've been so bad?" the nannies said, or, "There are wolves in this city who eat wicked girls."

As they grew older, it was the nannies' insistence, and not their stories, that frightened the girls, and fear won out.

Some terrors were fiction; some were not.

There were no monsters in the streets, but if they misbehaved, their father would be angry.

They didn't know quite what it meant, but whenever they asked their nannies what the punishment would be the nannies went silent, and the girls all knew that they must never, never cross their father.

For Jo's tenth birthday, her mother was in bed (a son, both nannies were praying), and her nanny was instructed to bring Jo to the theater to celebrate—after the lights went down, so they wouldn't be noticed.

(Their mother, invisible as she was, sometimes effected little intercessions in strange places, where their father could be most easily convinced it didn't matter.)

At the opera house, Jo sat forward, her head on her folded hands along the balcony. The nanny frowned.

"If you're tired," she said, "we'll go home."

But Jo was the farthest from sleep she'd ever been, sitting in the uncomfortable plush seat, feeling the violins under her hands, the rumble of voices floating up from the figures onstage, who did this and that wild thing, and pretended to love one another.

And in between grand gestures, there were parties, and dancers took the stage.

It was a reel in the second act, and a waltz in the third, a half-open embrace, the women grasping their skirts in one hand and spinning in their partners' arms.

In those minutes Jo woke deeply, eyes wider with every clasped hand and turning head and reaching arm.

The slippers of the women flicked through their skirts as they danced, as they sank and rose with the music, and Jo, watching them, was so tightly alive she thought her heart would pound through her chest.

Lou was awake when they came home. (Lou was always awake.)

While Jo got shepherded inside their room and shoved into a nightgown and scrubbed, Lou's jealous, gleaming eyes followed her.

Jo wasted no time. As soon as the nanny had closed the door on them, Jo was out of bed, pulling back the curtains to let in the light and clearing away dolls and books in careless handfuls.

"Those are mine," hissed Lou. "Leave them. I'll hit you."

"Come down," Jo said, like the bed was a citadel.

"No."

"Come down," said Jo, "and I'll teach you to dance."

After a long moment, Lou slunk out of bed and stood in the center of the room, frowning, her arms crossed.

"Liar," she said, but when Jo held out her hands, Lou unfolded her arms and took hold.

They were so busy practicing steps, and making up the ones Jo didn't remember, that they didn't sleep. It was the first time Jo had thought of Lou as a partner and not an interloper.

At dawn they called Ella and Doris to make a proper square for the reel, and the day (minus two resentful half hours walking in the fresh air) was given over.

They asked the nannies, quietly, if they knew any dances. The older one told them never to mind dancing, since that was for loose girls. The younger nanny waited until the older one was gone, and then she sat on Ella's bed and said, "I can show you the polka."

So that night was the polka. The next night was back to the waltz, and after that the reel. After a week they had grown tired of them.

"We should have real lessons," said Doris, after the third time Lou snapped at her about being in the wrong place.

"Yes," breathed Ella. "Lessons! Oh, how divine."

Ella had picked up some style from the older nanny, who went to the pictures too much.

"I don't know," said Jo.

Dancing was outside, and outside they must never go, for fear of being overwhelmed, or being overwhelming.

Lou raised her eyebrows. "Why not? You afraid of him?"

"Yes," said Jo. "Aren't you?"

None of them answered.

But despite everything, once the Hamilton girls set their minds to something they were hard to shake.

It was a mistake from the start. At ten years old, Jo was already drawn and solemn, with eyes like flint chips. She was tall and had come up looking tough; none of it was calculated to please.

Their father had a weakness for beauty and docility, which Jo might have known if they'd seen their mother when their father first married her, before she began to disappoint him.

Better to send Ella, who had their mother's eyes, who would have smiled through her lashes; their father might have given in to anything she wanted.

But they didn't know, and they sent Jo, who knocked on their father's study door like a solicitor and asked for dance lessons.

"I think not, Josephine," he said. "Dance lessons are expensive, and you have no use for them."

That seemed to be stacking one insult on another.

"Still, we would love lessons," she said. "Father."

He seemed to think for a moment. "Perhaps for your birthday."

"Perhaps?"

"For your birthday," he promised.

After her eleventh birthday, Jo learned never to take a man at his word.

At first it was just Jo and Lou and Ella and Doris in the tight knot of the reel, but the sisters kept growing older, and another one always came.

With so many trapped in the upper floors, it hardly surprised Jo how often they fought, or how fiercely. When you didn't have one room to yourself in the whole world, you laid claim to every inch of whatever you could.

(For them, the wide, winding town house was all narrow halls and narrow beds, in rooms that got narrower by the day, and the board in the center of the floor demarcated for each girl the line that, in honor, her sister could never cross.)

Left to themselves they were a pack of wolves, but when Jo summoned them they filed like soldiers into Jo and Lou's room, on the top floor, where they were least likely to be heard. They slid off their shoes and lined them up along the wall, and waited for Jo to call steps.

Once, early on, during a fight about the waltz, Lou called Jo "General." It stuck.

Later, Lou would tease her about getting big ideas.

It was more as though the name slid into the empty spaces between Jo's fears and habits (she was young, but she was already a jailer). "General" was the mortar that let her stand in both places at once and not fall.

By then Jo was fourteen and looked older than some of their first nannies, with the same air of being overstrict and underpaid.

When she walked down the back stairs with Lou one afternoon, that year's cook never even looked up. All the nannies came that way when they brought those upstairs girls for exercise—no need for them to make a spectacle of themselves, going through the front way.

(A young maid, new to the house like the maids always were, might have looked up as they passed, and seen two girls close to her age, and thought, Poor things.)

They saw a picture.

Jo hardly remembered it; the walk to the theater on Broadway was too long by half, and the park was a wilderness, and the streets were all a rush of carriages and cars and people skittering past them, and Jo raced through the middle of it all thinking only, We have to make it safely there.

And once they were inside the sheltering dark, she thought more about getting home than the movie, and she was watching Lou more than the screen. Lou was smiling, for the first time Jo could remember.

She only knew to pay attention when Lou said, "Aha."

It was a foxtrot. The leading man was supposed to be drunk, but it was the right idea—enough for Jo.

The leading man closed his eyes, and the heroine curled her fingers tight around his fingers.

"It's lovely," Jo said.

"Doris will hate it."

"She can hate it after she's learned it right."

When the wedding proposal came at last and the leads kissed delightedly, Jo watched with a pang in her chest. It was over, and she'd have to take Lou back to the house, because what else in the world could she do?

"Is that what women wear to get married these days?" Lou asked, making a face.

Jo looked at the door and sighed.

• • • • • •

They snuck back into the house just before dusk, where five girls were lined up on Jo's bed, fighting and fidgeting and waiting to dance.

"Foxtrot," Jo said, and they grinned.

Jo and Lou kept it up.

They slipped into theaters inside larger groups—harder to check tickets. Sometimes, when it was slim pickings, Lou flirted their way in. For someone who'd never really met men, she was an excellent flirt.

They sat in the sweet, sticky heat of the cinema, toes tingling as the piano rattled the floor. They brought home ragtime, the grizzly bear, the waltz.

("A new waltz?" Ella sighed. "I liked the old one."

Doris groaned.

"That one's out of date," said Lou. "This one's just like the old one, only with less dress."

"And more hands," said Jo, and Ella went pink.)

The nannies and the governess began to be dismissed. They had chosen the girls' clothes and books, and with them gone, Jo decided Father would have to be convinced, somehow, to give them a living allowance.

When Doris said, "So who do we send?" Lou said, "Not Jo. She's been in those trenches already, for all the good it did us."

(Lou tried to sound clever; sometimes it came out bitter.)

But Jo had learned a thing or two since the first time. It was Ella who went.

Jo coached her to stand with her toes pointing inward and knock on the doorjamb with one timid fist.

It worked; Ella was a natural actress.

A year later, it was five-year-old twins Hattie and Mattie who climbed his chair and teased until he almost laughed and agreed to give them pocket money for magazines, when they went for walks.

Jo saved. "You never know what you'll need," she said, as if they'd break out and hop a train at any moment.

But the younger girls bought candy, and most of the older girls bought rouge and lipstick. Doris bought a booklet on the canals of New York, to general bafflement.

Lou hoarded her money for weeks and then bought a cigarette holder.

"You never know what you'll need," she said to Jo, and smiled, her mouth a little thin.

(It stung, and it must have showed; when Jo turned back to her book, Lou sat beside her, and rested her head on Jo's shoulder, and turned the pages.

How Lou knew Jo had finished reading, Jo never figured. Lou had a knack when it came to Jo.)

At last there were twelve, from Jo all the way down to Violet, who was born after Jo had already turned thirteen and who still slept in the nursery.

As soon as Violet was out of diapers, their father dismissed the remaining nanny.

"The older girls," he said, "can watch the others."

The decree made its way through the house before it came at last, by accident, to the girls it was about.

Jo heard it from Nanny Harris herself, who was giving the littlest girls, Rose and Lily and Violet, a last scold as she packed.

"And because you've been so bad," Nanny Harris was saying, "I have to go away, and where will I be when you want someone to tuck you in at night?"

"You'll be lying to other children, I expect," said Jo from the landing. "Girls, come down."

Harris packed the rest of her things alone, with Doris standing guard in the doorway.

Back in her room, Jo put on a dress and combed her hair until she looked respectable.

She had decided to speak to their mother.

It was terrifying—it had been ten years at least since she'd seen her mother's room, and almost a year since she'd seen her mother, coming into the nursery to try to smile at the toddling Violet—but these were desperate times.

This couldn't be. The older sisters couldn't replace the nannies as overseers for the younger ones. It wasn't fair to force them into this captivity forever; surely even their mother, who saw so little, could see that.

But when Jo had summoned the courage to go down the front stairs to the second floor and knock on their mother's door, the frothy white bed was made up, and the inlaid oak wardrobes were empty.

That was how Jo found out their mother had, at last, given up on producing a son for the Hamilton patriarch.

Jo let herself cry for two minutes, to mourn a mother she'd hardly known, who could do no good for her daughters ever again.

Then she set it aside.

(She set everything aside. There was some hollow place inside her that grew and grew.)

Jo called Lou and Ella and told them, so they would have the crying over with.

Ella was tenderhearted enough to weep for their mother and not for herself. Lou dashed tears from her eyes as if ridding herself of a bad habit.

"We could tell them she ran away," suggested Ella, after the first flood.

Jo said, "I don't want to give them impossible ideas."

Lou said, "Then divide them. Let's get it over with."

Jo spoke to Hattie and Mattie, and stoic Rebecca. Araminta and Doris fell to Lou; Araminta took it badly, mostly because it came from Lou, and Jo wished later that she'd known enough to give her to Ella instead.

Ella went into the nursery and gathered Sophie into her lap, and dried her tears with a threadbare cuff. Only after Sophie was sleeping did she do the same for the little twins, Rose and Lily, who had started asking when their mother would visit.

(Violet was too young to understand; she'd never ask, assuming her mother must have been Ella. Rebecca would eventually set her straight, but so late an intercession of the facts had no effect on what Violet really thought.)

When the cook delivered dinner, she mentioned their father had asked what all the noise was about.

"We can't go out any more," Jo told Lou when the lights were out. "If he catches us now, there'll be no mercy. We're to stay inside, with the others."

That was when Lou cried.

That Christmas, as a reward for good behavior, their father had parcels delivered.

It was a generous year, from their father: sewing kits and books, dolls and music boxes.

The dolls were discarded. Araminta picked up the sewing kit. Jo picked up the books.

Each room (they occupied six) received a music box; the melody was the same, not even right for dancing.

The party dresses (cruel, Jo thought) were the wrong sizes for anyone but Rebecca and Ella, and too long, but they looked almost like they should, and everyone declared it a good Christmas.

With her savings, planning for disaster that might never come, Jo ordered a handful of flimsy coats.

(Ella had chipped in enough to buy hair ribbons; the ribbons went over better.)

She handed them to six girls, one for each room. No one said they were cheap or ugly, though they were; anything that had to do with outside carried power. They cast glances out the window.

"Never wear them unless you have to," Jo said, and they all nodded without asking why.

By then, their father was a myth; Jo was the one you worried about.

Ella was the first to ask Araminta if she could do something with the length; soon Ella's coat had a mostly even ruffle at the collar, made from leftover hem.

The others lined up, and Araminta—barely old enough to thread a needle by herself—did what she could.

In their rooms they'd slip them on, grinning as if at the beginning of a great adventure, as if when Jo rapped on the floor to summon them for geography or history or dancing (dancing, dancing), what she really meant was that they were going somewhere, anywhere, at last.

For years they lived that way, doves in cages, peering out and shaking the feathers of their wings; with every practice they were dancing along their perches, just waiting for a door to open.

One night, when Jo was nineteen, the house next door had a party.

They were frozen by the music. They had no gramophone (they'd never been good enough to earn that at Christmas), and humming and music boxes hardly counted.

To have music so close was overwhelming, and above the songs rang the laughter and voices and the scrape of three dozen pairs of shoes echoing off the walls, through the stairwells, right through to their rooms like a telegram.

When Lou realized, she laughed too sharply.

"Sounds like they can't even dance, the clodhoppers," she said, and then burst into angry tears.

Jo was startled into silence.

She didn't comfort Lou—there was no comfort—but when Ella and Doris came in, Jo motioned them aside.

Doris whispered, "But what if Father hears?"

"Let her cry," Jo said.

They sat on Jo's bed, watching Lou grind her fists into her brows, waiting for the storm to subside.

As soon as Lou had recovered air to speak, she said, "I've had it. I don't care what happens to me. I'm getting out. I'm running away and he'll never find me."

Doris said, at once, "Then so am I."

(She was fourteen, then, and still shadowed Lou as if she couldn't help it.)

"Wait a second," said Jo, but Lou was up from her chair and pacing, her long hair twisted behind her.

"He can't keep us prisoner," Lou said. "It's not right—he got Mother, he doesn't get us, too. I don't care if I die in a ditch, so long as it's out of this house!"

"I'm coming with you," said Doris, her eyes shining in a way Jo had never seen, and vanished out the door.

They meant it. Lou and Doris would walk out, the music drowning out their footsteps, and then they would be gone.

Jo went cold all over.

At least twice a year someone threatened it, natural in imprisonment (and that's what it was—Jo had no doubt, even then).

When it happened, Jo calmed the older girls or silenced the younger, and that was the end of it until the trees changed and someone else cried to be let out.

But that night the music from the party beat against the walls, echoing in Jo's fingertips, and she understood.

Even Ella was looking toward the window as if trying to decide whether she had the strength to walk out.

(They all had the strength to follow if one of them ever led; Jo knew that much.)

Jo watched Lou shoving dresses into a pillowcase and imagined what would happen to her, if she and Doris ran. If any of them followed suit. Separated, without money to live on, without any knowledge outside their neighborhood, or even coats that could keep them safe from the cold.

She guessed what the world would do to a few girls all alone; for a moment she despaired.

But Jo remembered enough of the movies she had seen to have some ideas. Desperate times called for grand gestures. Girls who stuck together did all right, and there were always places where a pretty girl could dance.

She knew from Lou's magazines that there were laws about drinking, new places to dance where people would be inclined to stay quiet about who came and went.

This might be the only chance she'd have to keep them from vanishing.

After a moment, Jo told Ella, "Go get Doris. We're going dancing."

four
POSITIVELY, ABSOLUTELY

Years later, Ella and Doris would remember it as Lou's idea.

(Lou, who knew it had been Jo, never corrected them. Some stories worked better if they weren't true.)

They remembered fastening their dresses with shaking fingers, gone down the back stairs with their shoes in one hand and into the cab the General hailed by magic.

(The long and terrible wait in the alley behind the house, as Jo waited, they don't recall.)

They don't remember that it had been the General ("Don't call me Jo—no names, for God's sake!") who told them to dress, who handed Lou some ugly catalog shoes, who asked the cabbie the best place for a dance and a drink, and as far from here as they could get.

(Once or twice, Doris says, "Don't you think it might have been Jo? She's bossy enough about everything else."

But Ella says, "That would make it a terrible story," and Doris is still young enough that she thinks you should try to be like the sister you're living with, so she never argues.

By the time she understands otherwise, the story's been told so many times it might as well be true.)

They remember the blaze of lights along Fifth Avenue—for Doris a blur of too many streets before they reached any place worth having; for Ella a constellation of delight in every window with a lamp behind it, every streetlight that illuminated a storefront long enough for her to get a glimpse of all the things inside that a lady could choose to buy, with money of her own.

(Of that first night, Jo remembered slipping free of the park and into the sudden open square, and seeing a palace, a block wide and ablaze with light, and holding her breath as if they'd taken flight.

But no one asks her, so she never says.)

It was Jo who guided them into that first club, Salon Renaud, where the air made a dim, smoky wall.

They were young and shouldn't have been within a block of the place (which was just what the cabbie told them, before he took off).

But girls who looked like boys in lipstick were coming into fashion, and the doorman hesitated.

"You looking for your old man, girlies?"

"We're meeting a friend," Jo said.

The doorman raised an eyebrow. "That so?"

He must have expected a smart answer, or a flirt, or for them to lose their nerve and bolt, but Jo (in a drab navy day suit, like their chaperone) smiled and looked him coolly in the eyes until he stepped aside with a shrug.

(The nightlife chewed up plenty of girls; if these four wanted their turn, it hardly mattered to him.

It had occurred to him in his time at the door that girls who could bully their way in could probably fight their way out; it was only that so few girls worked together that the theory had never been tested.

After Salon Renaud got run out by the cops, he moved to the Kingfisher. When the girls found it, he was more pleased than he'd admit. He guessed it was that oldest's doing—she looked like someone in charge—and every night, it was she for whom he opened the door.)

The answer was always, "Lou took us."

It didn't seem, later, like something Jo would have done. She ran the operation, sure, but she didn't like it. She owned hardly any dresses and wore them nearly to her ankles, so out of fashion it was embarrassing.

Jo rarely drank, and she never danced.

All of them but Lou thought Jo came only to be stern and snap her hand at them when it was time to go.

(Lou knew better, but if Jo didn't want to say, Lou would keep her confidence.)

Ella and Doris remembered the burn of champagne, the music under their shoes like a heartbeat.

They never thought of the general who shepherded them back and forth, her eyes narrowed across the crowd, the tether that kept them from getting swept away.

Lou's biggest memory of that night was coming home.

She'd smoked; she'd stolen drinks; she'd danced whenever she could get a man, not that she had trouble. An hour in, Lou figured she must be good-looking. (She took it the way she'd taken the thick-heeled shoes Jo gave her—it was better than the alternative.)

And all night—dancing or sitting, drinking or flirting—Lou could feel Jo keeping an eye on her across the room. It was spiteful. Lou wasn't Ella; she had two thoughts to rub together. Jo could keep her rotten eyes.

As the taxi pulled up two blocks from the house, Jo was still barking orders. "Doris, the money. Ella, go last, and don't make any noise with the door!"

Lou remembered hating Jo that night.

But Lou also remembered looking down at her shoes, seeing she'd worn the sole down almost to nothing.

She thought about what she'd tell Araminta, who had begged for a report as soon as Jo had explained where they were going, and the twins, who'd stolen her lipstick as revenge for not being invited.

It struck her suddenly how close she'd really been to running away and never seeing her sisters again. She'd have done it, in her anger—she'd have disappeared and been lost; she'd been desperate to the breaking point.

But Jo had seen it and done the only thing she could think of, and it had been enough.

Lou clutched her worn-out shoes to her chest all the way up the back stairs, like she was preparing for the grave and bringing them along.

In less than two years, Jo ran such a smooth operation that the girls were able to sneak out three or four nights a week with no one the wiser.

It was an operation of absolutes, and the rules never changed, no matter how many of them went out.

1. You dressed when she gave the word. (If she never gave the word, God help you if you dressed.)

2. You were ready to go when she called, you were ready to leave when she called, and if you drank too much you'd be left behind. (No one drank too much.)

3. If you were unlucky enough to get sick, you stayed home. If you were heartsick, it was worse.

"I can't worry about you," Jo said. "Be quiet or be ready at midnight."

But home was awfully quiet when you were alone, and it was just as easy to lick one's wounds in the arms of a handsome young man.

Araminta stayed home half a dozen times with an imagined broken heart, for one boy or another, but the rest got coldhearted. Young men were always proposing to Ella, and to Hattie or Mattie (men could never be sure which), and the sisters thought it was sad stuff proposing to a girl whose name you didn't know, but it was nothing to miss dancing over.

Jo, of course, had never missed a night.

"No heart in there to break," Ella said, and no one argued.

five
THE BALTIMORE

Salon Renaud had been a decent venue, as first dances went.

It was a dance hall well-enough known for the taxi driver to think of it; it was well-enough known to have a photographer at the door to catch starlets who had paid for a little publicity.

(Jo never knew about the photographer. There were only four—not enough to draw attention, yet.)

Inside, Salon Renaud was bright and had a bandstand big enough for a philharmonic.

They made a shabby picture in day dresses and catalog shoes amid the silk and velvet.

("Very Bohemian," one woman said, giving them the benefit of the doubt.)

The murmurs stopped once they started dancing.

Jo spent the night asking her partners where else they danced. It was something to talk about that didn't require flirting, and she already knew this wasn't going to be any kind of home. It was too gleaming to be real, and it worried her.

"Is that other place smaller?" she asked, frowning at the electric lights. "Less conspicuous than here?"

Halfway through the evening she wised up and switched from "less conspicuous" to "more romantic," which got her a lot more answers than the first round had. After the first night, they never went back. Big and bright were the last things they needed.

(Two months later, Doris got word that Salon Renaud had been shuttered.

"He told me they practically burned the place down," Doris said, tightening the straps on her shoes. "Now the owner's in jail, and they've locked it up tight as a tomb."

Ella said, "I don't know how you can get so much talking done during such a fast dance."

Doris grinned. "I'm a lady of talent."

They were at the Kingfisher by then, and feeling safe as houses.)

The next morning, the young maid brought up the breakfast trays.

When she reached Jo and Lou's room, she hesitated a moment, then said, "If you have any clothes that need washing, just let me know directly."

Lou blanched and looked at Jo.

Jo managed a reasonably calm, "I see. Does anyone think we need laundry done?"

The maid shook her head. "You're very quiet. It's just that sometimes I have trouble sleeping. And if anyone else has heard, I'm sure no one thinks the worse of you for getting some fresh air, even at a strange hour."

There was a little silence.

Then Jo said, "You're very kind," and paused.

"It's Mary," the maid said, wrinkling her nose like she shouldn't have spoken.

But Lou grinned and said, "Mary, you're a peach."

After that, Jo insisted they stay at the edge of the stairs, to avoid creaking, and anyone with beads had to coil her skirt in her hands so it didn't make a sound.

One maid might be sympathetic. You couldn't risk more.

• • • • • •

The second place they went was some supper club so far down-town that even if Jo had known her way around the city, she'd probably have been lost in the maze.

It was darker than the Salon, which suited Jo; it had a cramped band and whiskey that tasted like dust, which didn't suit anyone; and it had a name that was doomed to obscurity the moment Doris stepped inside and said, "God, it's like someone died in here."

They lasted two weeks at the Funeral Parlor Supper Club.

Jo and Lou got another name from a bartender with sleek, dark hair and high cheekbones that made him look like the star on a movie marquee. He was young and impatient, and apparently just traitorous enough to go other places on his nights off.

"It's nothing much," he warned, "but if they ever get some decent drink I might consider it."

"See you there, then," said Jo, and the bartender smiled at Lou with dark eyes and said, "I should be so lucky."

The flirting didn't do much to endear him to Jo (they weren't there for men), but Lou didn't seem to mind it; she took her time coming back with her drink, and she was glancing over at the bar again long before the champagne was gone.

"Just scouting for partners," she said when Jo caught her eye, and Jo said, "Good," already knowing better.

The place was the Kingfisher, and almost from the first moment Jo could tell it was going to be home.

By the end of the night, she was sure.

(Partly, it was that the Kingfisher was small enough to be out of mind and dark enough to slip into; there were faces of all colors on the dance floor and sometimes two men cheek to cheek, and she wanted a place that could keep secrets.

Partly, it was that Jo had a moment of weakness with someone she shouldn't have.)

There was a table near the back door that was big enough for all of them, with a few seats to spare. The spare seats filled with young men trying to trade drinks for dances, with varying degrees of success.

Even Lou approved of the place, which was saying something, and the next night when they scrambled into a taxi, Jo didn't hesitate.

They'd been going there only six weeks before the bartender from the Funeral Parlor appeared before the rows of bottles.

Jo pushed through the crowd to thank him.

When he saw Jo, he grinned and waved, already looking ten years younger than the last time she'd seen him, and she felt disconcertingly welcome, as if for a moment the nightlife had opened its arms to her in earnest.

She fought the feeling. Vanity wasn't going to get them all back home safely, and the last thing she needed was to get carried away.

"Hey there, Princess," he called over the crowd of men clamoring for drinks. "What are you having? I'll start a tab until the gentlemen start buying them for you."

A few of them glanced over their shoulders, as if sizing up how long it would be. She ignored them. As soon as they saw Ella, it would be taken care of.

"I'm surprised to see you here so soon," she said, smiling, when she managed to belly up to the bar.

"Ditto," he said, and slid the glasses across the bar with a sidelong glance at Lou.

By the end of the night, Jo knew three things.

First, his name was Jake.

("Oh," she said—she'd expected something different—and he smiled and said, "I have a name back on Mott Street, but Jake suits me in this neighborhood," and she wasn't going to question having a name you kept at home.)

Second, he already knew her sisters well enough to pick them out from the crowd.

(Lou smiled at him a little too long.)

Third, "Princess" was going to stick.

That suited Jo. It was as close to a real name as the men would get; maybe it would keep them from asking.

The Kingfisher was the first place Hattie and Mattie (two years later) and Rebecca (the year after) ever danced.

"They have it so easy," Doris said, sighing, "they don't know any other way," as if two weeks of dancing halfhearted grizzly bears at the Funeral Home Supper Club had been a crawl through the trenches under enemy fire.

"You're hopeless," said Lou, yanking the triple knot on her laces.

(It was the only way to keep them on. Later, they learned to look through the catalogs for ugly, thick-strap shoes that would last a little longer before they started to wear thin.

"It's amazing we ever get called Princess in these," Rebecca said sometimes as they flew down Fifth Avenue on Ladies' Mile, and a streetlight would illuminate a shoe store as if to remind them of what they couldn't have.)

Lou stood and tugged at her skirt. "Right. Jake can't get away, it looks like. Doris, show me that boy you were dancing with. Let's see if he's better at the waltz than the foxtrot."

"Come on," said Doris, blushing at the edges, "Sam does his best. People can't be good at every dance."

"Certainly not him," said Lou.

("Those girls have tin hearts," someone had told Jake. Jo was pleased when he passed it on—she'd worked to keep them a little cold.)

They lasted nearly four years there, before the bust.

The night the Kingfisher got raided was rainy. Jo had almost kept them home.

The weather was Jo's second thought when the bouncer banged on the door and the place erupted into chaos and she grabbed Rebecca and bolted out the back, through the alley and out to the street.

(Jo's first thought had been for Lou, but that wasn't a thing you ever admitted. She had a job to do; she couldn't afford to play favorites.)

From the shadows, Jo watched the police vans rattling away with her heart lodged in her throat.

When she saw a glimpse of red hair two blocks down—Lou, it was Lou—she clapped a hand to her mouth to keep from crying out.

Behind her came Ella, Doris, the twins, and Jake.

Jo's knees nearly gave out.

She and Rebecca crept around the block to meet them, and Lou was already looking when they came into sight.

"See," she told Ella, "I don't know why you worry."

"Where were you?" asked Rebecca, jogging over to Doris and lost in the glorious practicalities of engineering an escape. "Where's the secret door? Is it a tunnel? Where did you go underneath? How are you?"

"It's a long tunnel," said Doris. "I thought we'd run to Vermont already, and I'm covered in spiderwebs, but I'll probably be fine."

"It's just a precaution," Jake told Jo. "Tunnel's been there for ages."

Jo was trying hard not to shake. "And how often does that come in handy?"

Jake shrugged. "Generally the cops leave the place alone—out of sight, out of mind. It's more lucrative busting my neighborhood than some two-bit operation like ours. I bet Simmons just forgot to pay protection this month."

It didn't feel like "just" anything, but in front of the others Jo didn't dare look worried.

Lou came over, brushing the last of the cobwebs off her elbow, stopping just within Jake's reach.

"You can show a girl a good time, I'll give you that."

"Hope this doesn't scare you off the place," Jake said. "I know you sometimes disappear."

"You're a nosey parker," said Lou, but he shrugged with his hands in his pockets, met her eye, smiled.

Lou's face fell.

(Jo knew Lou knew better than to make men promises.)

"We should get home," Jo said.

In the cab, Lou said, "We're not going back, are we."

She sounded sadder than Jo expected, and Jo was kind when she answered, "No."

Pete's: at the seaport, where a man got rough with Ella when she wouldn't dance with him.

Hattie and Mattie appeared as if by magic.

"Not sure what port you're from," said Hattie, and Mattie said, "But when a lady says no, stop asking."

He frowned, spat out, "You girls have a pretty high opinion of yourselves," and dropped Ella's wrist with a flourish.

"Let's go home," Hattie said when he was gone.

Jo said, "That's up to Ella."

Ella looked around the room (which was slim pickings, and a lot of guys who looked like trouble), but then she squared her shoulders and said, "I want to dance."

Jo was pleasantly surprised. "Then we dance," she said, and cast a look around the room that dared anyone to make something of it.

And dance they did, all night, to spite the devil.

Still, that was the last time they ever saw Pete's.

The next time they drove past the palace (the Vanderbilt house, she had a name for it now; people knew the oddest things), all the lights were out, the rows of windows like empty eyes shrinking back from the life on the street.

It's not a sign, she told herself, and hoped it was true.

Fine Imports: a basement off Fulton Street, with shipping crates stacked to one side and a subbasement from which gin magically appeared. It felt, somehow, like dancing in an old tomb.

Not that there was anything wrong with old tombs, until you tried to dance in one.

"If this place gets any more cramped," Doris said, "I'll have to dance on my knees to keep from knocking my hair off."

They didn't last long at Fine Imports.

The Baltimore: half a block away from a print shop in Chelsea, just far enough west that the Flatiron Building blocked the moon.

The machines shook the sidewalks for three blocks in every direction.

"You're joking," said Jo, before the cab even stopped.

Doris laughed so hard it nearly drowned out the presses.

They never set foot in the Baltimore.

The Swan: a supper and music club nestled three blocks from the Waldorf-Astoria, with a double-door entryway, and a stream of businessmen and their respectable mistresses going past the doorman in his smart coat.

This time, Jo saw the photographer.

The cabs didn't even slow down.

By then, Araminta was starting to hover at the mirrors, watching them with big, hungry eyes.

She never asked—Araminta wasn't reckless enough to ask Jo for favors—but Jo knew what was fair.

Araminta had earned the right; there had to be a place for her to dance.

Two weeks after the raid, Jo told Ella, "Tell Araminta to bring up a dress and some half-decent shoes."

A minute later Araminta appeared, clutching a catalog dress and a pair of thick-strap shoes, smiling so broadly Jo hardly recognized her.

Araminta powdered up in the crowd alongside Rebecca, applying rouge with shaking hands until Rebecca took pity and did it for her.

"You're such a ninny," Rebecca said, "it's a wonder they're letting you out. Hold still."

Araminta said, "No need to be a wet blanket, Rebecca, it doesn't become you any more than your dress does."

"Don't be mean to the girl who's doing your makeup," said Mattie, and Hattie said, "You'll end up looking more like a clown than Mattie, even—ow!"

"Where are we going?" Lou asked.

Lou had probably guessed, Jo thought; for girls who had to wait as long as they did, who had to strike so suddenly and then vanish, where else was truly theirs?

Jo sighed. "Home."

Lou grinned.

When they nodded their way past the doorman ("Been a while, Princesses!"), the others vanished onto the dance floor. Lou made a beeline for the bar, where Jake looked up and saw them.

By the time Lou had crossed the room, he was already pouring the first of their drinks, and when she leaned against the bar with folded arms and tilted her head as if she was wishing him hello, he grinned, gave her a look that held.

Soon the only sisters left at the table were Jo and Araminta, who was shyly marveling.

"What now?" she asked Jo.

Jo said, "You know how to do this. Now find someone who can keep up."

For a moment Araminta frowned, and Jo realized with a pang of dread that she'd sounded like their father.

But it was all right; Araminta didn't know what their father sounded like, and her shyness disappeared as she evaluated the floor with the eye of a collector.

By the next waltz, she was off.

So Jo sat at their table and watched her sisters wildly dancing, and thought that maybe, maybe, things would turn out all right.

six

AIN'T WE GOT FUN?

Lou will dance anything, with anyone; she needs only a partner to be happy. She'd wear out a pair of shoes a night, if Jo would let them stay long enough.

Lou drinks like a fish and never gets drunk, as if her body burns it just to keep her going.

Lou kisses her first boy when she's eighteen. He says he's an actor, which Lou can tell is a lie (so much for acting), but she likes the look of him, and he isn't the only one who forgets the truth in a dance hall.

She avoids the bar for two nights. Jake shouldn't be upset—he has no right—but still, the next time he hands her a drink, his fingers brush hers and hold on.

"Let me know if you need anything," he says. His eyes are dark and still. "Some of these men aren't to be trusted."

He's not jealous; he's just earnest, and willing, and somehow that's worse. She's never promised him anything.

"As if I've ever trusted a man," Lou says, and takes the drink too fast.

(When the Kingfisher was raided, Jake grabbed for her wrist without looking, and the idea that he had known where she was made her heart tight in her chest for a long time after they were safe again.)

Better to kiss boys she doesn't really like. She sees how badly it can go; no thank you.

Lou misses the old waltz, when the leader's fingers just

touched her waist, the way Jo taught her back when they were the only two.

(Lou sometimes hates that Jo taught her first. It's tied them together some way she can't shake.)

"It was sweeter," she tells Jo, once. "Grander somehow, to be held that way. But you can't get something back once it's out of fashion."

She sighs, breathing smoke through her lips. "Might as well dance."

Ella loves foxtrot. She's not above begging the bandleader for one more, just one, before they have to go. She's the prettiest, with bow lips and blond hair, and she smiles so sweetly that the band obliges.

(Ella knows that when you ask for a favor from a man, you must always be smiling.)

If the girls have a mother, it's Ella, who's handy with a blister or a broken heart, and who can charm their father into little intercessions.

Jo sends her; Jo's the one who warned her to smile.

The Christmas the dolls come, Ella takes them all.

("You're kidding," says Doris.)

She pities the dolls. They have empty eyes, blue and heartless, and when she looks in the mirror and sees the resemblance, she worries.

(It's a fear not even the dance floor can shake; growing up with Jo and Lou makes you worry about getting heartless.

Jo sends her to the bar when the Kingfisher's full of strangers and they need a round of drinks: she's the ringer, every time.)

Ella sneaks Shakespeare from the library and acts to them, sometimes. They're the only audience who sits still—the trouble with sisters who care only for dancing.

She likes Shakespeare something awful.

She falls in love every night for a while. Then she learns that if you're quiet, they talk, and you can find something to dislike about anyone.

But sometimes a young man will look like a *Photoplay* cover, and she wants to ask about movies, if they're as wonderful as the papers say they are. She hopes so.

Because it was never any good seeking favors from Jo, she never asked to go to the flicks. Then it was too late.

Ella's learned. Now she asks for foxtrots.

You can't expect people to give you the things you love, unless you know how to ask.

Some man calls Doris "old girl" the first time they go out, even though she's fourteen, maybe not even that.

Doris almost likes it—she's so young that looking older is the best thing she can think of—but he seems so smug about it that she stops the dance early.

You can't let a man get the better of you; she learns that in a hurry.

On one of their first nights at the Kingfisher, a quiet young man asks her what he should call her—the first time anyone's asked for her preference, instead of pushing for her name.

"Whatever you call everyone else," she says.

(She'd wanted to give him her name—she liked him already, something awful—but Jo had given orders.)

The first time a man calls her "Princess," she smacks his arm.

"What am I, a Hapsburg? Watch your mouth. And pick up your feet, would you? This is twice as fast as you think."

About some things, Doris has always been picky.

At the table, Ella tells her she was rude. (Not news.)

"At least my hem isn't up to my knees," Doris says, and watches Ella turn red and tug at her skirt.

Doris's hems crawl up with everyone else's, eventually, but only because someone else makes her hand a dress to Araminta or Sophie for tailoring.

Doris never pays much attention to the fashion papers. When Jo asks her to make her choices in the catalogs, Doris would be happy to close her eyes and point.

If Doris can't be dancing, she'll settle for reading. Beyond that, she can't think of much to care about.

(Doris never thinks what she'd have done if there hadn't been dancing. She just remembers wanting to be free, and then being free.)

She isn't caught up with men. Sam, the quiet boy from the Kingfisher, is her only favorite, and even then she doesn't mention it. She knows she'll never hear the end of it from Lou.

Lou wants Doris to be wilder and rougher, always, and Sam smiles too much for Lou to think he has any flash.

(When he stops coming out a few years later, Doris doesn't let Lou catch her missing him. Lou's as bad as Jo when it comes to broken hearts.)

Doris doesn't stand for smooth dances. Doris has to be moving, as fast as possible, as much as she can.

"Oh, Lord no," she says when a man asks for a waltz. "Come back and chase me for the Charleston, that's a boy. God, this music is sad stuff!"

Hattie and Mattie live for the Charleston.

It's fine in partners, if a man can dance it really well, but they love being each other's mirrors more than anything in the world.

("Charleston!" they begged, as soon as they were old enough for the word.)

They have the look of the age—striking, bold, with large eyes and heart-shaped faces and dark bobbed hair in combs.

They have the look for the Charleston. When they take the floor, their feet flash and their bangles clang together as they pass their hands back and forth in the air with the abandon of rioters.

They wring joy out of anything. They rise late and laugh that they're not stuck in school—Doris made them do their math and

Ella makes them read, but in every novel schools are dreadful things, and every girl's out to poison you. Better to be here, with only Jo to poison you, and dancing every day.

They partner each other in practice with grins that look like they're hiding something.

(They are. They're the real twins—the younger ones don't have what they have.)

They fight. They wring joy from that, too, pulling nasty faces and cuffing each other like it's choreography.

To the world, they're a pair of clockwork dollfaces who dance like a dream, if you dare to ask.

If you're unlucky, they'll send you away. If you're really unlucky, they'll run back to their marble-faced sisters and laugh so hard the whole place can hear.

(It's from Hattie and Mattie that people start to get the idea that all the sisters are cruel.)

Hattie and Mattie, when they're dancing with each other, feel they're the only ones who matter, the only two girls in the world at all.

Hattie and Mattie, when they aren't dancing, still feel that way, despite themselves.

Rebecca is precise.

When the music boxes come that Christmas, Rebecca opens each one, sitting through the same song six times, just in case.

Even at five years old and barely reading, she picks up dances the first time Jo demonstrates—they roll out ahead of her as if Jo's left a map.

When Jo finagles a library out of their father, she appoints Rebecca the librarian, and she places orders twice a year with their father. They don't get all they ask for—"Father says money is getting tighter," Jo reports back every once in a while, in a tone that says she doesn't quite believe it—but they get enough.

(Once their father sends the message "I expected worse from

your book choices, but you seem to be handling it." It's the highest praise any of them has ever gotten.

She replies with a request for reading glasses.)

Rebecca's first night out, she takes pains not to look overwhelmed by it all, and makes up in the mirror the way she's practiced for months, red sliding over her lips with a practiced flick so that the others will be impressed by how prepared and mature she is.

(Araminta's shaking hands embarrass Rebecca more than she can ever say. The day after their first night out, she makes Araminta rouge her face beforehand, so no one will see her.

"Someone has to keep you from looking like a silly fool in front of Jo," Rebecca says. "She'll keep you at home if she thinks you don't have the nerve."

Araminta raises her eyebrows. "I didn't realize you were my keeper."

"I'm not," says Rebecca; she's never stopped wondering if it's true.)

Rebecca doesn't think of herself as romantic—she'll leave that to Araminta, thank you—but still it disappoints her when the first man she dances with doesn't know what he's doing. He holds her too tight, and falls behind the beat, and steps on her toes.

She gets back to the table and cries.

Jo allows it for half a song. Then she says, "Enough, it makes your eyes red," and hands her a hankie.

(Never a lot of comfort in Jo, but it was hard to deny she gave practical advice.)

The little burn of disappointment never goes away, and Rebecca gets picky, fast.

(She brings out the reading glasses, sometimes, so she can peer over the rims like a contest judge.)

For a while, she doesn't do much dancing. Then the men start to take it as a challenge.

The results, by and large, haven't impressed her; it's a pile of boys fighting for a spinning top. She still hasn't found a man she's willing to kiss. Sophie's starting to ask if Rebecca's turning into Rose.

Whenever pocket money comes, Rebecca makes note of how much has come in. (Nothing goes out. She's saving all she can, because you never know.)

She has two dresses: one gold, one blue. The blue one she inherited from Lou.

("You should have something that doesn't make you look like a pauper," Lou says. "Do us all a favor.")

Rebecca's favorite dance is the quickstep; she looks too serious for it until she takes the floor, but then her smile is blinding, and it's all a man can do to keep up.

Rebecca has the fastest feet of the sisters; of all twelve she's the only one who's never misstepped, not once.

Araminta's eighteen and hates it, and acts like a dowager countess because she thinks it makes her seem older. None of them can bring themselves to tell her it just makes her young and sweet as a fairy tale.

(Doris blames Araminta for the "Princess" nickname sticking so hard.)

There's nothing Araminta can do to shake the idea, with her long lashes and big eyes and the dark hair she refuses to cut. She pins it with gold nets and thin wound scarves, and fixes it all night.

"You'll never find them, it's like a pincushion back there," Hattie sometimes says, and Araminta tilts her chin and says, "Thank you for your concern, Hattie." Teasing is juvenile. They should know better.

They don't tease her too badly, though—she can sew.

She wishes Rebecca wanted more, since they're in the same room, but it's hopeless. Rebecca has always been hopeless, really. Doris is nearly as bad. Araminta would be out of a job if it weren't for the twins.

(Araminta thinks of Hattie and Mattie as "the twins" and never remembers Rose and Lily; most of the others do the same.)

Araminta only ever dances the waltz. The rest of the dances are undignified. They muss her dresses.

The men don't seem to mind the wait; they say it's romantic, and they'll wait an hour, sitting quietly one table over or bringing champagne from the bar.

She can ignore them, she's found, and talk only to her sisters all night, and the men still listen as though every word is meant for them.

It's made her careful.

She waits, talking to her sisters and ignoring the men, their gazes on the long column of her neck, where she wears a string of green glass beads wrapped tightly round, like the high collar of a captive queen.

Sophie doesn't remember their mother. (Ella's become her mother, in any way that matters.) She's never seen their father. She floats through childhood, into her dresses, into the dance halls.

She never pressed to go; she was just as happy to stand in Jo and Lou's room (against the wall—she's afraid of Jo) and watch her sisters getting ready.

When Araminta took up sewing and needed a set of hands, Sophie was happy to learn the needle. Sophie has a talent for smoothing fabric through tricky seams.

Sophie is Lily's favorite partner—"You know just how to follow," Lily says, as if it's something Sophie thinks about.

Sophie likes dancing with Lily; why not? Better Lily than some of the men. Sophie gets nervous around men who are too young or too handsome, and hates to sit out. Lily's perfect until the right men ask.

The right men do, eventually, and there's nothing Sophie likes more than an older man, less handsome than refined, coming to the table and holding out his hand.

Jo glares, but if they don't mind, Sophie doesn't.

Sophie knows from the way Jo studies the atlas and Lou practically claws the drapes that she should feel like a prisoner, but she doesn't. At night they go dancing, and Sophie doesn't worry for more. She's happy just to be happy. Sophie dances like a dream; she does just what you ask her to do.

Lily and Rose dance tango.

The Argentine style is a scandal at first, even underground, where the ballroom style's already known. A couple from Paris is brought in for an exhibition. The sisters watch, calculating; by the time the couple is taking their bows, they already know how it goes.

They bring it home.

"And you dance this with strange men?" asks Violet, the youngest, in a doubtful voice.

In Doris's arms, Ella is grinning and swooning like the performer did at the last moment, one arm flung out like a swan's wing.

It's two nights before the Kingfisher plays one. Rose and Lily tap their fingers on the table and sigh.

"Please, can we?" Lily asks, finally.

"Not with men," says Jo. "It's trouble we don't need."

They don't argue. (Jo's never made anyone sit home from spite, but she could, and they aren't taking chances.)

But it isn't disobeying Jo to dance with each other like at home, faces pressed cheek to cheek, arms outstretched, making fish faces at the sisters who are sitting.

(They act like twins whenever they can, even though they don't often feel like it. Sometimes they hate Hattie and Mattie for their ease; they'd never say it, even to each other.)

"When are you going to get a fella?" Lily asks Rose after a year or two of dancing. "I have one who wants to take me kissing, but I think I should wait for you to have one."

Rose flushes. "I don't think I'll ever have a fella."

"Why not?" Lily bristles. "We're plenty pretty."

"I don't like the look of them," Rose says.

Lily purses her lips at the dance floor, appraising.

After a moment longer, Rose says, "Any of them."

Lily looks at her a long time, as Rose tries not to hyperventilate.

Then Lily shrugs and says, "Well, then it's you who should have learned to lead, isn't it?" and when Rose clasps Lily's hand, she clasps it back.

It's the closest they've ever been.

Rose is happy to dance tango with men as soon as Jo gives permission. Rose is happy to dance anything with men; it's perfectly safe, and most men are perfectly nice, and the music is perfectly nice.

If, between songs, she looks too long at bob-haired girls smoking at the bar, that's nobody's business.

Lily keeps leading, dragging this sister or that one onto the floor. (Sophie is the first to offer her hand, after Rose stops dancing with her.)

In her second year, she gets up the courage to hold out her hand to a girl at the bar.

"It worked," she pants, back at their table, flushed from the thrill and smiling wide.

She tries more often, chatting up girls by the bar until they sigh and agree to just one Charleston—just one—and spend a dance laughing and kicking up their heels. Then they spend another, and another.

"Why won't you dance with men?" Araminta asks, just short of pique. The men crane their necks, waiting.

"None of them have the nerve to ask," says Lily. "Rebecca, quickstep or not? If not, I'm asking the blond."

"Stop it," murmurs Araminta. "You'll get a reputation."

"Too late," Lily says over her shoulder, and picks up the blond on her way to the floor.

Rose doesn't know if Lily does it to cover Rose's secret for her, or to spite her for it.

Rose doesn't know much about Lily at all.

••••••

Violet thinks sometimes about being a boy.

It would've made their father happy, that's for sure, and would have spared them a bunch of this junk.

(She's never seen the front door of their house. Whenever she thinks about it, she itches everywhere.)

She's thirteen when they start taking her along.

"Remember," Jo says in the cab, "don't tell anyone your name. If any man gets fresh, push—some of us will see you."

She never says what they would do, but somehow Violet never doubts the man in question would be sorry.

(Violet doesn't doubt much that Jo tells her. It doesn't seem wise.)

Jo says, "I'll be at our table. Make sure you can see me, wherever you are."

Behind Jo, the streets are flying past them, a tangle of lights and cars and storefronts lined with evening gowns and the roar of a city that's alive in every corner. For a moment Violet struggles to pay attention.

"Watch out for men without a cigarette in their hand," says Doris. "They're looking to pinch your rear."

"I'll crack *them*," snaps Violet, and Doris says, "Good girl."

"We're here," says Jo.

Violet's night is a blur of sound and noise and smoke and champagne, men like catalog cutouts, and Violet in the center in a green dress, feeling like she's shouting so the world can hear, like she's one of them at last.

A man tries to pinch her on her way back to the table. She slaps him hard enough to leave a mark, and when she turns, she runs into Jo, who's appeared as if by magic.

"Beat it," says Jo to the man, and the hair on Violet's neck stands up.

The man backs into the crowd. All night, he stares like a whipped dog from the bar, where the bartender Jake (who Araminta says is soft on Lou) looks like he wouldn't mind making the fella disappear for good.

Hattie and Mattie laugh at him, and Violet laughs, too, shrill, because didn't she hold her own?

Violet's still laughing (and dancing with a handsome young man with dark skin—Charleston or Baltimore, she doesn't remember, something fast and wonderful) when Jo raises her arm and snaps her hand like she's snatching a key from the air.

It sucks all the sound out of the room until Violet can't even hear her own breathing, and even as she weaves her way back to the table, she moves like someone in a dream, because now it's over.

Violet realizes for the first time that she's never hated anyone before, that she can't imagine hating anyone as much as she hates Jo tonight.

The anger fades in the quiet cab ride home, Violet watching Jo's face across the dark seat. Jo's looking out the car window; her head never moves.

Violet pities Jo, who can't ever have felt anything wonderful, to pull them home so heartlessly; poor Jo, who's never felt anything at all.

seven

SOMETIMES I'M HAPPY
(SOMETIMES I'M BLUE)

Jo was standing in the fourth-floor hall at five of midnight, at the back landing of the servants' stair.

She had a bathrobe over her frock, just in case her father came up, and she tied and untied the belt for something to do with her hands.

As the clock in the front hall struck midnight, Lou and Ella and Doris stepped out of their rooms.

They were soundless, dresses gleaming in the feeble moonlight that turned them all to ghosts.

Lou went down first. After Doris vanished, Jo saw a brief flash of gold that meant Rebecca was following, and then came the rest of the girls from the third floor, dots of white and green and purple that took their places on consecutive stairs.

(This was a dance all its own; Jo had trained them for this, too.)

Jo waited, so she could make sure they were safely in the stairwell without anything crashing down. If there was any sound, it would be Jo running down into the kitchen to make some excuse about being hungry, tugging her robe around herself as if she'd caught a cold.

(Mary had, once or twice, left a ribbon tied to the banister when she knew Mrs. Reardon, the housekeeper, would be up late in the kitchen.

Mary had been dismissed a few years back, when the household had retrenched. Violet, who called her Aunt Mary by then, had cried.

Jo was surprised she'd been allowed to stay as long as she had.)

All the years they'd been going out, Jo had only had to make that lie once; the girls were quiet when they had to be.

Lou was waiting by the door that opened to the alley. When Jo was down the stairs, Lou disappeared into the dark. Ella and the twins followed—they made up the first cab.

The other eight waited for the rumble of an engine.

A few minutes later, it came and went. A moment later, Doris motioned to Sophie, Rose, and Lily, and they slid into the alley.

Fifteen minutes passed. Violet sighed softly, once, and shifted. This wait scraped at her patience.

A car came and went, at last. Then it was Jo's turn to slip into the alley, slip on her shoes (not bothering with straps), walk down the block, and look quietly fetching until a cab pulled over.

Often it was quick, but she'd waited an hour, sometimes, for a taxi to take them.

The last three girls were in the alley, a tight and terrifying wait. Violet was at the door, holding it not quite shut—if something happened and they had to run inside, they couldn't risk being locked out.

After less than ten minutes, a cab appeared.

Jo waved him over and gestured behind her until the girls appeared, their stocking feet damp from the grass.

In the cab the younger girls talked to each other—Jo was chaperone, and they knew better than to gossip with her. Jo caught Rebecca telling Violet, "Keep talking like that and I'll marry you to someone myself," but didn't intervene. Let them tease, if it helped.

Once, Araminta said, "Jo, I wish you'd let me take up your hem. It would look so pretty at your knees."

"I'll take your word for it," said Jo.

· · · · · ·

Though Jo had started everything, though she had given her sisters the hunger, Jo didn't dance any more.

Dancing made Jo nervous. She knew what it could do.

Jo had almost run off with the first man who danced a good foxtrot with her.

She was nineteen, too old and too young for her age, and still getting used to going out at night.

He was a deliveryman, sneaking barrels into the Kingfisher's basement; then he was staying to dance with her, and staying, and staying.

His name was Tom, and he was just shy of handsome, and when he smiled she felt like an only child.

She'd never told him (thank God she'd never told him), but he'd talked about being the only living person on the road at night like he knew she wanted to hear about being alone.

Then he'd said, "Come with me."

"Where do you go?"

He smiled, drew her closer in. "Everywhere."

Jo rested her forehead on his cheek and imagined sitting in the car beside him, driving down a road that had no end.

She thought about what would happen to her sisters (a reflex), but in her daydream she was free—she had served her time as overseer, and the world was wide and waiting.

(It was only a dream, she thought; what was the harm?)

She danced with him for months, caught up in the music, the sharp smell of sawdust and bourbon that lingered on her hands where she touched him, the tips of her fingers tucked under his collar as they danced.

"When I'm finished here," he murmured into her hair, "won't we have a time!"

One night, he didn't come.

She waited three weeks for any sign before she got up the nerve to ask Jake.

"Is this the same stuff you always have?" she asked as she picked up a round of champagne.

"New stuff," he said. "Our alderman changed, and suggested a new distributor. Just as well—that other one was a racket." He paused, as if she had her ear to the ground and he hoped she'd approve.

"Huh," she said, when she could speak. "Well, if that's the pace of politics, I guess it's for the best I stick to dancing."

"Come on, you know all the real deals happen after dark." Then he frowned. "Is it no good?"

"Oh, no," she said. "It's lovely. I could hardly tell."

The first thing she felt was a sharp stab, a sudden loss.

The second thing she felt was relief.

By the time she got back to the table, Jo had hold of herself. The future had narrowed until it was only Lou and Ella and Doris waiting for sips of champagne so they could cool off for a moment before going out to dance.

It was lucky. It was the luckiest strike in the world she hadn't had a chance to get carried away over some boy. If dancing was going to go to her head, she'd sit things out until she was less foolish.

Two weeks after that, Lou sat out a waltz with her. Doris was at the bar, trying to get a drink out of Jake with what looked like a presidential address, and Jo and Lou were alone.

"Go on," Lou said. "That milk truck is never coming back."

Jo had never mentioned him. Still, no surprise Lou had seen. They kept sharp eyes out for each other.

"It's probably not a good idea," she said.

She had to keep control of herself. Everything depended on her.

Lou frowned. "You might as well dance," she said. "Unless you want to sit here and get old."

She wondered if Lou was being cruel or kind. With Lou you could never tell.

(Jo had kept a canvas bag packed, just in case one night she got up the nerve to be free.

Long after Tom disappeared, Jo kept the bag, a reminder that a Hamilton girl should never take a man at his word.)

Jo didn't dance much after that.

Even in those first wild years she spent out dancing, with Lou and Ella and Doris, she'd never danced like they had, a T-strap seared onto the tops of their feet like a brand. She'd never gone so wild for a dance that men started to remark, or that she'd lost track of what time it was.

She'd never gone overboard, except the once; she didn't dare get taken off guard again.

Sometimes a girl would drag a young man to the table and say, "General, you must dance, truly, he's divine."

Jo would give in for a waltz, and they would say he must have been something if she was willing to break her rules and dance.

It got easier just to have rules that never broke.

Once, Rebecca asked the others if they thought Jo was just embarrassed because her dancing wasn't very good.

"Watch it," said Lou.

No one asked after that. Lou was the other sister not to be crossed.

Lily had asked Jo for a tango once or twice, with no luck, but Lily had a feeling Jo was holding back. Jo could teach the lead perfectly; you didn't come by that by accident.

Jo hadn't danced at all in three years.

Every night they snuck out, the sisters slid on their spangles and their pearls and their sequined headbands, a tumble of girls against the two good mirrors.

("Sophie," Hattie snapped, "those are my good shoes, you sneak!"

"I need them! The colonel stepped on the others."

Three of them groaned.)

Jo, who put on her lipstick in the reflection of her bedroom window, felt that sometimes, even this close, her sisters were like a foreign country whose language was always changing before she could learn it.

All night they beat feet with this fellow or that, and Jo waited quietly in the corner, keeping an eye out, just in case.

It was only ever when they pulled up in front of the Kingfisher that Jo felt she was home.

It was home when the men raced out to greet them, five men escorting the girls across the pavement, ready to offer in case any of the princesses wanted carrying.

It was home when Jake had a tray of drinks ready as soon as they took a seat. (Lou gave him a smile that sent him pink at the temples.)

It was home when the girls buckled their shoes and slid their bangles up their arms so they wouldn't lose them during the Charleston, and met the waiting men.

It was home as the band struck up a tune nearly as old as Violet, and the sisters sighed and smiled at one another and clapped before they took their partners' arms, moving under the lights in sharp, glittering strikes, because there was nothing like old times.

It was home, until that night, when the cops came.

eight

THAT'S WHAT I CALL A PAL

The cops burst in just after a quickstep.

Most of the sisters were making their way back to the table. The sisters who abstained from the quickstep (Araminta and Lily) were at the bar, and Jo was in her place, watching them move through the room.

Their booth was the same one they'd had since the beginning—close to the back door that led out the alley to the street. It had become Jo's favorite table ever since those first days; men knew to look for them there, and Jake always managed to keep it for them, somehow.

It served them well when the cops knocked down the front door.

There were only three at first—too anxious for the score to wait for cover—and over the last brave chord from the band, two of the cops fired into the air.

One of them shouted, "Everybody on the floor!"

"Beat it," breathed Jo.

(She knew they'd all hear, even over the chaos; she knew when they were listening.)

The sisters scattered like leaves.

It was a matter of seconds—Lou leading a contingent out the back door, Jake shoving Araminta and Lily and Violet into the cellar tunnel. Sophie, who'd been dancing with an older gentleman they'd known for years, got hustled out under his arm like his daughter or his wife.

They were all so good at disappearing that the only one of them left, when the dust cleared and the cops had flooded the room, was Jo.

By the time she was sure the others were safe, it was too late to run. They had a cop stationed outside the back door, and she wasn't about to try anything with cops.

There was nothing to do but stay in the booth with her hands in plain sight and watch as the Kingfisher's patrons, staff, and musicians got arrested one by one.

It seemed, at least, to be a business-hearted affair rather than someone in the precinct setting an example. Jo knew about raids that went sour. (Salon Renaud was dust.) This was just reminding a delinquent about payment due.

There were no shots fired after the first warning round, and they were taken out by tables rather than dragged to this side or that side of the room. Most of the women were brought out without handcuffs, and aside from a few unnecessary comments to the prettiest, there wasn't much roughhousing. Even Jake got by with only two or three clobbers, when he didn't take the stairs fast enough to please the cop escorting him.

(Still, Jo watched them carefully—she could guess what the police were like when they knew they could get away with it.)

Eventually, an overgrown boy in a police uniform stopped by Jo's table (gun in the holster).

"Miss, you're under arrest for—for imbibing."

Imbibing. She debated a crack about arresting everyone in New York who'd ever had a drink of water.

Then she thought what would happen to her if she disappeared for mouthing off to a cop, and she couldn't get word to the others, and her father came looking for her.

When she stood and offered her wrists, he flushed; instead, he kept his hand hovering just above her elbow as he escorted her outside.

She risked a glance under the streetlights—someone might have stayed behind to look for her—but she didn't see anyone.

Panic rose in her throat. She forced it back. If the others weren't within sight, it was because they were out of reach of the police, already on their way home.

"I'm really sorry about this," the young officer said as he passed Jo into the police van with the dozen other women who hadn't gotten out in time.

"You and me both," she said.

At the precinct's holding cell, Jo sat in uneasy silence with the other women who had been picked up.

Two policemen took turns bringing them for the bail-money call at the sergeant's desk at the end of the hall. One by one they clicked away on their dancing shoes, and laughed over the line with whoever was awake at three in the morning and willing to come to the station.

One of the women, a sharp-looking lady with a curly black bob and a dress studded with sequins, walked out with a grin and asked the desk sergeant to dial a Fred for her.

He gave her a look up and down that made Jo want to shrink back in her skin, but if the woman noticed, she didn't say.

"Darling, come and bail me," she said into the line. Her voice rolled down the hall.

There was a short pause, and then she continued, "Well, if he won't bail me out, would you mind? Thanks a million, doll."

"Who was that?" asked her friend, when she was back.

"My husband's girl on the side," said the woman, brushing some invisible dust off her skirt.

The friend gasped. "Myrtle, no! What will you do to her?"

Myrtle shook her head. "She's bailing me out. She's not the one who's in deep with me."

When Jo's turn came, she asked the officer (a new man, older and kinder) if she could have a little while, just to make sure someone would be home.

"Maybe even until morning," she added hopefully.

"Sure thing," said the officer, but he added, "Your mister's bound to be angry no matter what. Better just call him and get it over with. This is no place to spend a night."

Jo didn't have much choice. Even if Lou could make it to the house, there might not be enough savings for bail (she didn't know how much bail was for imbibing), and Lou still had to find out where she was. It could take a day just to visit every jail in the city, assuming you were allowed outside at all.

Jo decided she might as well get comfortable; she'd rather take her chances in jail than ever call her father's house.

But what would happen to the rest of them if she was discovered missing?

She fought against tightness in her chest. They were clever. They'd come up with an off-putting illness for Jo, if anyone asked for her. It would give them a day, maybe, before she had to find a way to get home.

She pressed a hand to her sternum—it felt as though some air needed forcing.

Over the next few hours, the other women went home. They went out joking or yawning, shuffling out in unstrapped shoes. One girl, still drunk, gave the officer a kiss on the cheek as he walked her down the hall to meet the man who'd come to bring her home.

Jo watched them going, her panic growing. Was their father even now sending a message upstairs that Jo should come to the library? When he found out she wasn't there, he'd think she'd run away. What would happen to the rest of them, if he thought his oldest and steadiest offspring had made a mockery of his authority?

He'd bar the back door. He'd give them all away to the first eleven men he could find.

Jo leaned her head back, the cool brick wall scratching her clammy neck, and closed her eyes.

When the kinder cop came back and called for Myrtle, the woman with the curly black bob stood up.

"Who's outside for me?" she asked.

"A young lady."

"Alone?"

"Yes, ma'am."

Myrtle nodded, unsurprised, and adjusted her headband before the walk down the hall. Jo guessed it wouldn't do to show up disheveled in front of the husband's new girl.

"Myrtle," called her friend as Myrtle moved past the bars, "I'll come down to the store tomorrow and hear about it?"

"You might as well," Myrtle said. "I'll probably be selling her T-straps at a discount when you get there."

Her friend gasped. "You wouldn't!"

Jo wondered what shoes were so delightful that the idea of a discount was so horrifying.

"I'd say she's earned it. At least she's smart enough not to play around close to home, which is more than I can say for myself." Myrtle shrugged. "Get home safe, Agnes."

The kind cop came back four more times. At last, Myrtle's friend was called up.

Then Jo was alone.

"You want to make that call now?" he asked.

He was a middle-aged man, a career uniform (the nameplate that read CARSON was well worn). Some of the younger cops were gruff when they took a woman out, as if they were embarrassed on behalf of the boyfriends outside and were making sure the women felt suitably sorry, but Carson had walked Myrtle out to her husband's girl.

"I don't have anyone to call," Jo admitted.

Officer Carson didn't seem surprised.

"Well," he said, "the sergeant is the one who made the bust, so I can't just shuffle you out of here off the books. He'll have my head."

She was touched it had even occurred to him. "I understand."

He frowned and gnawed on his lower lip, where a little salt-and-pepper stubble was beginning. "Tell you what. Why don't you sit in the lobby while I book you for your overnight stay? I'll take my time, and you can see if a friend might be around to pay your fine."

It would have been a more useful trick several hours past, when people's husbands' mistresses were swarming the place looking to post bail left and right, but Jo was grateful for the sentiment.

"That would be lovely, thank you," she said, and managed a smile around her sour stomach.

The front of house was still pretty busy for four in the morning. Apparently when a man called his wife telling her he had been out drinking and dancing, it took her a while to find the energy to bail him out, and the penitents piled up.

The place was a crush of made-up women in morning suits walking from the front desk to the collection area and back, with rumpled, sheepish men following behind.

Officer Carson got her settled on a bench in the center of the room and said something in a low voice to the desk clerk, who seemed to be even younger than Violet. Carson hooked a thumb in her direction, then disappeared into the crowd.

Jo smiled at him as he rounded the corner. This wasn't quite a ticket home, but it was nicer than cuffs.

She watched the crowd, regretting that she didn't dance much. She was a stranger to all the men here. She'd have to hope that one of the dozens of men in love with Araminta was willing to do her a good turn in hopes it would work in his favor.

After half an hour of scanning the room for anyone who might be inclined to part with twenty dollars for her sake, the panic began to rise in earnest.

Oddly, without this chance she might have been more stoic (it was easy to be stoic in a cell all alone), but to look at every face and see a stranger who might have helped her, except except *except*, was more than she could bear after a sleepless and terrified night.

Their father got up early, and he never hesitated when it came to business. If he called for her before the girls could disguise her absence—

Across the precinct, someone laughed.

It was a man's laugh, carefree; someone who had come to rescue, rather than be rescued.

The man was saying to the desk clerk, "What, you wanted him to pour you a drink?"

His voice fell out of her hearing, but a moment later the desk clerk laughed, too.

The man was wearing a long black coat and a fedora that cast shadows over his face. Between Jo and the man there was a constant stream of strangers that blocked any glimpse of his face, but something about him caught her attention, held it.

It was too loud, she couldn't place the voice, just knew it was familiar—

Someone beside Jo cleared his throat.

It was Jake. He looked a little worse for wear, a dark circle under one eye where he'd been socked.

"You all right, Princess?" he asked, frowning.

Relief washed over her, and she gave him a smile that felt like it would split her face. "Not really. I thought your boss had worked things out with the cops."

"Me too," he said. "Either they upped their rates, or the boss got on the wrong side of a congressman."

"Are *you* all right?"

He half-shrugged. "Around cops is a bad place to be Chinese, sometimes."

She had wondered before about his parentage, and how it had brought him to the Kingfisher, but never asked; she was sorry this was the way she'd been admitted into confidence. She tried a smile. "Guess nobody at the Kingfisher knows the mayor?"

"The mayor's even worse," Jake said with a rueful smile. "You got a ride home?"

"I don't even have a ride out the door. There's no one to pay my fine."

Jake didn't seem surprised. (Jo felt like the only person in the world who was ever taken by surprise any more.) He nodded, glancing across the crowd.

"I'll get my friend to post you," he said. "He's got money to spare, and he likes playing the gentleman." Jake waved over his head at the clerk's desk.

The man in the fedora seemed to cross the room by magic — one moment he was standing at the desk, and the next he was in front of them, laughing and shaking hands with Jake.

"Told you to come work with me instead," he said. "The police call me in advance when someone's out to look righteous. This low-blow stuff is a waste of everybody's night."

(Jo couldn't breathe.)

"The bosses like a little excitement, I guess," said Jake, shrugging. "Say, I have a friend who needs bail. Could you spare twenty?"

"Sure thing, you sly dog," the man said, and absently looked over at Jo.

After a second, he recognized her.

His shoulders stiffened under the coat, and he shifted his weight evenly onto both feet.

It was his nervous habit; that much she remembered.

She said, "Good to see you, Tom."

nine
BIG BAD BILL
(IS SWEET WILLIAM NOW)

It was a relief that Tom had changed.

He'd gotten broader in the shoulders. The hawkish lines of his face had settled, less out-of-place than they'd been when he was young and gaunt. His eyes were ringed with lines that were turning to wrinkles. He moved more cautiously (though maybe it was just that she'd never seen him when he wasn't dancing).

Maybe he was just out of practice; maybe it was only that he hadn't done so much running from the police in the last eight years.

His eyes were dark green. She hadn't really known; in the dance hall they'd looked gold, because of the lights.

He stared at Jo as if he couldn't believe it, like it was Christmas, or like he'd expected her to pine to death when he went away and he was shocked to see she'd made it to this ripe old age without him.

She could slap him.

She could kiss him.

She had to get home.

"Tom?" Jake prompted. "Would you mind? It's only twenty. I'm good for it, if you don't have cash to spare."

Tom shook himself a little, glanced between Jo and Jake as if trying to figure them out.

"Not at all," he said. "Happy to help a friend of yours." He looked back at Jo. "What's your name?" he asked, too innocently.

He'd asked that question a lot, years ago; late at night, breathed against her hair.

She'd almost told him, once, the first night he asked her to come with him. But as foolish as she'd been, she knew better than to break their cardinal rule (*her* cardinal rule) for some boy who could dance. She'd shaken her head no, every time, and he'd smiled and dropped it until some other night.

Now he was looking at her with a Cheshire grin.

She returned it.

"Jane Doe Six. I was the last Doe in line."

He frowned for a split second before he smiled. "Be right back," he said, talking to Jake, looking at her.

When he was gone Jake turned to her, arms folded. "I didn't realize you knew each other."

"We don't," she said.

There were no taxis.

By the quality of light it was close to sunrise, and Jo wondered how fast she could walk eighty blocks in her heels. (If she didn't take a wrong turn; the city looked so different in daylight.) She could feel the chilly steps through her soles.

"Let me give you a ride home," said Tom, who had come up beside her like they were friends, like they were just picking up where they'd left off the night before.

"I'll be fine. Thanks for the bail," she added, not quite looking at him. "I owe you."

"You could start with your name."

She looked over. "What would you do if you had it?"

He seemed a little uneasy, his eyes moving over her face like he was looking for something. Jo realized that (of course) the years had changed her, too. She was older and heavier, with lines creasing her forehead from years of concern. Her hair was laced with a pinch of gray, and she answered questions with questions.

He was facing a sour old woman he'd never expected to see again.

This was like meeting someone you'd seen once in a movie when you were a kid—as unreal, as impossible to find what you were looking for.

She must have looked sad, or disappointed, because he frowned and glanced away.

Finally he said, "Jake tells me eleven girls follow you around at night now. Where do you find all those strays?"

"It's amazing how quickly you collect people when they stick around," she said, glancing down the street at the sound of a motor. She couldn't stand here any longer. She had to find a cab or a bus, beg or borrow. She had to get home.

He shifted his weight. "Yeah, well, some absences aren't your own fault. It's easy for a guy to land in jail, just for being in the wrong place when the cops show up."

This morning, she couldn't argue.

"It's good to see you," she said. "Glad you're doing all right. Now I've got a cab to catch."

"I'll drive you," he said again, quietly, earnest. "Cabs don't hang around at this hour waiting to take broke drunks home. You'll walk twenty blocks just looking."

It was already lighter. Any minute the sun would be up. Jo had only a few minutes before her father was awake and looking for her.

Tom waited, holding very still. He smelled like whiskey and soap now; gone was the cedar from when he unloaded barrels and boxes into the cellars of the Kingfisher.

"Swell," she said.

When the police station dropped out of sight behind the jagged teeth of low buildings that lined Houston, and they were flying north over the cobbles, he settled back into the driver's seat with a smile.

It was almost how he had been, and for a moment she was dangerously close to being that girl again, her face pressed to his lapel.

She fought it. It was a bad habit; it was a problem when you had too much nightlife and no daytime occupation. No one hung on this long to some crush they had when they were young and stupid. She was just tired, that was all.

"No luck on your name, right?" he asked, glancing at her when they stopped at an intersection.

She looked at him sidelong, and he laughed.

"Can't fault me for trying. Not like it's a strange question to ask."

"Or a new one."

He didn't argue. "Where are we going?"

"Eighty-Second and Fifth," she said. She'd slip through to her place somehow.

There was a little silence.

He drove the car effortlessly, which didn't surprise her. Once he'd told her how he'd had to shake some cops downtown, driving through streets that weren't meant to handle cars. He'd grinned as he told it, eyes gleaming, and she'd thought he was magic.

She'd been young.

"You still bootlegging?"

The question was sharp, but he only grinned. "Nah. That's a dangerous business for a guy my age. I have a dance hall of my own, these days. Just traded for it with the old owner—he gets my place in Chicago."

She wondered what had driven him from Chicago to New York. Probably a warrant.

"How long were you there?"

"Long enough to start missing things in New York."

She knew better than to take the bait and look over.

"This is Eighty-Second," he said a few minutes later, taking a corner onto a row of stately, silent houses whose windows gaped black. "Which house is yours?"

"The stone one, thanks," she said, swinging the door open before the engine was even off.

He sprinted around the front of the car to help her out of the seat and made it just in time to take her hand once she was already on the sidewalk.

This close, his eyes were startling, and his hand was warm. She fought against tightness in her chest.

"I missed you," he said, so low her heartbeat in her ears almost drowned it out. "I've wondered a lot about you, since we met last. How have you been?"

"Stock market and hemlines both went up," she said, pulling her hand back and turning down the street. "Thanks again for the ride," she said over her shoulder.

"Do you always go dancing at the Kingfisher?"

She should say yes, and never go there again. She should say no, never to look for her. She should say she hardly remembered him, that this was getting him nowhere.

"Sometimes," she said.

She ignored the smile that spread over his face, and turned on her heel and rounded the corner before he could get it in his head to follow her.

He was dangerous, and she was off guard. No good could come of it.

She slid into the alley between two houses and, suddenly panicked by her proximity to home, ran fear-blind to Eighty-Fourth, where the loose gate latch on their neighbor's fence led to the narrow scrap of common yard, and then the welcoming alley, where the new milk bottles were still waiting to be taken inside, and then (finally, finally) the back door of the house.

Inside, she took her shoes off with shaking hands and scaled the stairs in stocking feet, forcing herself not to run, listening at the second floor for any sound.

The house was silent.

What if they had all gotten picked up?

Oh God, what if no one else was home at all?

There was nothing on the third floor either. She took the last flight slowly, her breath short, feet heavy with dread.

Finally, with shaking hands, she opened the door to her room.

Eleven girls were inside, baggy-eyed and too wrung out to even greet her when she stepped inside. They just grinned nervously and slumped back against the walls.

Jo sympathized.

Lou, who'd been pacing the room with a look of having done it all night straight through, nodded.

"I was giving you until dawn before I started looking for you in jail cells," she said.

Jo didn't question it. Lou had resources when she set her mind to something, and she was wearing a face not even Jo would argue with.

"Who got back first?" Jo asked.

Sophie raised her hand. "Mr. Walton put me into a cab and paid the fare. I was home in twenty minutes."

Araminta, Lily, and Violet raised their hands next.

Jo looked over. "Lou?"

"It took some doing," said Lou, "what with all seven of us, but it was still dark, and we managed."

Violet spoke up. "Did you really get caught by the cops, General? We thought you were right behind us, but when I turned—"

"It was fine," said Jo. "Over and done."

Lou frowned. "How did you get sprung?"

"It took some doing," said Jo. "Now come on. Everyone back in bed. I have to get into a nightgown before breakfast comes."

They went, whispering about all the awful things that hadn't happened to them but could have.

Lou closed the door and turned to Jo.

"How did you get out? Are they looking for you?"

"No, the fine's all paid." Jo peeled off her stockings and hid them under the mattress.

"Who paid it?" asked Lou, with narrowed eyes.

"Jake took care of it," said Jo. "Now help me out of this. They'll come up with breakfast any second."

Lou eased the silk up off Jo's shoulders. "Jake got picked up, too," she said. "We saw it as we came around. He couldn't have paid your fine from inside."

Jo sighed. "Let it alone, Lou. It's done."

"Jo, are you in trouble?" Lou was frowning into their reflection in the mirror, Jo's dress a pile of fabric in her hands. "When I got home and didn't see you, I could have just—well." She hooked the slip on the mirror's edge. "How come you couldn't run out with the rest of us?"

"There wasn't time for everyone to get out," said Jo. "Someone had to make sure the rest were safe."

She pulled a nightgown from her wardrobe. Lou sat on the edge of the bed, staring at the floor.

"There were seven of us," she said, her voice tight. "We took two cars, and it couldn't have been more than half an hour to wave them down, but the whole way home my heart was in my throat like it was trying to jump into the other car. I don't—I don't know how you do it."

Jo sat beside her, Lou's warmth seeping into her skin. "You get used to it."

Lou sighed. "You're out of your mind, Jo. If I'd been left alone, I'd be halfway to Boston by now."

Jo didn't answer.

Lou leaned closer in. "But I'm glad you're home."

Jo smiled.

Jo had a fondness for practical Doris, for proud Araminta, for brainy Rebecca. But it was with Lou that Jo had made her first waltz figures on some dark, quiet night in their room, nearly twenty years ago.

It was for Lou she had first taken them out dancing, so Lou would stop her talk of leaving.

Of all of them, Lou was the one Jo couldn't lose; Lou was the only one of them who knew her.

"Help me clean up," she said at last. "Breakfast will be here any second."

The note came on Jo's breakfast tray.

Please bring two downstairs for interviews this afternoon. Love, Father.

ten

YOU WOULDN'T FOOL ME, WOULD YOU?

After breakfast, Jo got herself in decent shape with rouge and powder, put on day clothes, and knocked at Doris and Ella's door.

As she read them the note, Ella frowned, as if finally realizing their father's plan wasn't a bad dream and that he intended to go about it with exactly this amount of empathy.

Then Jo folded the note and regarded them levelly.

"If you don't want to go with me, I'll ask a couple of the younger girls," she said, "but you two are the oldest besides Lou, and I'm not sending Lou."

They didn't ask why not; they knew.

Jo looked from one to the other. "Doris, you know how to keep your head in the middle of something this stupid. Ella, he likes you most, and you know how to handle him. What we do today will affect the younger ones. I hope you'll both come with me."

"Sure, General," said Doris.

Ella sighed. "Of course, if you need me. But this is horrible, Jo, what he's doing."

"I know," said Jo. "I won't let him marry you off to anyone if I can help it, but I need to come up with something that will get us out of this, and I'm asking you two to buy me some time. Can you?"

They nodded, Ella a moment sooner than Doris.

"Wear something plain," Jo said. "If you're going to sell something, you need a product people are willing to pay for. We'll give him the dullest girls on the island."

"What if it doesn't work?" asked Doris.

Jo shrugged. "Then we pile on the ruffles and send in some twins."

Jo met them on the landing at one minute to two o'clock.

Luckily, catalog shopping had given them plenty of chances to collect ugly, ill-fitting dresses that looked fine on paper and like monsters when you opened the mail. Some things not even Araminta could save.

Jo was wearing a gray dress with a limp ruffle at the neck that made her look like a secretary. Doris had a dull-blue sack a size too large and had combed her hair so it clung harshly to her skull. Ella still looked lovely—she couldn't help it—but she'd tried her hardest; the pale yellow suit almost washed her out, and it was an unfortunate length that made her look short.

"Josephine," Ella ventured, "what do I say to him to make him stop?"

As if Jo knew what you said to a man like their father to get him to change his mind. If logic didn't work, Jo was at a loss.

Ella was better with their father than any of the others; if Ella didn't know what to do, they were really in trouble.

"Whatever Mother would have said," she answered.

No one looked comforted.

Jo went first. It seemed only fair.

Walters was waiting, and to Jo's surprise he led them to the sitting room, where their father was seated in front of a modest tea spread for four.

She had never been in the room, but Jo realized at once that it must have been their mother's. The room, as pale and scalloped as a frosted cake, bore a woman's stamp, and their father was perched on the very edge of his armchair, as if their mother had told him he must never ruin the furniture and he'd taken it to heart.

That would have been one of the few wishes of their mother's he had ever listened to.

That thought bolstered her resolve, and as she stepped through the doorway she remembered there was no mother any more, no one at all to speak for them; Jo was their only line of defense, and this was an interrogation room, nicely furnished.

There were footsteps behind her. Ella came in slipper-soft, Doris in four-four time like a marching band.

"Father," she said without turning, "this is Doris, and you remember Ella."

He half-stood, his hand out to shake like this was a business meeting before he thought better of it. When they came forward, he kissed them on the cheek instead.

Doris and Jo sat on the couch that faced the windows (the curtains thoughtfully drawn against prying eyes), and Father took hold of Ella's hand and guided her to the small settee, the seat closest to him. Ella sat, and let their father keep her hand, and smiled and smiled.

Maybe Ella could manage something after all, Jo thought. A charmed man would agree to anything.

Ella could plead the case for the ones who weren't yet eighteen; they might go to school. He'd long been deaf to Jo, but maybe he'd listen, if there were concessions, and if there was Ella.

"So," said Father to Ella, "Jo's told you why you're here?"

"Yes, sir."

"And what do you think?"

Ella blushed and cast her big blue eyes down. "I'm not sure, sir. I haven't thought much about—young men. I'm a little—a little afraid of it all . . ." She let her voice trail off, twisted her hands in her lap.

Father frowned and leaned forward.

"My dear girl," he said softly, "I would never make you do something of which you're afraid. I'm not a monster."

Doris and Jo exchanged glances without moving.

"I only think, Ella," he went on, "that you don't wish to stay in this house forever, cooped up with your sisters and never really growing up." He was stroking her hand now, gently, like she was a frightened animal. "I thought I could find you a nice young man, a man I can be sure is well suited to you, that's all. I thought you might like him, and if you like him, well, then marry him."

Jo watched Ella and worried. Ella was a great pretender, but their father was just as great—he'd gotten their mother, after all, and tricked her into twelve of them. Ella couldn't afford to believe, even for a moment, that their father was thinking of her happiness.

Who had trapped them in this house to begin with?

Jo made fists in her lap. Ella could *not* forget.

Ella looked up through wet lashes, a frown on her perfect forehead. "But what if I don't like any of them?"

Father chuckled. "Surely you'll like one?"

"I don't know. He'll have to be awfully nice. I mostly know the storybook princes; they're always nice."

Doris pulled a face. Jo pinched her leg.

"I'll make sure, my darling. Come, let's have tea, and we can talk about what you like to read—"

"Could I meet them?"

Father frowned.

Jo froze and glanced at Ella. Don't push, she thought desperately, you've got him, don't be direct, don't lose.

(She had as much will as their father, if they would just listen.)

Ella caught the glance; then she smiled and said, with the air of one who knows she's being silly, "It's just that I worry about the others, too. I want to know all our husbands can be friends, and we can still be together sometimes."

Father seemed to be thinking it over. After a moment, he looked at Jo.

"It's not a bad idea," said Jo, as if she was only now considering the merit of letting someone meet more than one candidate for husband. "Perhaps there could be some dinner parties for the older girls. We'll get used to chatting with men, and look out for the younger girls while we're at it."

As she spoke, he slowly closed his mouth over a negative answer.

"We could, I suppose, have a few small parties at home. How many of you would be participating?"

"The three of us," Jo suggested, "and Lou. Hattie or Mattie, too, if you like, later on."

He nodded. "There are some suitable men in our social circle. I'm in correspondence with them now. Jo, perhaps you'd be willing to oversee a small dinner party?"

"Of course," said Jo, as if she'd ever planned a menu. She'd never seen her mother's china. She'd never seen the dining room. "I'll speak to the cook on any day that suits you."

He spared Jo a smile. "You're a good girl, Jo—odd, but a good girl." Absently, he glanced past Jo to Doris, looking stodgy against the white couch.

"I like boats," said Doris blandly, and crossed her legs at the ankles.

At the third floor, Ella slapped Doris on the shoulder.

"I can't believe you! I worked so hard! 'I like boats,' " Ella mimicked in basso profundo, dissolving into giggles, and they made the last few steps smothering their laughter with their hands.

Lou was in the hallway, leaning against the wall, looking out over the balcony to watch them coming.

"What's so funny?" she asked. Her face was a set of hard lines.

"Ella was the cat's meow," said Doris through her snickering. "You should have seen it. She played Father like a violin."

Doris assumed the bland face and gave Lou the same mono-tone she'd presented downstairs. "I like boats."

Lou cracked half a smile. "That'll land you a prince, won't it?"

"Or a pirate," Doris said. "They say you'll never get bored with an adventuring man."

"Well, all four of us are in for dinner parties now," said Jo. "We'll have to see what we can do. Doris can put off any number of men—"

"Gee, thanks."

"—so this could drag on for months."

"We should celebrate, then," put in Hattie from the doorway to her room, where the top of her bob was visible through the crack between door and jamb.

"Sure," said Lou. "That's a perfect setup if you're trying to snag a cop husband. Get your shoes on."

Ella took in a breath as the notion hit her. "General, does last night—does last night really mean we're not going out any more?"

Jo raised an eyebrow. "Well, I hadn't thought much about it, since I'm still recovering from all the fun of spending a night in jail, thanks for asking."

"But that's only ever happened once," Doris argued. "Remember what Jake said: the boss just got somebody angry, is all. We could go to one of the other places—"

"I said no."

"Now you sound like Father," accused Ella.

Lou tensed. Jo wondered if that was what they all said, behind her back.

She managed, "We'll think about it in a few days."

Ella pulled a face. "With all this going on, sitting in our rooms and stewing? I'll go crazy in a few days!"

Doris said, "We'll go without you—"

"No," said Lou, sharply, before Jo could say it.

The defense was so unexpected that even Jo went quiet. Hattie disappeared for a moment, and there was a quick flurry of whis-pers behind the almost-closed door.

Lou was watching Jo.

"Jo will take us," she said. "I know she will."

Jo walked past the little crowd into her room without saying anything. She couldn't come up with anything *to* say; there was a knot in her stomach, suddenly.

She sat on the edge of the bed and pressed her open palms into her gray skirt. She remembered sitting on the edge of this same bed before her feet touched the ground, quietly waiting: for the governess to begin lessons, for their mother to visit, for the cook to bring dinner, for news that they had a little brother at last.

She'd spent a lifetime waiting, powerless to do anything— except at night. At night, she had managed to build them a world.

They couldn't go dancing without her. Whatever was in store for the sisters, it would be better if they weren't alone. There would be something Jo could do to help them, no matter what happened.

She was their general. It was her job to help them best fight what they were up against.

Soon they would all have to go their own ways, if they were going to make it out—but not like this, not on the heels of some fracture, with their father downstairs waiting to snap them up.

"Some of them might not mind, I think," said Lou.

She closed the door, and as the lock turned, Lou's face softened. (She was always more earnest when they were alone and she had less to prove.)

She went on. "Not all of us are terrified of it. Some of them wouldn't want anything more than to be married."

"Married to some stranger that Father's chosen by post?" Then, with emphasis, "One of the men he counts among his *friends*?"

"I know." Lou sat on her bed. "Too awful."

"Sophie might not mind," said Jo. "Araminta. Rebecca, if he's a college man. Doris, if he's a dancer."

"They'd all have to be dancers," said Lou. "We'd die otherwise."

Jo didn't argue; they'd gone out almost every other night for years. If that ended, they'd be anchorless. They'd have to find men who could dance—

Jo went cold. "Oh God, what if these men are men we've danced with? What if they tell Father?"

Lou took a breath. There was a small, horrified silence as they thought it over.

"At least it won't be a dull evening," Lou said at last.

Jo smiled despite herself.

Lou leaned forward. "Nothing's going to keep me in here at night," she said. "Neither cops nor Father. I want you to take us—it's best—but if you don't want to go, I'll do it myself. I'm not going to stay here and rot because Father wants it."

Lou had been a blur of red in Jo's memories of this room, the bright spot of color in the endless waiting white.

Jo knew better than anyone how much Lou needed to be out; Lou, too, thought jail was better than sitting in the white room all night. But Lou had never been separated from the others. Jo knew better now; she knew enough to be afraid.

Still, there was something you could learn every night, and Jo knew some things she hadn't yesterday.

(She knew that, for all her hard work, her sisters needed only the word from Lou, and they would rise up and disobey her. That stung; it stung her palms, where her nails had curled in.)

There were options. It would be embarrassing for her, but it would be enough to keep them safe, for now, and that was worth a little pride.

Jo could let them dance one more night, at least.

"No one leaves their rooms until I give the word," she said. "Cabs leave at midnight."

She remembered that spring, the night they'd been detoured away from Fifth, and as they turned she'd looked out the window and seen the remains of the new Sherry-Netherland tower burned out, bare and smoking, and felt as sick as if they'd all been trapped inside, though no one had been, though it had worked out all right.

She expected disaster. It was a habit. You got used to planning.

When the cabs pulled up in front of the Kingfisher, Jo leapt out and gave the two other cars the sign to hold tight.

She snuck through the dim club, marveling at how quickly some things returned to normal, and trying not to let any of the men catch sight of her; if they did, there would be a rush outside to greet the others, and then she'd really be stuck.

Jake was holding court, sliding highball glasses to either end of the bar, and when he saw her he grinned and pulled a bottle of champagne. A corkscrew appeared in his other hand, and he called over the crowd to her.

"Hey, jailbird!"

She edged her way through until she could brace both hands on the bar. Jake was smiling at her—a coconspirator.

"Drinks are on me tonight, Princess. What can I get you?"

"The name of Tom's place," she said.

eleven
FORGETTING YOU

The Hamilton sisters entered the Marquee together.

It was bigger and better appointed than the Kingfisher; the staircase could accommodate all twelve of them, in stocking feet, their shoes dangling from their hands.

Without knowing they'd be going someplace new, all the sisters must still have sensed that the beautiful times could end any night. They must have known they had to enjoy themselves while they could.

They had dressed like it was New Year's Eve in a movie, the last night they'd ever have.

The effect of all twelve of them standing on the stairs was striking enough that the room paused as the crowd caught sight of them, and even the musicians dropped the volume for a beat, as if the wind had been knocked out of them from twelve girls with glittering, dance-hungry eyes appearing all at once.

Jo was the most subdued, in a fawn dress bordered with purple beads. It was the nicest she had; she hadn't worn it in years, and it was too long for the fashion, but she felt more comfortable with knees covered. She held her shoes in one hand, her grip white-knuckled around the heels.

Behind her came Hattie and Mattie with headbands of tight-pressed feathers over their caps of dark hair, each in a gray dress spangled in silver, and carrying matching pairs of silver shoes.

Sophie, Araminta, and Rebecca came next, their chins up like the Three Graces: Rebecca in her gold, Sophie in green, her blond hair curled. Araminta's long neck was wrapped in the pale green beads, and her white dress fell nearly as long as Jo's.

Rose was in red, Lily in black with a necklace of paste pearls. Doris's dress had a black hip sash that hid the ragged edges where it had been cobbled together.

Violet was in a simple dress the color of an orchid. Ella wore pale blue and looked like spring.

Last was Lou, in a copper dress, her shoes hanging around her neck, fastened by their ribbon ties like a pair of rabbits from a hunting expedition, and she had her cigarette holder already clamped in her teeth.

The Charleston picked up seamlessly (good musicians were hard to rattle), and the bouncer closed the door behind them, dropping the room back into false twilight. Still, the crowd seemed to hang back from the stairs, waiting for them to burst into song or pull out revolvers or throw their shoes at the unsuspecting.

Jo was already scanning the crowd, looking for Tom, dreading it.

He was a consummate host, at least—two breaths after she'd started looking, he was already out of the shadows and moving through the crowd to meet them, wearing a slightly awed expression at the pileup on his stairs.

"Ladies," he said, including them all with the word. "Welcome to the Marquee. I didn't know you were coming"—he glanced at Jo—"so there's nothing reserved for you tonight, but I'll get you settled in with something that I hope will be all right, and then we'll see about drinks. You must be thirsty. Henry at the bar will be happy to help you."

Hattie and Mattie moved to keep pace with him, and the others followed. Jo hung back and let them go. Rebecca called it "sheep counting," and it wasn't far off, but it wasn't hard to lose one in the shuffle; best to make sure everyone was safe inside before they scattered.

(Once the sisters hit the dance floor, all bets were off.)

Lou was last, and she stopped next to Jo long enough to pluck her cigarette holder out of her mouth.

"You meet the nicest people in the clink, Jo. I should have figured something was up. Were you planning to hit the road with him in your fancy frock after the party?"

"Oh, I don't think he'd look very good in my fancy frock," said Jo, and moved to catch up with the rest.

There were two empty tables on a mezzanine just off the dance floor, and with the materialization of a few extra chairs, there was enough space for them all.

Within seconds, the younger girls had strapped on their shoes; before the older girls even had a chance to fasten their buckles, the first tray of champagne was being delivered. Henry, the young man behind the bar whom Tom had pointed out, had bleached out his hair stone-white, and when he looked over, Jo watched his pale head pause, counting them.

The Marquee was a sharper establishment than the Kingfisher. Besides the waiters moving back and forth behind the bar, the wood floor was polished and the red curtains newly made. It was half as large as any other place they'd been, except maybe Salon Renaud.

Jo guessed that Tom's deal with the police meant he could afford to spread out a little.

The space allowed for tables and chairs tucked off the dance floor, in front of the mezzanine, where a stray kick could knock a glass off the table and into someone's waiting arms. That was another good sign; you had to trust your clientele to arrange things this way. There would be some decent dancing here.

There were already two hundred people milling around, maybe more. Jo wondered how they ever heard of a place like this when there wasn't even a street number to mark it, when you had to count stoops and knock on a plain red door and say "Curtain up" to the man who answered before you could go through the second door and down the stairs into the dance hall. It felt like a place she would have liked to know about a long time ago.

From beside her, Tom said, "Penny for your thoughts."

She thought Tom had a bad habit of standing too close to her; she had a bad habit of letting him.

"It's lovely," she said instead. "How long have you had it, did you say?"

It was strange, thinking that he'd been so close to her for so long.

He shrugged. "I've had it almost two years, but it hasn't been open long. I had the deed, but I had to shake a lot of hands before I had the safety to open up shop, and then I had to get up the nerve to open it and declare myself a businessman."

Jo remembered one or two nights when Tom had shown up with his hands shaking and his face drawn, and had pulled her onto the dance floor without a word, as if he was afraid that if he opened his mouth he'd tell her what had happened and frighten them both.

Whatever it was he'd been hiding, Jo suspected he had been paying for it for the last eight years.

A waltz was playing, and most of the girls were out on the floor with blissful-looking men who held them as if they were porcelain.

Sophie and Lily were dancing together, and Doris was waiting it out at the bar, laughing with the bartender and casually spinning a highball glass that had appeared in front of her.

When Jo looked at Tom, he was watching the flow of the room, quietly satisfied, a smile flickering over his face.

She knew that expression. It worried her.

The night she met him, he'd been unloading barrels into the Kingfisher's cellar under Jake's orders.

He wasn't much older than Jo, and he wasn't carrying a gun or making a nuisance of himself to Jake, but still, Jo kept an eye on him all night. (There was something about him she didn't understand; she couldn't help looking over.)

When there were no more barrels, he'd come back inside, looked around for a girl to dance with, and immediately seen Ella at the bar.

Jo moved closer—Ella could handle herself, but you never knew when there could be trouble.

He came up to Ella smiling, gestured at the dance floor as he spoke. Ella ran her finger around the rim of her glass, which meant she wasn't interested.

Jo decided to cut in before this went farther. Some men had a bad habit of staying interested in Ella long after Ella was tired of them.

"I promise not to step on you—I only look like a clodhopper," he was saying when Jo reached them. He winked at Ella, who glanced away and blinked, as if surprised that he'd come so close to guessing what she thought.

Jo slid up to the bar behind her sister, planted a stiff arm on the ledge, and raised an eyebrow at him.

He glanced up and saw her.

She expected him to blanch, or bristle, or pretend he'd just forgotten someplace else he had to be. A lot of men did that, when they realized that the girl they thought was alone had brought friends to look out for her.

But instead he only said, "Oh," softly, his smile so wide and earnest that crows'-feet appeared at the edges of his eyes; he smiled as though she was an old friend, as though he had been waiting for Jo a long time and was delighted to see her at last.

"Or I can dance with you," he said to Jo, "if you'd rather. This is too nice a foxtrot to waste, is all."

It was a joke they were sharing, somehow, and she smiled without meaning to.

(She could have told him he was wasting his time with Ella. Ella liked matinee idols, and he was too lived-in; there was a little stubborn sawdust still clinging to his jacket, a little distinction lacking in the line of his jaw.)

"I promise I'm not as dull as I look," he told Jo, half-laughing. He ran a hand through his sandy hair; when he smiled, his eyes turned into crescents.

Jo gave Ella the go sign. Ella flashed a grateful smile and disappeared into the crowd.

He didn't turn to watch her go.

Jo wanted to tell him he was wasting his time. They came out to dance, not to make goofy eyes at young men. If he was looking for a girl like that among them, he could hit the road.

But he was still smiling, soft eyed, like she was a welcome friend.

(It made her feel as though she was really his choice; it was the first time she'd felt that way.)

And what Jo said instead was, "So let's dance."

He smiled wider, and it was just like the first time she had seen people dancing when she was a girl, just like the first time she and Lou had crept into the movies, and her heart turned over.

They danced almost every dance, all night; turned out he wasn't very good at the breakaway, so they sat those out at the bar.

(It was the only time they sat at the bar. She felt too exposed, she could hardly see the dance floor, and she worried about her sisters seeing them together. That was her first hint, later, that things had gone too far.)

"You can dance it with someone else if you'd rather," he said. "Not fair to make you sit just because I can't figure out how to do it."

She didn't know how to explain that it was all wonderful even if she was sitting out, that she had as much happiness watching her sisters dance as she did dancing herself. There was no point, anyway, even if she'd had the words. It wasn't as though she could tell him a thing. She had sisters to think about.

"It's all right," she said, "I never figured out how to do this one without losing a shoe," and he laughed.

She caught him looking at her a lot that night, in a way she wasn't used to seeing. A lot of gents looked at you a certain way when they were guessing their chances for a kiss (zero), but this wasn't it.

He watched her like he had come home after a long absence and had missed her most of all.

"You made a good trade from Chicago," she said. "This place is really something."

Tom nodded without demurring or boasting. After a moment, his gaze dropped to her shoes, and he frowned.

"The next dance is a foxtrot, if you'd like to?"

Jo was a little ashamed that the question could still surprise her.

It was the Charleston now, and in the middle of the floor Hattie and Mattie were holding court, their silver shoes a blur moving in time to the trumpets, bracelets sparkling as they threw their hands into the air.

"We'll see," she said. Then, "What brought you back from Chicago?"

He shrugged, tried a smile. "There's only so much you can do in a city like that. I did it all. I wanted something a little quieter in my dotage."

"And that's New York?"

He laughed. "You ever been to Chicago?"

"No."

Something about the way she said it must have struck him, because he didn't ask why not.

They stood side by side looking out at the dance floor, the only people in the place standing still.

Doris and her partner were pressed cheek to cheek, popping up and down on their toes. Lou was tapping a rhythm on the floor with her free foot, her arm curled around her partner's back;

Hattie and Mattie skipped side by side, laughing brightly, white teeth behind red lips.

Dancing was the only time any of them ever really smiled. They were never alive until the music was shaking the floor under their feet.

She wondered, sometimes, if they would still have been this way if they'd had a world of freedoms, or if she had sculpted them as surely as their father had.

The first, she hoped; she hoped desperately.

The band finished with a last bright chord, and the place applauded (either for the band or for the twins), and laughter swelled up in pockets from the dance floor, the buzz of a satisfied crowd.

The next dance was a foxtrot after all. Tom had the band well trained.

Jo knew better than to say yes; she knew how bad an idea it was to dance with him after so long. She had stopped dancing because it so easily overwhelmed her. What would happen to her if she agreed now, and danced with him after eight years? Did she even remember how, or had her feet rusted over?

What would the others think, to see her dancing after so long?

The singer stepped up to the microphone and sang the first bars of "Forgetting You." There was scattered applause, and then the shuffle of finding pairs. Doris was in a corner begging off, but Ella and Violet and Sophie and Rose were being scooped up by ecstatic young men and being absorbed into the crowd.

A gentleman at a table on the floor smothered a yawn. It was getting late. Soon the night would be gone.

When Jo looked over, Tom was watching her. She got the feeling he'd been watching her for a long time, and she tried not to flush. She was too old for it.

"So let's dance," she said.

twelve
IF YOU HADN'T GONE AWAY

On the dance floor, Jo had a heart-stopping moment of worry that she really had forgotten how to dance.

Her shoes didn't quite fit (catalog shoes never did). Her dress was too long and too old. She had put on some perfume without examining why, but it had gone sharp in the bottle in the last year or two, and now she smelled too much of bergamot.

This was a terrible idea.

She opened her mouth to say she'd changed her mind, but he was already standing in front of her, and his arm was already around her, and he was looking at her with the same smile she remembered.

She slid her hand into his waiting one, and they were dancing.

He was a careful dancer; without falling behind the beat, he still took his time. It was a rare thing. More often than you could bear, you raced around the floor trying to keep up with a leader who forgot a dance required a partner.

Not Tom. Tom moved around the line of dance with measured steps, never bumping another couple even on the packed floor, and though he kept an eye on the crowd, she still felt his gaze every now and then.

When she'd first met him, that night he was giving Ella the eye, she'd tried to dismiss him as fickle, as reckless. Then she'd danced with him.

That was her first mistake.

This was a close second.

Tonight he smelled faintly of smoke. She closed her eyes and fought the urge to rest her forehead on his cheek, or lower her head to his shoulder, where his lapel trapped the remnants of his cologne. (He'd never worn cologne on his neck; it was aggressive to a partner's nose. He wore it on the skin under the right side of his collar. Jo remembered just where. She could have rested her fingertip over the spot.)

She wondered if everyone was so marked by what they did. Maybe, despite any perfume she'd ever put on, she smelled like a dusty book locked up too long.

"Your friends are looking," Tom said.

She didn't open her eyes. If she thought about them, the dance was over. She'd deal with it after the song.

"I don't dance much," she said, half an explanation.

He made a wondering noise that hummed through her hand on his shoulder. "You really cut a rug, back when I knew you."

When he'd known her, she was younger, and barely taking charge. When he'd known her, only four of them were going out to dance.

When he'd known her, her fawn and purple dress was just coming into style.

(Then, Tom had smelled like sawdust and asked her to leave everything, and she might have. No telling.

She tried not to think about it.)

"People change," she said.

She must have sounded sad, because he didn't answer; he only curled his fingers around her fingers, wrapped his arm tighter around her.

She must have been sad, because when he pulled her closer she sighed into his neck, tilted her forehead until it rested on his jaw.

The hem of her dress swung gently against her ankles as they danced, a feeling she'd forgotten. Every so often, when the trumpet trilled, his fingers tapped against her ribs as he kept time.

When the song ended, and the crowd clapped, Jo startled. For a moment she'd been nineteen again.

It was a feeling she couldn't afford.

He was still a stranger, and she was no longer a stupid girl whose lapses were forgivable.

When the waltz began, she dropped his hand and pushed away, gently. He frowned and let her go without a fight, though his fingers brushed her waist as she stepped back.

"You don't like the waltz any more?"

She smiled tightly. "I just want to sit down awhile."

"I could keep you company?"

It was a question but didn't sound like it; he'd already guessed something was wrong, and that he was probably it.

"I brought company," she said.

As she turned to go she added, "Thanks anyway," and winced at how it sounded.

She didn't look behind her again; she picked up her hem and pressed her way through the crowd to the safe darkness of the mezzanine.

She stayed in a little alcove, her eyes closed, until the waltz was over.

Back at the table, Doris was already parked, drinking from Ella's champagne (you could tell by the lipstick) and bumming a smoke off one of Araminta's men.

"Wait one dance and I promise I will," she was saying as Jo climbed the stairs. "I just can't stand these droners. Got a light?"

Jo sat. The others were all dancing—even Rebecca had found a man she liked the look of—and Jo sat as far back in the shadows as she could and tried to get hold of herself.

It was foolish, this whole business. Her dress, the dance, the whole night. The plaintive notes of the waltz sank into her skin, and she folded her arms like she was fighting a chill in the sweltering, smoky room.

"You still look good on the dance floor," said Doris, exhaling smoke when she smiled. "Nice to see you come out of retirement."

"Thanks," Jo said.

She wondered how much Doris remembered of Tom. Doris had been a baby, and caught up in the thrill, but maybe Doris had seen more than Jo had guessed, sitting out the slow dances, sizing up the room.

Doris took a sip of something new, set it down. "Lord, that's strong. One of us is a lush, you watch and see."

"That's mine."

"Well, you're welcome to it, you big lush," Doris said. She took a puff of her cigarette and a sip of champagne, which seemed a bit much just to get a taste of whiskey out of your throat.

Doris sat back and sighed contentedly. "Not a bad night. How'd you find this place?"

"He paid my bail," said Jo. "He's a friend of Jake's. He's in good with the cops, so I figured we're safer here than the Kingfisher, for now."

Doris nodded. "He looks familiar."

"He was around for a while when we were first going out," said Jo. "Then he disappeared."

Doris dropped her eyes to her drink. "That happened a lot with boys back then," she said.

That struck Jo. Doris wasn't moony, and Jo had kept a sharp eye on them all for a long time now, but that first year she hadn't seen what she might have seen. Had Doris's heart been broken?

Before she could ask, the song was over and the other girls descended like a flock of birds.

Sophie said, "Nobody dance with the one in the white vest, he's got wandering hands."

Lily gave the white vest an appraising look. "When you look like that, your hands are welcome to."

Araminta frowned. "Lily, that's disgusting. Don't let him get away with anything."

"I won't! I've found one I like. He's a lieutenant."

"In the Two-Left-Foot Army?"

"Very funny, Rebecca."

Hattie and Mattie were laughing too hard to speak, but they both pointed their votes to Rebecca.

Lily smoothed her hair in the reflection of the brass trim of the booth. "As if I'm dancing with him for his floorcraft," she said as she moved for the stairs.

"Oh lovely," Hattie said, and Mattie said, "You're the queen of good taste."

"Everyone's judgment slips," said Lou from the edge of the crowd, not quite looking at Jo.

Jo didn't answer. She didn't like being on shaky ground when it came to things like this; it was the reason she'd retired.

She kept her eyes on the dance floor, tracking her sisters one by one as they skipped across the dark wood, wearing out their shoes with dancing shines. Hattie and Mattie were so rough on their T-straps that they had to tie ribbon knots where the leather was most likely to give out.

Jo pretended she didn't know when Tom's eyes were on her; she pretended not to know when he was behind the bar or at the door.

He didn't dance with anyone else.

The music thrummed under her feet, and she didn't look at him, all night long.

Jo summoned them just after three.

By the time Ella and Hattie had undone their shoes and scrambled last up the stairs, three cabs were waiting.

"I thought you'd prefer not to linger," Tom said.

It was halfway between hospitable and hurt; Jo didn't want to know.

Rebecca blinked at the cars. "That one's not letting the grass grow under his feet, is he?"

"Ladies," said Tom. "Does anyone require carriage? There are a dozen willing men inside, or this one, until his achy old knees give out."

"We've got it handled," said Jo.

Hattie frowned. "But my stockings—"

"Move it."

"Yes, General," Hattie said through gritted teeth, and began to pick her way across the sidewalk. The other sisters followed.

Tom looked over. " 'General'?"

"You try getting eleven girls to do what you say and see how long you stay nice," she said.

He bit back a smile.

Doris stood outside one of the cabs, Lou outside another, shepherding three girls into each, and in ten seconds they were all in place, and Jo moved to the last cab, which had an empty seat.

Tom followed her. When he offered her a hand up, she took it without looking. (She hated that she knew he'd be offering.)

He closed the door and the cabs pulled away from the curb, and a breath later they were gone.

"That was a genius night," said Rebecca. "Well chosen, General. How'd you find the place?"

"He sprung me," said Jo. Outside, unfamiliar streets sailed past.

Hattie smacked Mattie on the shoulder. "Told you," she said. "You owe me a dollar."

"Not yet," said Mattie. "General, is that why you danced with him, though? He sprung you?"

"I owed him one, I'd say."

"Ha! Hand over the dollar."

"I don't have a dollar!"

"Then don't make bets," said Rebecca.

"Useful advice four hours ago," muttered Mattie.

The buildings had the corona of morning that streetlights sometimes gave, the white stone fronts looking iced over in the retreating dark. Jo counted the streets as they climbed closer to home.

She could still feel the press of his fingers from the moment he'd gripped her hand, just before letting go.

They crowded up the back stairs, the rasping of their dresses the only noise in the house.

At last, it was only Lou and Jo left.

"Saw you dancing with the delivery boy," Lou said. "You looked pretty comfortable for someone who hasn't danced in a while."

In the dark hall, Lou's hair was an angry halo, but her face was in shadow, and Jo couldn't see her expression.

Jo shrugged. "Just like old times, I guess."

"That's what I'm afraid of," said Lou.

She disappeared into the bedroom.

When Jo rubbed her forehead, where a vicious headache had begun, the crook of her elbow smelled faintly of cologne.

thirteen
IS EVERYBODY HAPPY NOW?

It's the second night she's known him.

It's an unbearable day between seeing him the first night and seeing him the next, his eyes skipping over the crowd looking for her.

(Looking for *her*.)

She's dancing with someone else, and when he sees her, he grins, slows down, reshoulders his crate, and half-turns to keep her in sight until he reaches the cellar door.

He makes an endless number of trips. She takes dances—she's not about to waste a minute when songs and partners are good—but underneath the din, she can hear the cellar door opening and closing, little ticks marking time.

Eventually she gives up, sits, and watches her sisters. It's a good night; they're deliriously dancing, betraying a panic they never quite get over. (By the time the younger ones began to come out, there was a sense of order, but the four oldest always knew how close they'd been to the edge.)

He appears at their table, still brushing sawdust off his jacket.

"I hoped you'd be here," he says. "Care to dance?"

She's out of her seat before he's finished talking; he has her hand before she's out of her seat.

"Missed me, I guess," she says, half-teasing, but he doesn't deny it.

She closes her eyes against the smoky air, smells the cedar and whiskey that cling to him.

"Where did you come from?"

"The back alley?"

She squeezes his hand, and he laughs into her hair. "Near Philadelphia," he says. "I picked up this route as a favor to a friend."

He doesn't say *I won't be here long*. She doesn't ask.

They dance for a long time. Sometime after two, he offers to show her his truck in the alley.

She pulls back a little, meets his eye.

"You picked the wrong girl for that line," she says, not as cruelly as she could—not as cruelly as she has, with other men.

He nods seriously, apologizes with a flush at his temples, and doesn't suggest it again.

(She'll be the one, weeks later, who leads him into the dark cellar. It's summer, sticky even underground, and she'll comb her damp bangs out with her fingers just for something to do with her hands.

He'll stand a few inches away from her, and wait a few moments after she drops her hands before he leans forward and kisses her.)

Later that night, he'll ask Jo her name for the first time, and hear no.

(Ella has already perfected "Don't you like calling me Princess?" and Doris likes "You can't pronounce it."

Jo favors the level look and "Does it matter?"

That one she doesn't try; to Tom, it matters plenty.)

Her father's note arrived with breakfast.

Dinner party this evening, eight o'clock. Four guests expected. Have already spoken with Mrs. Reardon about menu. Love, Father.

So much for Jo seeing anything ahead of time.

There was no mention of which guests were expected, or for whom these upstanding young men would be intended.

Jo handed the note to Lou and sat down at their writing desk to reply.

Lou frowned at the note as if she'd accidentally read it upside down. "He told you he spoke with Mrs. Reardon about the menu, and not one word about the guests?"

"Well," said Jo, "I suppose he doesn't want us to worry about the menu."

"I hope you have a brilliant plan to get them out of this," said Lou, perching on the edge of her bed. "I'm more than happy to get out of here alone—I'll find something—but that still leaves plenty."

"All suggestions welcome."

Lou narrowed her eyes. "I suggest you come up with a brilliant plan to dissuade Father before all of us end up married off and locked up tight along Park Avenue."

"Very helpful," said Jo, and turned her attention to her note.

Dear Sir,
I would very much like to speak with you regarding plans for this evening. Please call for me at your earliest convenience; I will make myself available at whatever time suits you.
                                                                Josephine

It suited their father that Jo meet with him at two.

She wore the gray dress that made her look secretarial and (she hoped) would suggest to their father that she was capable of handling all the weight and import of a four-person guest list.

Walters left her at the foyer where it led to the pale front parlor. The pocket doors to the gold-and-green dining room had been pulled open at the far end of the room, an uneasy contrast that looked, at a glance, like a white beast opening its vast mouth.

(It would devour them just the same, she thought.)

From where she stood in the foyer, she watched her father overseeing as two women bustled back and forth from the butler's pantry, arranging plates and bowls and thin-stemmed glasses at nine settings around the enormous oak table. They looked up as she entered, one assessing glance, and then turned back to their work.

There was no light of recognition; if they had even been at the house when Jo and Lou were sneaking out to the flicks, they'd paid no notice back then, either.

When Jo cleared her throat, their father turned and smiled cheerfully, waving her over.

"Josephine, come and have a look at this. Your mother selected a beautiful china pattern, don't you think? It's so like her."

It was white porcelain with a filigreed and gilded edge an inch wide, fussy and impersonal—the sort of thing a woman chose when she was afraid to really choose.

It looked expensive, too, which was probably what he liked about it.

Jo said, "It's lovely."

"It looks very sharp with the crystal," he said. "Tonight should be a great success. Mrs. Reardon, if you please, could you wash the champagne flutes as well? I think we'll serve some from the cellar with dessert." He turned to Jo. "No harm in bringing out a little something you've had on hand."

That sounded close to home.

"Of course, sir," said the older woman, and disappeared into the kitchen.

So that was Mrs. Reardon, with whom she might be expected to be lady of the house for the dinner parties that would follow this one, as soon as their father tired of the novelty.

"About tonight," said Jo. "I was hoping to speak with you about the gentlemen guests who are coming."

He blinked. "What about them?"

Jo balled her fists.

"You can't expect—" she said too sharply, swallowed, and tried again. "You can't expect us to sit down with them, without knowing what they know about us. That's—that's—"

Her father frowned, pulled back an inch, and she remembered what it was to be ten years old and really fear him; she went cold.

"Hardly sporting," she finished, and attempted a winning smile. (She should have sent Ella. Damn, damn.)

He didn't return it. Jo held the smile until her mouth ached, not knowing what else to do.

Finally he raised one eyebrow and turned back to the table. "I suppose the guests can know a bit about each other beforehand. I don't really know party manners these days."

Jo wasn't surprised. "It would be nice, sir," she said. "For the other girls."

He considered it a moment longer, unused to arming them with knowledge of anything at all; then he nodded, as if satisfied it wouldn't actually arm them much.

"Bring me the business cards from my office desk, there's a girl."

Well, Jo thought as she crossed the foyer, at least the secretary outfit worked.

Their father's desk was covered with papers and items neatly stacked: the business cards in a small pile off the edge of the blotter, and the day's paper folded in quarters at his left elbow, his magnifying glass resting on top of a small advertisement on a back page.

ANY MAN W/INFORMATION ABOUT DANCING SOCIETY SISTERS INVITED TO APPLY DIRECTLY TO 3 E 84TH ST.

She read it twice; she'd seen the front of the house so rarely that it took a moment for their address to register.

Then she grabbed the cards and moved deliberately back to the dining room, a small smile fixed to her face, wondering how many times it was possible to feel sick in a single afternoon.

Rebecca was sitting on the landing of the third floor when Jo took the stairs back up.

"What did he say?"

"Round them up," said Jo, not slowing.

Rebecca scrambled out of the way and swung into the doorway to Rose and Lily's room. "Come on, she wants us!"

Rebecca was only a step behind her all the way up the stairs, and by the time Jo was in her room they were coming, taking positions on the bed, the desk, the floor. By now, they all had places; this was their war room, and they were soldiers.

"Last in close the door," said Jo, and someone did, the key turning with a satisfying clack.

When Jo pulled the cards out of her pocket and they realized what she was holding, there was a collective intake of breath.

"I want information on . . . Robert Foster," she read, and glanced up.

"Oh God," said Araminta a few moments later, one hand pressed to her cheek, "I know him. He's been out a few times. I don't think he's ever been sober enough to put a sentence together. Father can't mean for us to marry a flat tire like that."

"If he can afford to get blotto, then he can afford to buy up one of us," said Lou.

"We can hope he passes out in the soup," said Jo. "Next is Michael Prescott—the Fourth, heaven help us."

A couple of the girls groaned, but nobody offered any information. Either he was too square to go out, or he was too discreet to give his name to girls he met in dance halls. Bad news either way.

Jo read out, "Samuel Lewisohn."

There was a little silence as the girls realized that their father had no intention of keeping them all in the same social register, if he was bringing in Jewish suitors.

But Doris started at the name, and smiled.

"Yes," she said. "Sam. He used to go to the Kingfisher a few years back. He was nice—one of my firsts. After a while he stopped coming."

That didn't sound good. "What happened to him?"

"He said his father was putting pressure on him to take over the family business? Something about clothes. He was a sweetheart, no trouble, if that's what you mean."

"Yes, now I remember," piped up Ella. "He couldn't waltz, but he was very nice."

"Handsy?" asked Araminta.

"No," Doris and Ella answered at the same time.

"Nice enough to keep his mouth shut?" said Jo.

"I hope so," said Doris with a slightly stricken face.

Jo let it be. Sam wasn't the worst news she was carrying.

She looked at the fourth card a moment longer, as if hoping the name would change.

At last she said, "And we have David van de Maar."

No one volunteered; they were watching Jo worry the edges of the card in her fingers.

"You all won't know him," she said finally, glancing up at Lou and then at Ella. "He's one of Father's business associates. Lou, Ella, you might remember. I see him here, from time to time."

Ella and Lou exchanged blank looks.

Araminta made a face. "Father's age? He'd be sixty!"

Jo didn't answer—his age was the least of her worries—and the significance of the silence passed from girl to girl.

At last, Jo slid the cards back into her pocket. "So, this is who we're up against. Four rich men—two old men, one stranger who may know who we are, and one man who definitely knows. Doris, Lou, Ella, and I will be representing us, with the expectation that each of these men will find a wife under this roof."

Rose went white. "But, Jo—I mean, you won't—"

"That will be all," Jo said, so sharply that Rose swallowed the rest.

"I'll have more to tell you tomorrow," Jo said, more calmly. "Lou, Ella, Doris, please stay."

They filed out in despairing silence, until only the four oldest were left.

As soon as Jo closed the door, Doris whirled on her. "Jesus, Jo, why not just slap them all on their way out?"

Jo sighed. "What am I supposed to do, Doris, tell them four handsome princes are coming to dinner? They're in serious trouble. There's no point lying about it."

"You could make it sound a little less horrifying," said Ella.

"It *is* horrifying," said Jo. "They're not stupid. They deserve to know what they're up against."

"But—oh, it's all so awful."

"Don't worry, Ella," said Lou. "At least it won't be dull. Nothing worse than a dead party. We'll have plenty to tell the others on the way to the Marquee."

"We're not going out tonight," said Jo.

They looked at her.

"There's too much risk now," she said, the secret of their father's little newspaper ad leaving a metallic taste in her mouth. "He's suspicious, more than ever. Just, take my word. Please."

They waited a moment longer for an explanation she didn't know how to give. She couldn't risk their knowing—Lou wouldn't be able to keep it off her face if she knew.

"Well, I'm going to get ready for dinner, then," said Doris finally, pushing Ella out the door ahead of her.

When the door closed, Lou turned to look at her.

"I'm frightened," Jo said, a whisper that got caught in her throat.

It was like dropping a heavy coat, and when Lou moved closer, Jo leaned on her more than she'd ever admit.

The four sisters met at five minutes to eight, in the front parlor adjacent to the dining room, where they arranged themselves in a line to receive the visitors.

Once they'd taken their places by birth order, they waited in taut silence, hands folded like witnesses outside a courtroom.

Jo's dress was black with net overlay, like a housekeeper at a costume party.

She'd worried how the girls would appear (if they would dress beautifully), but they knew better than to look too fetching just to spite Jo.

Lou was in a dress of Araminta's, high-necked pink with long sleeves, her hair glued down; Doris was in an ill-advised dress and reading glasses she must have borrowed from Rebecca; and Ella was wearing a dress the color of mustard that made her look ill.

Their father came down the stairs as the clock struck eight and surveyed them, looking slightly disappointed.

"You look well, I suppose," he said at last.

Doris bent her head to hide a smile.

His tuxedo made him look even taller and slimmer, and his hair was pomaded. Jo could see the sort of man he must have been out in the world, elegant and reserved and admired, and no one ever thought to ask about the daughters he'd been so unfortunate as to collect at the expense of his departed wife.

The doorbell rang, and Walters materialized to answer it and get the name of the gentleman at the door.

"Robert Foster," Walters announced.

And the auction begins, Jo thought.

Robert Foster had a round, tight face that seemed younger than forty-five, but Jo knew that alcohol sometimes acted as a preservative for the right kind of man. His tux was custom cut to fit the beginning of a paunch, and he smelled slightly of brine.

"Ladies," he said, and smiled with shining eyes.

"Foster," their father greeted him. "These are my daughters: Josephine, Louise, Doris, and Ella."

Jo held her breath, but Foster smiled politely without any light of recognition. He shook hands just as blankly with Lou and Doris; he paused only in front of Ella, whom he kissed on the cheek.

"Come and have a drink, won't you?" their father suggested, a hand on Foster's shoulder to guide him away from Ella and toward the sideboard.

"Well, now we know who's reserved for the youngest and hand-somest gent," muttered Lou through her teeth.

Michael Prescott came to the door a few minutes later, looking like a catalog ad for a Rolls-Royce.

"And now we know who he is," said Doris.

Young, tall, blond, and crisp, he kissed them each on the hand with an "*Enchanté*." Lou rolled her eyes as he passed. He, too, lingered over Ella, complimenting the house and asking how she was finding the spring.

"I'd hardly know," said Ella, and he smiled like there wasn't an edge in her voice, and talked about driving.

When Prescott joined their father and Foster, the men shook hands pleasantly.

"I recommend the sherry," said Foster, winking at Prescott.

Jo's stomach sank.

After as many years of nightlife as she'd seen, she knew that when women were involved, old men and young men didn't get along.

For these young men and old men to both be pleased, their father must have pledged to the older men that they wouldn't go empty-handed in favor of the young.

Without moving, she said to Lou, "He's already promised each of them something."

Lou held her head higher, as if she hadn't heard, but her jaw trembled.

"David van de Maar," called the butler.

He was of their father's make, at least sixty, at least as cold. He looked them over impassively. Then he kissed them on the cheek like an uncle, murmured his hellos, and moved through the parlor without a second glance to shake hands with the men.

"Disgusting," said Lou.

Doris shushed her. "Not as bad as some. You could go to Paris for a month and he'd never even notice you had left."

Jo doubted it; if van de Maar was anything like their father, he liked to keep count of all his possessions.

The gentlemen came back with sparkling fruit punch for the ladies. Lou, on her best behavior, silently accepted a glass from Foster, even though Jo knew she could probably drink him under the table with straight gin.

"So," Foster said, addressing Jo but glancing back at Lou, "lovely of you to extend the invitation. Your father didn't mention an occasion?"

"He's putting some things up for auction," said Jo.

Lou coughed into her punch.

"Samuel Lewisohn," announced Walters, and Lewisohn, garment-factory owner and onetime hoofer carrying a secret that could ruin them, stepped into the room.

He was tall and scrawny, impeccably dressed in clothes that didn't suit him, and he looked like he'd been sent on a distasteful errand—the only one of them who seemed to think it at all strange to go to a man's house and shop for a wife.

At the threshold, he pulled himself up and smiled politely around before he recognized the four of them.

Then he went white as a sheet.

(He was nearly as white as Lou had gone.)

"Lewisohn," called their father, "not a moment too soon. Good to see you! Come in, come in. These are my daughters, and we have sherry at the sideboard. Come and have a drink before we go in to dinner."

Lewisohn blinked at the style of the introductions and cast a sidelong glance at the four of them, as if waiting for a cue as to what to do next.

Jo shook her head tightly, once, trying not to shout—He doesn't know about us, don't tell him, please don't tell him.

Lewisohn let out a breath and stepped forward, grinning.

"Sam Lewisohn," he said, sticking out a hand. His expression was comically polite. "Pleased to meet you."

"Likewise," said Jo, meaning it for the first time that evening. "Josephine Hamilton."

"Louise," said Lou, shaking his hand with better grace than she had managed for any of his predecessors.

When he got down the line to Doris he grinned even wider.

"Hello," he said, sounding like he had just barely swallowed "again."

"Hiya," she said. "Doris."

When they shook hello, he held her hand tightly, and she smiled so hard she wrinkled her nose.

Lou and Jo exchanged a look.

He met Ella with no kisses, which was refreshing, and then their father was ushering them into the dining room.

Doris and Sam Lewisohn walked in side by side, talking quickly in low voices.

"I'll be damned," said Jo.

Lou said, "The night is young."

As they entered the dining room, Jo saw the long rectangular table had been laid out with their mother's elaborate china—in places for ten.

She didn't dare guess what it meant. Problems would have to take their turn tonight.

Each of the girls had a seat next to a man and away from her sisters, so there would be no way out of making charming conversation, unless you were Lou and didn't mind putting up a wall of silence for three hours.

Jo saw she was meant to be seated next to Sam Lewisohn, which was awfully generous on their father's part—he was young and pleasant—until she remembered how Doris had acted at their meeting with him. Of course, then, their father would be setting Doris up with the stupidest man in the bunch and be hoping that Jo could keep Lewisohn entertained.

(For Lewisohn to be on the ballot at all, he'd have to be a man of means; their father was no progressive, unless it would benefit his bottom line.)

"Do sit, Doris," she said, easing Doris down into her own chair before Doris could ask any questions. A glance around the table told Jo she'd be spending the evening with Foster.

Ella had, of course, been seated next to Prescott. Jo wasn't worried about that pair; Ella could handle anyone, and Prescott's evil was bland enough.

It worried Jo most that Lou was next to van de Maar. A drunk was one thing and a bore was another, but their father's friend was doubtless the richest man at the table (excepting their father). If Lou lost her head, it could mean more than just their father's social standing.

Their father and van de Maar were business associates. Their father relied on van de Maar's discretion, but Jo knew that a man with wounded pride was capable of anything. If things went sour, they'd really go sour.

Be good, Jo mouthed as she took Doris's seat next to drunk Foster.

Lou raised an eyebrow at Jo, looked away pointedly, and held up her glass for wine. She got back a glassful of water.

"So," said Foster, smiling vaguely, "your father tells me you like boats."

"Very much," said Jo.

"Lovely. I've got two, you know, one that I keep at the cape, and then one on the Danube, for when I do business abroad."

"What sort of business?"

"Oh, anything," said Foster. "Pass the wine?"

Across the table, van de Maar was filling Lou's water glass. "And what is it you like?"

Lou said, "Sovereignty."

After a moment (too long), van de Maar smiled. "Very clever. Have you been to England?"

"No," said Lou.

"I think you'd love it. There's so much history there. Everything about America is still so young, you know."

"Oh, not everything," said Lou.

When van de Maar frowned and looked over, she said, "I've been reading some geology," and smiled blandly.

Jo wondered about the tenth place setting through the first and second courses, eating without tasting anything, listening to Foster talk up the treasures of the Danube (mainly liquor, as it turned out, which sounded more interesting in theory than in execution).

The empty seat pressed on her, and Foster wasn't helping. By the time the entrées were delivered, Jo was almost willing to drag Doris out of her chair just to have a decent conversation for five minutes.

Not that she would; Doris and Sam had forgotten there was anyone else at the table, chatting as if they were old friends rather than near-strangers at a cattle auction of a dinner party.

Lou must have finally frozen out van de Maar, Jo noticed when she looked; he was speaking with their father as though Lou wasn't there. (Or that was how van de Maar thought of women. Jo couldn't tell.) And beside the pristine Prescott, poor Ella looked ready to drop.

Jo hoped their father saw it. If nothing else stirred their father's sympathy, seeing Ella suffer might. It hadn't helped their mother, she thought, despairing, but even ownership, if it could be stirred up in him, would be better than—

The doorbell rang.

The tenth guest, Jo thought, and went cold.

She gripped her fork and knife like it was a call to battle.

Their father was out of his seat with only the barest excuse, striding for the door.

"I'll answer it," he told Walters, who had taken a few steps out of the shadows and now hesitated.

The butler frowned. "Sir, are you expecting—?"

"Oh, yes, Walters," their father said, half a smile on his face. "The gentleman has been expected all afternoon."

With no other sign of surprise, Walters pulled the door open, letting in a pool of night-darkness that had a stranger in it.

The man in the doorway stepped out of the shadows quickly and had his hat in his hands before he was fully across the threshold.

"Mr. Hamilton," he said, out of breath, "I'm so sorry for the late hour, but I thought you'd want to hear this tonight. I've got some information about those dancing girls."

It was Tom.

fourteen
WHAT DO I CARE
WHAT SOMEBODY SAID

It was Tom.

Jo didn't even notice she had moved until Lou stood up. Then Jo realized Lou was rising to meet her, because Jo was already standing, her knife and fork still clutched in her hands.

Doris and Ella stood up a moment later; it looked like they were all rising to greet the guest. Almost.

"You've seen them?" their father was asking.

"Yes," said Tom.

Jo's fork fell to the table. (Her hands were numb.)

At the noise, Tom looked up and saw them.

Only his shoulders went tight—he gave no other sign of recognition, and Jo felt the numbness creep to her elbows as she saw what an actor he really was.

(She'd never doubted that those long-ago nights when he hadn't wanted to speak, he'd done horrible things.

Now she wondered about the nights he'd come in smiling.)

Her father was focused only on Tom. "When have you seen them? Do you know them?"

"A little," said Tom to their father. "I've seen them from time to time."

"How many of them?"

"Must be more than ten," Tom said, "when they're out in their full numbers."

Jo heard Lou down the table, breathing in and out through her teeth.

"What do they look like? You would be able to recognize them, I take it?" Their father sounded impatient at having to ask what he felt should be freely given.

"A few are blond, a few are darker," Tom said. "Two or three still have long hair. Pretty girls—mean, too, if that's your poison."

Poison. The word filled Jo's mouth; her heart was thudding against her ribs, sluggish, half speed.

"I'm paying you for information, not raptures. Where do they go? I need to find them. As quickly as possible."

"Ah, I didn't realize the time," said Tom, all pleasant apology. His voice was shaking, just at the edges, like it did whenever he was about to give in.

Don't, Jo thought, don't, don't, how could you do what you're doing to us? She couldn't swallow.

"They go anyplace that will have them, I hear—"

"*Names.*"

Jo's heart slammed against her bones like it could send her flying—once, twice.

"The Kingfisher," Tom said. "Usually."

There was a moment without sound, where Jo thought she might have drowned.

(Some unconscious engine inside her thought, It's the old place, the unsafe place, he's given you a reprieve by saying it, you can build your story around it if you have to—as if she could be making plans, watching Tom in her father's house, in her father's confidence.

"Usually," he'd said—could they escape through one word?)

Then Tom was saying, "They're out dancing now. I was on my way out to see you when they were on their way in."

Their father frowned, just for a moment, like he was disappointed. "How many of them?"

"I counted seven," said Tom. He didn't even glance at the dining room.

Jo couldn't move, couldn't breathe.

The girls upstairs wouldn't have disobeyed her. They disliked her sometimes, they saw her as a tyrant, but surely they knew when it was important to obey. They wouldn't have gone out alone, she was sure. They wouldn't have—he wouldn't be—they couldn't.

She gripped the knife harder, her hand aching.

"Hamilton, what's this about?"

The four girls jumped.

It was van de Maar; the men had given up their conversations and gotten up as well (Foster a little more slowly than the rest), and now they were peering into the hallway at the evening's entertainment.

"I'm so sorry," their father said over his shoulder. "Forgive my manners. This is a small professional curiosity. It won't take a minute. Please, have a drink."

Then he beckoned to Jo. "Josephine, if you would come here a moment."

Without thinking, Jo obeyed, walking around the table like a woman dreaming.

(Tom was blinking, like hearing her name had stung.)

As she passed, Ella plucked the knife out of her hand.

"If you wouldn't mind," their father said when she was close enough, "I'd like to see your sisters."

She blanched. "Now? In their nightclothes?" She lowered her voice. "In front of strangers?"

She didn't look at Tom. He was a stranger now, more than any of the others, and all strangers could be equally ignored.

"I did not offer it as a topic for discussion," he said. "I will meet them on the second-floor landing, so our guests are not inconvenienced. But I want to see them all. Now."

Out of the corner of her eye, she could see Tom was watching them with the detachment of someone waiting to see who would win a tennis match.

Too bad about the knife, Jo thought. She could have put it to good use.

"Yes, sir," she said finally. Her throat was dry.

She took the stairs as calmly as possible, slowly, her legs shaking. She didn't dare look back at the dinner table, where the low voices of the chatting men highlighted the silence of her three sisters.

Seven girls. If they had gone, if seven of them had gone to Tom's place because she'd told them it was safe (oh God), then one of them was still sitting upstairs—too afraid to go out, waiting for Jo to return. Rebecca? Sophie? Would it be better or worse for that one girl, having stayed?

Rounding the second-story landing, Jo had a terrifying premonition of opening doors to empty rooms; she imagined walking right to the end of the fourth-floor hall and out the back stairs, out to the streets, never stopping.

At the third-floor landing (dark and quiet; it could mean anything), she had to search for enough breath to walk forward and knock on Rose and Lily's door.

Her blood pounded in her ears so loudly she couldn't hear if there was noise from inside. She forced herself to count to ten before she panicked—tears would muddy her powder, and she didn't dare give her father the satisfaction, no matter what happened.

(Her eyes were stinging. She blinked once, hard.)

On the count of eight, Lily opened the door.

Her hair was sleep mussed, and she frowned blearily at Jo. "What's wrong?"

"Is everyone here?"

For a moment neither of them moved, breathed.

Then Lily frowned. "Jo, I don't—"

"Lily."

Her voice was thick—Lily flinched away from it.

"Yes, of course, you said we shouldn't—"

"Get them up," Jo said. "Line up on the stairs to the second floor."

"Jo, what's hap—"

"Up," Jo snapped, still too panicked to even be relieved. She was taking the stairs to the fourth floor, moving by rote.

Hattie didn't even bother to ask questions when Jo knocked; she and Mattie grabbed their robes from the foot of their beds and followed Jo.

Lined up on the stairs in nightgowns and bare feet, they looked like a collection of orphans, and Jo walked between two columns of girls toward the first floor as if she wielded the willow switch.

(Perhaps all of this, all these years, had only given their father what he'd always wanted from Jo—an instrument.)

"Father," she said at the landing, the flint in her voice surprising her. "You wanted to see them."

Tom was still in the foyer, looking at her with something that might have been sympathy. She didn't bother meeting his eye. He could keep it.

Their father seemed taken aback by the speed with which she had rounded them up. He cleared his throat and excused himself again, smiling, to the gentlemen at the dinner table.

"Back in a moment," he said.

There were soft noises from the dining room as the older sisters fidgeted in their seats.

Tom looked over at the dining room, smiled encouragingly. Probably at Lou.

He'd better hope Ella took Lou's knife, too, Jo thought.

Jo couldn't look at the girls behind her, didn't want to look at their father, refused to look at Tom. She fixed her gaze on the front door, wishing for nothing more than a head start to reach it.

Their father took the first few stairs, then hesitated. Jo wondered if things were going to get worse—if he could even do any worse, unless he called the men over and told them to take their pick.

But he didn't move for a moment, and then another, and suddenly she realized what the matter was.

He'd never seen them all together.

He must not have seen more than three of them at a time, ever since Ella was young. He was about to meet some of his daughters for the first time, and all at once, and if he was suspicious enough to be willing to buy information about some girls going out, then he must suspect his daughters' hearts were set against him.

He was a fool. He'd ordered himself into confronting eight strangers he'd fathered who lived like mice in the attic above his house. He hoped to sell them off one at a time as untouched goods who had never been so wild as to go out dancing; his only concern for them had been for their reputations, and now he was standing before them, afraid of what he had made.

He was afraid.

Good.

"You'll have to come a little higher," Jo said, and after too long added, "sir."

Tom took one step closer to the bottom of the stairs. It was just enough that their father would have to excuse himself if he turned back; there was nothing for it, now, but for him to stay where he was and meet them.

Jo met Tom's eyes for a moment. Then she turned like a society hostess and swept her arm to the girls on the stairs.

She opened her mouth to introduce them one by one, but her father held up a hand.

Jo swallowed.

He didn't want the guests to know how many more girls there were, that there were other girls being saved for someone better.

Jo wanted to look over at her sisters (this was horrible, even more surreal for them than for her, and though she wasn't Ella they needed comfort from someone), but she couldn't tear her eyes from her father's open palm, held out like a talisman against them.

He didn't look any of them in the eye. He glanced over just long enough to count them, and then he was back down the stairs, as unflappable as ever, tugging gently on the hem of his jacket and looking at Tom.

"Well, I appreciate the information," he said. "And I appreciate your discretion on this matter—though, as you can see, should anyone insinuate, loose girls who go out dancing are no daughters of mine."

Tom's face was inscrutable. "I can see that."

"Unfortunately"—and their father gestured to the table—"I'm not in a position to leave my guests waiting any longer. Come by tomorrow—I pay a fair price for good information. Of course, you can join us for dinner, if you like. My daughter Josephine is hosting"—and he indicated Jo—"and her sisters, Louise, Ella, and Doris are entertaining some associates of mine."

From the dining room came the sound of three people shifting in their chairs to stare at the man who had come to give them up, and a thick, tense silence before Tom nodded acknowledgment. Probably Ella's gesture, Jo thought. Manners ran deepest in her.

Tom looked levelly at all of them, and Jo tried not to think that his gaze was sympathetic as he looked at her sisters, and harder as he locked eyes with the men.

(It was, though; it was like looking into a mirror, watching him look around the table and wonder what was going on.)

Their father went on. "I had a place set out for you, just in case. You're welcome to join."

Tom's placid smile when he shook his head was only a mask over his panic and bewilderment. Their father didn't see it, but oh, Jo could.

"I'll have to decline," Tom said. "It's getting late, and I have work to do yet."

Jo motioned for the girls to get back upstairs while they were safely forgotten.

She ignored the hateful looks she got from Rebecca and the twins, the fearful ones from Sophie and Violet. They could hate her all they wanted, so long as they obeyed.

She glanced down the stairs to make sure their father wasn't watching; when she looked back at the staircase a few moments later, they had vanished. (They knew, by now, how to disappear.)

"Come by as early as you like," their father was saying to Tom. "I'll have compensation ready."

"You're very kind," said Tom, shaking hands like they were friends. "Tomorrow morning. Have a good night, sir. Enjoy your party."

On his way out, he glanced into one of the narrow windows beside the door, trying to catch Jo's eye in the reflection.

Her throat was tight. She looked away.

Then he was gone, and their father was smiling and closing the door.

"Come, Josephine," he said, holding out his hand for her as if nothing had happened. "It's time for dessert, and we're neglecting our guests."

The guests went home more than an hour later, after dessert, and coffee, and one last drink to toast the Danube because it was a shame to waste good sherry, and a round of extended farewells.

Van de Maar had talked business with their father. Lou had been resolutely silent. Ella had also been quiet, but Prescott seemed happy to answer his own questions, and she needed only to nod and agree to keep him happy.

Doris and Sam Lewisohn had recovered best. They made small talk about his business and her favorite books; if she hadn't known better, Jo would never have guessed they'd spent nights at the smoky Kingfisher, zooming through the room whenever a Charleston played.

Foster was a drowsy drunk. Jo was worn thin with second-guessing and dread, and was happy to have such an easy problem. She spent the rest of the dinner waiting until he nodded himself awake, head snapping upright, to ask him a question. He blinked and gave her a muddy answer, and dropped off to sleep again; she gathered several facts about bootlegging and decided his business was better off with him here, asleep.

When the last man (Lewisohn) had shaken all their hands and

been escorted out, Walters closed the door, leaving the sisters and their father alone in the little parlor. From the dining room came the soft sounds of china being cleared away.

"Well," their father said, "you girls must be tired. It's very late."

Doris grinned, managed to turn it into a yawn at the last second.

"Thank you for the lovely dinner, Father," said Ella, and kissed him on the cheek before she started up the stairs. Lou followed, fuming, and then Doris.

"Josephine," their father said as she turned to go, "we can discuss how the evening went in the morning."

"Sir," said Jo.

He leveled a look at her. "There are several matters to discuss."

He still suspects, she thought, but just as quickly she caught herself. Don't give anything away. Don't give in. If he's going to catch you, he'll damn well have to catch you in the act.

"I look forward to it," she said evenly. "Good night, Father."

On her way upstairs, she passed the younger girls' bedrooms on the third floor. Each door was open a crack, but she didn't slow down, and no one was brave enough to step out from safety and question her.

She must have looked as angry as she felt.

Lou was already shoving herself into her nightgown when Jo got there.

"So," Lou said, "how long have you been planning to have your boyfriend come over and meet the family? What did he need the money for, your elopement?"

Lou was in a panic and striking where she could, but still Jo felt something snap—a betrayal from Lou she couldn't bear, not on top of everything, not tonight—and she sucked in a deep and satisfied breath before she said, "Go to hell, Louise."

She'd never said anything like that, never to Lou, and it froze Lou solid.

Lou was still standing with fistfuls of nightgown in her hands, gaping at Jo, when someone rapped softly from the doorjamb outside the open door.

Without turning, Jo said, "What is it, Doris?"

Doris's cropped head appeared in the reflection from the window. "White flag?"

Lou let out a heavy breath and opened her fists, letting the nightgown fall. "Go on."

Doris grinned and slid inside, her hands shoved into the pockets of her robe. Jo turned to face her.

Doris cleared her throat. "General, I just wanted to say thanks, for earlier. Sam's much nicer than—well, nicer than I ever expected from any man Father picked."

Jo looked her over. "How much nicer?"

Doris flushed. "A lot nicer. I've always thought he was sweet."

So many things had happened that first year that Jo had been blind to.

"What does he think of you?"

"He's asked if he can see me again."

"No," said Lou.

"Good," said Jo.

Lou stared.

Doris grinned. "I really do like him."

"Fine," said Jo.

Doris looked from Lou to Jo and pulled a face. "Right. I'll just—Good night."

Jo closed the door behind Doris and waited.

"You can't let her marry him!"

Jo moved to her bed, scooping up her nightgown from under her pillow. "Why not? She likes him."

"And it would appease Father after that stunt tonight!"

Jo slammed a fist down on the dresser. Lou jumped.

Jo choked out, "You think because I'm playing for time I'm out to *appease* him? I have eleven girls on my hands with no education except the third-floor library and going out nights—where exactly shall I take them? Where would they have a life, if we ran from him now?"

"So what, you're going to hope a few more good men wander in the door so you can palm us off?"

"I haven't palmed anyone off! Doris isn't stupid. She knows him, he seems kind, and Father would be pleased—the rest of us should be *half* so lucky."

"Listen to you, telling us all to wait until you say, to go where you say! You're no better than he is!"

Lou might as well have hit her; the pain was sharp enough, deep enough.

Jo pressed a hand to her ribs and concentrated on breathing in and out.

After a moment, she looked up. Lou looked halfway apologetic, halfway defiant, waiting for the answering volley.

"If the girls ask where I've gone," Jo said, "tell them you can handle it."

And then she was moving down the hall, out the back stairs (quickly, avoiding the faint light from behind the kitchen door), through the alley and around the corner, out of sight of the house.

By the time she thought about where she was, she was already standing on a street she'd never seen before; she was alone and free.

fifteen
SHE'S SO UNUSUAL

Jo all but ran the first few streets, shocked at herself—General Jo, fleeing from the house without a friend in the world or a penny in her pocket.

She shoved her fists into the folds of her skirt and slowed down, forced herself to pick a direction, as if she knew where she was going.

She looked over her shoulder a dozen times in the first five blocks, uneasy and not able to articulate why, until she passed a shop window and saw her reflection.

Then she realized she was uneasy because she had never gone out at night alone before.

She was surrounded by sisters at night, the alpha of a little wolf pack in dresses.

In the apothecary window with the skyline of bottles inside, Jo felt anonymous, swallowed up by the city.

It was intoxicating.

She walked without thinking, past the house on Seventy-Ninth that looked like a palace in a Gothic fairy tale, turning onto Lexington when the sharp blue awnings of a chemist caught her eye, ignoring the ache in her feet. She was angry enough that it thrilled her to be lost, with no one to answer to, no one to keep track of, without anywhere to be or anyone to tell where she was going.

She should be going to the Kingfisher, she thought; but even as she thought it, she knew it wasn't true.

She knew exactly where she was going.

At last, she flagged a cab and put on her most winning smile as she gave the address of the Marquee.

The party was in full swing.

Girls had feathers plastered to their hair with sweat, and the men had already begun to unbutton their collars. The frantic conversation threatened to drown out the music, and a cacophony of clinking glasses sounded along the bar in a futile attempt to drink away the heat.

The bandleader seemed determined to drive the crowd into the ground; he was playing a quickstep in what felt like double time, and the couples flew around the floor, narrowly missing one another, arms pressing forward into the sea of people like the prows of glittering ships.

It sounded like Jo felt. Her heart was a drum.

I'd dance this with anyone, she thought as she stepped inside; just give me a partner and get out of the way.

Alone, Jo was just one of a hundred other girls who came out for a good time. She was still wearing the dinner dress, black with net over it like a shroud.

It was equal parts terrifying and comforting that without her sisters, Jo was unremarkable.

No one even looked up from their drinks as she came in, except Tom.

He was beside her before she even got her bearings.

"What's happened?" he asked, eyes searching her face. "What's wrong?"

"Can you pay the cab?"

He frowned. "Of course. Do you need anyth—"

"I'm fine," she said, and plucked the drink out of his hand as he passed.

The band struck up a foxtrot. Some of the dancers stumbled back to their tables to recover; the rest shrugged off the sweat and aches and kept dancing.

Jo knew how they felt—at the beginning, that first year, she had often danced to songs she hated, just to be moving, just to feel music under her shoes.

When Tom appeared beside her, she handed him the empty glass. She felt more than saw his eyes on her.

She was going to crawl out of her skin.

"Let's go someplace quiet," she said.

The second floor of the town house had a pair of doors just off the landing. Tom unlocked the left-hand one, and she let him turn on the light before she stepped inside, as if cops were lying in wait and he wanted to make sure they weren't in for another bust.

Of course they weren't. Like a good businessman, Tom had paid off the cops. This place was safe as a bank.

Under the stark light of the bulb, Jo saw this was only a studio apartment, not quite what she'd been expecting of a man with a deed to the place. There was nothing in it but a bed and a desk and a chair that looked ready to collapse. Tucked to one side was a kitchenette that looked like it had never been touched, the top of the cabinets an inch thick with dirt.

"Classy establishment," she said.

He pulled a face and closed the door behind them. "Can't say I spend a lot of time here. It's good if you need a quick sleep, but I don't like to be so close to work all the time."

Just in case the cops changed their minds.

"About tonight," Tom said, coming closer.

She slapped him.

The sound of her hand against his cheek echoed through the apartment, snapped his head around on his neck, and he had to take a half step to catch his balance.

After a second he looked back at her.

His expression was dangerous; the hair on her neck stood on end.

She would have been afraid, but she'd burned up the last of her fear for the night, and all she could think was, There you are.

This is who you've been for all those years. The junior-gentleman bootlegger and the suave nightclub host who's in good with the cops—those were only suits you put on and off.

She stood her ground.

Jo had guessed long ago that to survive in his business as long as he had, you probably had to be something more dangerous than you looked to be.

(She knew the feeling; it was the way you survived a dance hall, too.)

Even when she was young and foolish, she'd known there were things about him that she would never see in the false romance of a dance hall. There were things about him it would be better never to face.

This was the Tom she was meeting now.

(This was the Jo he was meeting now.)

He was quiet long enough for her to decide she was up for a fight, if he started throwing punches. She had the arms of a seasoned dancer; she could hold her own. Anything, anything to burn off this anger.

At last, he half-smiled as if accepting a compliment. "You're not quite as I remember you," he said.

"Good."

"Are you done, Josephine, or should I sit in the kitchen? I can, if you don't trust me."

He didn't say her name like a threat—it sounded more than anything like he was relieved to have something to call her—but she still crossed her arms over her chest to ward it off.

"Funny," she said, "I can't imagine why I wouldn't trust you."

He had the decency to flush. "Josephine, I—"

"It's Jo."

He blinked. "Oh. That suits you."

She ignored the little heat that flared in her belly when his smile came and went.

"Tom, what were you going to tell my father when you came to the house, if you hadn't seen me?"

She waited for him to lie.

She expected him to tighten his shoulders and grin and assure her he had never planned to say a word, that it was all a ploy, that he had known all along that she was in the house and had come only to rescue her.

But he didn't. He slid his hands in his pockets and was quiet for a long time.

"I don't know," he said.

It was closer to the truth than she had expected. She didn't know if that was better or worse.

She could punish a lie. She'd never anticipated the truth.

She didn't know what to do about any of this.

(Anything, she thought. She was here alone. She was adrift, restless, exhausted, wild. There was no overseeing General here; tonight she could be anyone she wanted to.)

She sat on the edge of the bed. He moved to sit beside her but thought better of it, and instead he pulled the desk chair to face her and took a seat.

He was so close their knees were almost brushing, and in the dim glow of the bulb across the room, her handprint on his face looked like a shadow play.

"I didn't even know who had placed the ad," he said. "I just thought—it was so close to where I had driven you, who wouldn't put two and two together—I wanted to see for myself what was going on. I mean, you never know what can come from these things. I got my job driving the milk truck because I replied to an ad for a barber's assistant."

He got an expression like a businessman hedging his bets. "I thought maybe there was some old banker who wanted to get those ten dancing girls to his place for a good time. I thought maybe there was some alderman sending you over from the King-fisher to spy on us, and some councilman was fighting back."

He looked up. "I thought maybe you had run, and there was a jealous husband looking for you."

She dug her palms into the bedspread.

When she didn't reply, he cleared his throat and sat forward, elbows on his knees. "I stay alive on information, Jo. Information is worth whatever it takes to get it. Whatever it was about you that you were keeping secret, I had to know."

"That's not your right."

"I know. But that's not how my business works."

A lifetime ago, that might have stung.

"What would you have told him?"

"I dunno. I figured I'd go looking first. Whatever I got faced with would prepare me for the man I was dealing with, and then whatever happened after that, I'd be able to handle it. I'd find you, finally, and if there was going to be trouble we could get a fix on anything before—"

"What would you have told him, if I hadn't been there?"

Now she was making fists in the blanket, crossing and uncrossing her legs at the ankles, pinned to the bed by the need to know.

(She knew, she knew, but she needed him to admit the danger he'd put them in.)

She stared at the flushing silhouette of her handprint on his skin, torn between the urge to cover it up and the urge to do it again.

At last, Tom shrugged.

"Whatever he wanted to hear."

And there it was.

At least now she knew how he'd made it this long in his line of work.

Her dress was tight, suddenly—she could hardly breathe—and she stood up, just to get some air. There wasn't any air left, where he was.

His gaze followed her, but he didn't move. She wondered if he expected her to run for it, and this stillness was his way of assuring her he wouldn't give chase.

She wasn't going to run. She had nowhere else to go, and they both knew it.

"My head aches," she said. "Do you have anything?"

"I can get aspirin," he said, standing.

"I was thinking something with a proof."

He grinned. "Attagirl," he said, and moved to the kitchen. One of the cabinets (the least dusty) had a bottle of something unmarked in it, and he took it down and wiped off the cork with his cuff.

She stood at the edge of the dust, arms folded, watching him.

"It puts hair on your chest," he said as he handed it to her. "Be careful."

She drank, carefully, and let it coat her mouth and burn down her throat.

"Better?"

It didn't feel at the moment like anything would ever be better again, but she said, "Sure thing."

He smiled. This close she could see some familiar sadness seeping into his eyes, and something inside of her twisted and stung.

"I missed you," he said. "I was worried for you."

There was no sweeping declaration of love, no impossible promise, which was why she believed it.

It was worse, knowing she could.

She'd missed him, too. She didn't say it.

"That so?" she said instead, and raised an eyebrow. "Poor Tom, crying into your pillow at night, having sweet dreams about that girl from the Kingfisher."

His teeth were white when he smiled. "Some of them weren't sweet."

She didn't have an answer for that. Her throat was burning.

(He's the enemy, she thought.

She thought, He's a survivor, and tried not to admit she understood how deep it went.)

"Well," she said, "sounds like you've kept busy."

It must have been his turn not to answer, because he only said, "You, too, with eleven at home." Then, more quietly, "I can't believe they were your sisters."

"What, you thought we were a circus act?"

He gave her half a smile, but his eyes were serious. "I hadn't thought about it. Now . . . I guess he must have locked you up something terrible."

"I guess he must have."

Her throat was dry from the drink.

"Well done," he said.

He was too close all over—standing too close to her, asking questions too close to the mark. She didn't want to answer him. She didn't know how.

He was like a song she'd heard years back, played again in a quiet room; there was no telling if the song was any good, or if she only remembered it fondly because of the person she'd been long ago, when she heard it first.

She passed him the bottle. He rested his fingertips on hers longer than he needed to before he took it back.

She licked her lips and frowned at the floor just past his feet. His footprints were outlined in the dust, except for the point of his shoe past his toes. He danced heel-heavy, for balance.

"Was that dinner party an engagement party?" He was watching her closely now. "Are you supposed to marry that man who was beside you at the table?"

She set her teeth and met his gaze. He was too close, much too close. She was practically against the wall as it was; everything smelled like dust and whiskey, and she could hardly breathe.

"I don't want to talk about it."

"So what will you do?"

It was the impossible question, but she was exhausted, and angry, and he was here and too close to ignore. She leaned in.

"I don't want to talk," she said.

Her voice cracked, but he was moving to meet her; then he was kissing her, so all she could think about was his hand against her neck, the sharp smell of alcohol (he must have dropped the bottle), his mouth on her mouth.

Then it was the bed; then it was the little puff of dust from the bedspread, his hands and his mouth and the sounds he made when she curled her nails into his back, because she needed to hear some other sound than the words pressing against her mouth, words she didn't dare say.

"How much is he paying you?"

It was the first thing she'd said since he'd kissed her.

Tom frowned at her, exaggerated. "Is this some kind of pillow talk? I have to say it's not my favorite."

"How much is he paying you?"

He sighed. "More than enough for information like that. Enough that it feels like hush money. Why?"

So you can pay what you owe us for thinking you could solve any problem you made, she thought.

"We get four dollars a month," she said. "It's all we have in the world."

For a moment he seemed on the verge of sympathy, but she didn't go on—there was nothing to say—and the moment passed. Instead, he kissed her shoulder, the inside of her elbow, her collarbone.

(He struck such a balance between manners and selfishness, always; even in bed he had taken precautions, and she still couldn't guess for whose sake.

His body was so warm.)

She closed her eyes, set herself against this. She couldn't give in.

The madness was over. She was herself again, and there were sisters at home, and there was work she had to do.

He slid one hand across her stomach.

She caught his wrist, set it back on the bed, her fingers just brushing his skin.

She looked him in the eye and said, "I need a favor."

• • • • • •

Tom drove her straight to the back alley after dawn. There was no point in playing coy any more about where she lived.

The ride was silent; everything had been silent after she'd asked for the favor and they'd fought.

("Do you have any idea how dangerous this is?" he'd shouted, after he'd stopped saying no, no, no; after he'd stopped trying to explain as he would to a child that what she was asking had risks.

"No worse than being trapped in that house," she said, buckling her shoes. "No worse than that."

If he thought she could be frightened into seeing the comforts of staying quietly at home, he'd picked the wrong fight.)

But either he felt guiltier than he let on, or he really loved her, because finally he fell silent and fastened his tie, and went downstairs to ask that his car be brought around.

From time to time, on the drive home, he looked at her as if he was hoping she might change her mind. Jo knew what that meant.

It meant that, against his own wishes, somehow, he must already have agreed.

After he'd turned off the car, she asked quietly, "How many men have you killed?"

He said, "Two."

"Would you do it again, if you could go back?"

He looked at her as if the question surprised him, but he nodded.

"It was me or them," he said.

After seeing him in her doorway, ready to betray them, sure he could rescue them later, she was beyond surprise at what he would do in his own interests.

It was such a terrible answer to be satisfied with, but these were desperate times; sometimes you had to pick and choose your vices.

He didn't kiss her. After the favor she'd asked of him, she wasn't surprised, but as she closed the door she could feel its absence in the way he looked at her.

Jo crept onto the third-floor landing just in time to hear the knock at the front door, and the butler scrabbling to answer.

Lou was sitting on the windowsill in their room, smoking a cigarette. She had upended a little tin compact, and a pile of butts balanced in a mountain inside it.

"Big show," said Lou, without turning around. "You had the girls worried."

(Lou had been her first and only; her very first friend in the world.)

"Promise me something," said Jo, her voice stuck in her throat.

There was no hesitation. "Anything."

"When they ask you, say yes."

Lou turned to her, her frown washed out in the dawn light against the red corona of her hair.

"Jo, what did you do?"

It was impossible to explain—it was pulling the first brick out of the levee that would bring the waters down.

Jo said, "Promise me."

Lou didn't answer.

In the early morning, the house was so quiet that they could hear their father's voice and Tom's floating up from the hall as they went into their father's office.

"And, sir," Tom was saying, "while I'm here, I wanted to ask— that is, I don't want to presume, but if your daughters are courting—"

Their father laughed. "An ambitious businessman, I see. It would depend, of course. They're traditional girls, you know. None of this running around with men. They're looking for homes, for real homes. You understand."

Tom said something in a low voice that must have been encouraging. (Jo wondered if he was too embarrassed by her father to say it any louder.)

Lou stood slowly, dreadfully.

"You did this," she said, so low she could hardly be heard. "You went out last night just to see him. You're leaving all of us."

"No," said Jo.

Lou took a step forward, her index finger jabbing the air, little attacks.

"You made us all promise, Jo. No men, ever—never go home with a man, no matter what he tells you. Now look what you've done—this man who betrayed us—this man who thinks nothing of turning his back on you—"

"I'll waive my fee," Tom said. "Call it a dowry."

Lou stopped, horrified past words.

From downstairs, their father cleared his throat. "Well, that's— a show of good faith. You're an enterprising young man, I'll say that much. I suppose there's no harm in seeing what the girl in question has to say about it. Which of my daughters did you mean?"

Tom said, "Louise."

sixteen
ME AND MY SHADOW

Of all the sisters, Lou was the most contemptuous of tears.

They were a weakness; Jo had taught them that much, and Jo didn't like them in front of her, but Lou despised them happening at all. The girls who ran to Ella were careful not to cry if Lou could hear; they'd catch a sharp remark if she ever knew they'd given in.

But once, when things had been too awful to bear and the music was slipping through the walls, Lou had gotten an angry, disbelieving look, and burst into tears.

It had been almost ten years, but it was hard to forget, and Jo could see Lou's tears were threatening now.

"Jo," Lou said. "Jo, what have you done?"

Jo entertained the idea of letting Lou find out on her own, just to make her sorry for doubting, but that was petty and dangerous. This wasn't a punishment; Lou couldn't look at it that way.

"It's only to get you out of here," she said, shucking the black dress. "Tom knows a place in Chicago that needs a hostess, some members-only club where men go with their mistresses when they're trying to look rich and respectable."

Even through her confusion, Lou looked wary of a place that sounded rough to manage. (None of them had patience for an unruly dance hall.)

"It's just about keeping an ear to the ground," Jo said. "This place is where the chief of police goes, so you're safe on that count, and it pays plenty to get you in a good way, living on your own."

"But, Jo—"

"I'd have gotten Jake for you if I could," Jo said, "but this chance came, and I took it."

Lou flushed a little at the temples, right where Jake flushed if you talked about Lou.

Jo pulled on the gray dress and smoothed her hair. "You'll be out of the house as soon as Father can get rid of you," she said. "If he's as desperate as I think he is, that shouldn't be long. He'll send you off to Chicago with Tom, and you'll start a life there."

Lou's expression was split between despair and hope; she looked like a different person.

Jo said, "It's the best I could think of for you."

Lou shook her head.

"This isn't right," she said. "It should be one of the others first. We're all in danger."

Jo said, "I chose you."

Lou's eyebrows sank down her face, and her mouth was tight beneath her welling tears. "Jo—"

"Don't," Jo said.

There was a little quiet, and Jo watched Lou measuring things out, narrowing her questions, trying to decide what else she needed to know.

(They looked the same, Jo thought, when they were trying to think their way out of a problem. It was the only time they looked alike.)

Finally Lou said, "What if Father insists we have a courtship before we go to Chicago? We don't know what he'll say. What if he insists we get married? What if I actually have to marry him?"

Jo shrugged. "You could find worse men."

"But I *know*. You and he were—what if he wants to—"

"Lou," Jo said. "Tom won't insist on anything like that. This is a favor he's doing for me."

Lou narrowed her eyes. "Why?"

There was no answer Jo could give. Even if Jo knew Tom's reasons for sure (and there was no telling any more, everything now was a series of gambles), the words to name his reasons were trapped in her throat, prisoners of the last seven years.

Best to let things like that lie. These were uncertain times.

"Josephine," their father called up the stairs. "Please come down, and bring Louise."

Lou startled and looked around as if their father had been listening. After a moment, she moved to her closet and grabbed for a suitable dress.

Jo smoothed her skirt, wondering why she was bothering. It didn't matter now what she looked like.

"Fix your hair before we go down," she said to Lou. "You'll scare someone."

Jo didn't ask what Lou had decided. She watched Lou scramble into a dress (a deep brown that suited her), comb through her hair with her fingers, rouge her cheeks, and guessed how Lou's decision had gone.

It was the best offer any of them was likely to get, and Lou wasn't stupid.

The other girls peeked out from their open doors as they passed, but they seemed so surprised to see Jo back that none of them so much as opened her mouth.

Tom and their father were in the study; apparently Lou didn't merit the parlor for so small a thing as marriage. There was a decanter on the desk, and one empty glass in front of each of the men. No provision had been made for Lou and Jo—naturally, they didn't drink.

"Louise," Father greeted them. "I'd like to introduce you to someone. This is Tom Marlowe."

Jo hadn't known his last name before.

"Mr. Marlowe," Lou said, and held out her hand for him to shake.

Tom rose, searching her face as they shook hands, looking for a sign that she knew what was at stake.

He must have found it; he smiled.

Jo didn't know where to look.

"Mr. Marlowe is a business associate of mine," their father said. "He came by last night and was quite taken with you, though I don't know if you met properly then. Josephine, you remember Mr. Marlowe."

"I do," she said, glanced at Tom, felt like the room was closing in around them.

"He's asked my permission to court you, Louise," their father said. "I trust you're amenable?"

Naturally, Jo thought; just as he'd trusted Lou would be amenable to van de Maar, before Tom had put ready money on the table as a gesture of goodwill and smuggled Lou right out from under him.

This was what Jo hadn't known—how much their father valued Louise.

After Lou's stonewall showing at the dinner party, Jo had gambled on "not much." Their father must have known that was a nonstarter and figured that in desperate times, something was better than nothing. Now he was letting her go to someone for less than a tenth of what a wife was worth to van de Maar.

Jo had gambled and won.

Lou glanced at Jo, then stared at their father as if the whole thing were only now coming clear, as if she realized for the first time what sort of man Jo had been keeping away from the rest of them.

Jo understood. Even now, with the outcome she'd put in motion herself, she felt as though she was trying to keep back an avalanche. She thought how impossible even a waiting game would be now, and was glad Lou wouldn't see what happened if Jo failed.

"Yes, sir," said Lou. "I'm amenable."

When she looked at Tom, Tom smiled, the genuine camaraderie of two people sharing a gallows joke.

Lou returned it. It was the first real smile Jo had seen from her in a while.

"Well," their father said, "that's nice to hear. Tom?" He poured the two glasses of liquor and toasted to Tom, with an absent gesture to Lou before he drank.

Tom glanced at Jo over the rim of his glass, just before he drank.

Their father set the glass down with purpose. "Now, why don't you two go on to the parlor and I'll have the cook send something out for lunch?"

"Lovely," said Lou.

As Tom and their father stood up, their father leaned across the desk, stone-faced. "Marlowe, I don't believe in extended courtships. It keeps things uncertain that shouldn't be so."

Tom glanced at Lou and nodded, the picture of a serious suitor. "I understand, sir. She's a swell girl; if she thinks well of me, I hope to be taking her back to Chicago with me before long."

"As do I," their father said. At the idea of a speedy courtship, he'd managed a smile. "Come with me into the parlor. Jo, thank you, you can go back upstairs. I'll speak with you later about last night."

As they passed Jo, Tom glanced at her sidelong and extended a hand to shake good-bye. She was too slow meeting him; he brushed the tips of her fingers, just skimmed her skirt.

A moment later they were gone, their voices filling the hall, fading as they turned the corner into the parlor. Tom said something Jo couldn't hear, and all the way from the parlor Lou's laugh echoed.

Jo wasn't surprised. Tom had that effect on a girl.

• • • • • •

On Jo's way up, Rebecca opened the door. She was only visible for a moment; when she saw Jo was alone she closed the door again, and the whispers began.

The whispers would spread—these girls could walk through walls—and within the hour all ten of them would know that Lou was downstairs with some man, and Jo had abandoned her.

Their bedroom was quiet and bright white without Lou in it. Jo went to the window—she needed air, suddenly.

In the morning light, Eighty-Fourth Street looked fresh and busy and open, as if leaving room for the wonderful something that could happen any moment.

Jo stared at the hats of the passersby, gripped the sill until her knuckles went white.

Twelve P.M. The upstairs maid brought the lunch trays. Jo's was set for only one; Lou was still in the parlor with their father and Tom.

One P.M. Jo went into the library to calm her nerves with the atlas.

One thirty P.M. She gave up. No matter what page she looked at—Russia, China, Mexico, Iceland—she thought of Lou on the road to Chicago, Tom showing her how to drive, the two of them laughing about their clever escape.

She was too restless, too uncertain, to speak to Ella or Doris. She was waiting for word from Lou or a summons from Father—anything that would put affairs in order.

Jo needed a new hobby. Araminta and Sophie remade dresses by hand; Jo should take up sewing. That was useful, and it made the time go faster.

Two P.M. Someone knocked at the door, the timid tapping of someone afraid to face her. (One of the little ones, then.) She didn't answer; there was nothing to say.

Three P.M. Jo sorted out her wardrobe, arranging and

rearranging her dresses: day and night. There were only eight of them—it was hard to convince their father that they needed many dresses, and they tended to wait until the last moment to ask for anything, so they could present something suitably shabby.

The black dress was still in the bottom of the wardrobe. She took it to the hall bath and washed it in the sink with a little white vinegar, which got the scent out without the color bleeding. (Mary had shown them, long ago, as if she'd known they'd need it.)

As she hung it on the wardrobe door to dry, her chest got tight for a moment. When it passed she felt foolish, and made her bed again just for something to do besides stare at the windowpanes like they were the bars of a birdcage.

Four P.M. Lou came up the stairs and closed the door with a firm click before she turned to Jo and broke out with a smile in earnest.

"I leave tomorrow," she said. Her eyes were wild with the terrified delight of the pardoned prisoner. "Tonight Tom and Father will go over Tom's finances, to make sure he can provide for me." Lou rolled her eyes. "Then it's straight on to Chicago."

"That's . . . very efficient," Jo managed.

Lou wrinkled her nose. "Tom didn't give him any reason to delay. Father started out talking a month or two, and Tom agreed, but then Tom kept talking and before I knew it my bags were practically packed. I don't think Father even noticed the runaround Tom gave him. Tom's very clever."

"I know," said Jo through a dry throat.

"Of course." Lou moved to the closet and began to sort through her dresses as if she had a hundred instead of ten and would have to leave some behind. There was a hint of panic about it, as if she was under surveillance and anything that went wrong now would lock her in the house forever.

"I've got to pack, somehow. Father said I should pull one of the trunks out of the old nannies' room and not waste any time."

Lou stopped and turned, as if she'd just realized how this happiness might look to Jo.

"I'm glad for you," Jo said. "Does he want to see me?"

Lou nodded.

It was strange to think that their father's office, which a week ago had been another country, was now so familiar that she knocked only twice before entering.

She plastered a polite smile on her face.

Tom was still standing in front of their father's desk, shaking hands, shifting his weight as if he was eager to be gone.

"Father," said Jo from the doorway. She watched Tom's shoulders go tense.

"Ah, Josephine. Come in, come in. Mr. Marlowe was just leaving. As a very happy man, I might add."

Tom turned and gave her the sort of smile a young man wears when meeting his beloved's spinster aunt.

"Congratulations," she said. "Best wishes."

She shook his hand. It ached.

His gaze was dark and unwavering. Her misery was probably palpable, but she met his eyes anyway. There was nothing to fear from him now; he could hardly kiss her in front of her father, and the next day he would be gone to Chicago with Lou. He wouldn't be back for weeks or months, and even then—

"I'll see you tomorrow, sir," Tom was saying. "Josephine, nice to meet you."

He perched his fedora on his head and was gone.

Their father sat back in his chair and laced his fingers over his slim stomach, the picture of satisfaction. "I knew this would work out in the end," he said, as if to himself.

Then he remembered Jo. "Now, about last night."

"Van de Maar will be disappointed," Jo said, taking a seat. Outside the study windows, Tom was revving the engine, hopping into his car, disappearing into the traffic.

She let her feelings disappear with him. There wasn't time to mope; she had to think sharp.

"Van de Maar will understand, I think," said their father, and Jo wondered if that meant there were other daughters in the wings who had been earmarked for van de Maar's understanding. "How did you like Foster?"

"I can't say I did," said Jo. "I don't know if I trust a man who"— she stopped herself from saying *can't hold his drink* just in time— "drinks so much in front of ladies."

Their father nodded. "A fair point," he said. "Foster has always been a little blind to excess. Well, if you don't like him, that's all settled, then. Have you spoken to Ella and Doris?"

It had been settled quickly—too quickly—and Jo suspected something terrible looming even as she answered. "Ella seemed very quiet at dinner," Jo said, "and she hasn't said anything to me this morning about Prescott one way or the other. He seems to be very refined?"

"He is," their father said. "He comes from a very influential family. Ella would be a lucky woman if she could become Mrs. Prescott—probably a chairman's wife someday. I trust she'll keep that in mind."

Because nothing seduced a girl like the idea of becoming the chairman's wife in a family even more ambitious than her father's.

"Yes, sir. When will he visit again, do you know?"

"Soon, I suspect. He seemed to like her. What about Doris? She and that Lewisohn boy seemed to get along. I wasn't expecting that."

"She likes him enormously, I think," Jo said, and managed a genuine smile. "She already told me she'd like to see him again."

"Excellent," said their father. "I'll start thinking about another small party next week, then. I'll tell Mrs. Reardon so she has time to get something decent. I didn't like the pheasant this time— nasty bird, pheasant, unless you know how to cook it. And Pavlova for dessert. Lewisohn will be for Doris," he said, like it was still a discussion of the menu, "and tell Doris she'd better lock him in before he gets wind of her strange thinking and changes his mind—and we'll get some of the other girls downstairs in the meantime. What are their names? The twins, I mean, next ones in line. Matilda?"

"Hattie and Mattie," Jo said, her skin crawling. "The twins." The older twins. She couldn't even imagine him succeeding so far down the list of them that he got to Rose and Lily.

"Right." He smiled. "That should be a joke, shouldn't it? You can just change them around until everyone gets along, and no one's the wiser."

Jo blinked at him and didn't answer.

"Well, that's all," their father said, taking up the paper. "I'll call you or Louise if you're needed."

She stood, feeling numb, and turned for the door.

"And tell Ella to make up her mind soon," he said. "If it's not Prescott it had better be the next one. We can't let word get out about a houseful of choosy girls."

Though she should not by then have been shocked at anything their father said, still the words stopped her in her tracks.

She had also rejected the first choice; would she now be bound to the second?

Carefully, she asked, "And what about me, sir?"

He waved a hand. "I have other plans for you," he said, "don't you worry. Now go along."

Jo could have hit him; she could have picked up one of the paperweights off his blotter and thrown it at him hard enough to knock him right out of his chair.

For a moment her hand felt heavy, as if she really could take aim and bring him down.

But if he got up again, God help all of them. That was the trouble. Even after all of this, there was still something to lose.

"Yes, sir," she said.

Jo had to give Lou credit for efficiency.

While Jo was gone, Lou had dragged a small trunk down from the attic. It had been mostly wiped clean of dust, except near the hinges, where she hadn't bothered. Now she was folding her dresses as fast as she could, as if nothing could backfire once her trunk was packed.

When Jo came into their room, Lou looked up, hugging a green dress to her chest as if she'd been caught out.

Jo had never seen her this way; Lou had never been hopeful before. She was a different creature.

It helped; not as much as it hurt, but it helped.

"Jo," she said, "I want to thank you. I—I can't believe I'm getting out of this house. I should be afraid, shouldn't I?"

Jo thought about Lou and Tom in the front seat of his car, driving through open country, and wondered what there was to fear.

"I should be terrified," Lou answered herself, "but all I can think about is what it looks like outside the city—what it really looks like, not just in pictures."

The green dress went into the trunk; a nightgown appeared in her hands.

"Your Tom is the cleverest cat I ever saw," she said, her eyes feverish. "He handled Father like it was a parlor trick! I could hardly stop myself from laughing and ruining everything."

Jo's black dress was still hanging on the outside of her wardrobe door. The late-afternoon sun filtered through the net, and the dress looked as if it had been covered with dust, forgotten for a hundred years.

Lou was inspecting pots of rouge, holding one up to her face in the mirror. "How was Father with you? You arranged everything, I'm sure, you're as smart as he is, that old bastard. Is everything settled for Doris?"

"Soon," Jo said, feeling like her throat was turning to mud.

"Good." Lou knelt to look through her pile of ruined shoes. After a moment the sound stopped, and Lou said to the inside of the closet, "I shouldn't have doubted you, Jo. I'm really sorry. Of course you know what you're doing. You've always looked out for us."

Lou sat back on her heels and looked over her shoulder. Jo saw she was holding a pair of gold shoes in her lap—one of her first catalog pairs, Jo remembered—so worn down that the strap had vanished and every last flake of glitter was gone.

Lou had bought them that first year at the Kingfisher, when it was still just the four of them dancing and Jo was in love with Tom.

"Once you're out, don't ever come back here," Jo said, quietly, and left.

She sat in the library a long time without bothering to turn on a light; there wasn't much, just now, that she wanted to see.

seventeen
SOME SUNNY DAY

Lou was almost done packing by the time Jo came back to the room. The bronze dress Lou wore out dancing was draped over her bedspread, the only thing of Lou's left.

"I want to go out," said Lou.

Jo felt too empty to argue anything except, "It's dangerous."

"I know. But the girls have been trapped like mice up here for two days, and this is the last time we'll all be together for God knows how long. I want to leave off like we started—dancing."

The difference between now and when they had started was that they were no longer invisible. Their father's suspicious eye was on them now, and he was determined to keep them unsullied goods in a busy market.

But Jo was too tired to be frightened, just now, and Lou was right. Who knew when any of them might ever see her again?

No. That didn't bear thinking about.

And under all that was something deeper and meaner and true; Jo wanted to see him, just once, before he was someone else's husband, and gone for good.

"Call them in," Jo said.

Jo had washed her face with cold water on her way back from the library—she had been flushed—and when she was alone she rested her fingertips on her temples for a moment, just to bring a little feeling back.

The room filled with them, primly, as if they'd been prepared for a scolding.

"All in, General," said Doris, closing the door. She moved behind the younger girls, rested one hand on Sophie's shoulder and the other on Violet's.

Then eleven pairs of eyes were fixed on Jo, and for the space of a breath she felt the impossible weight of protecting any of them, let alone all of them, and hated their mother for dying.

"This is how things stand," she said when she trusted her voice. "Lou is leaving us. She leaves tomorrow for Chicago, with a man named Tom Marlowe. You might remember him from the Marquee—he was the host there."

The silence was absolute. Jo could hear pigeons walking on the ledge, it was so quiet.

At last, Ella ventured, a hint of poison in the tone, "Tom from last night?"

"Yes," said Jo, and pressed on quickly, "he was very taken with Lou at the Marquee, and didn't like the look of the gentleman she was with last night, and so everything is already settled with Father."

A moment too late to be casual, Doris whistled and said, "Lord, you dodged a bullet, Lou. That other one's a mummy."

"But you—but Father called us down in front of him," Violet said, her voice shaking. Fear or anger, it was hard to say. "It was so awful."

You. Jo's throat went dry.

"He suspects us, from the papers," Lou said. "Tom put him off the trail."

"Then he has a terrible way of going about it," said Rebecca.

Hattie and Mattie exchanged unconvinced looks.

Sophie whispered, "Tomorrow? She's going tomorrow?"

Jo ignored it. Sophie wasn't deaf; if she didn't like it, that wasn't Jo's problem.

"Doris will be seeing Sam Lewisohn again, since she was so keen on him the first time."

Hattie and Mattie, who were recovering from the first round of bad news, snickered and kissed their own fists with relish.

Araminta blushed and whispered something to her, but Doris was grinning too hard to mind either the twins or Araminta's advice about dealing with teasing.

When the kissing noises died down, Doris said, "I liked Sam back when he danced, and I like him now."

"Yeah," said Lily, "but he's just some man."

"Hey." Doris lifted a finger. "He's just some man I *like*. There's a big difference. You be nice."

"You said he hardly dances now!" moaned Rebecca.

Doris flushed. "Well, at least he dances, and well enough for me. Who knows if this Tom fellow is any good at dancing, either? You're a bunch of nosey parkers."

"You'll have a chance to see for yourself," said Jo. "We're going out to his place."

A ripple of relief ran through the room.

It was too loud, too happy; it was a gloss over an unspoken thrum of mutiny so sharp that Jo felt like someone had snapped a rubber band against her wrist.

Lou hadn't been lying about the girls being ready to bolt, if Jo tried to hold them. If she had said no tonight, they might well have sneaked out from under her, even after everything.

Jo resented the undercurrent—as if she had chosen to give them a terrible father, and to be his envoy.

"Enjoy it," she said. "It might be the last time we go dancing for a while. It *will* be the last time we go out dancing all together. Tomorrow Lou leaves us. Doris won't be far behind her, and then it will be Hattie and Mattie's turn to be thrown to the wolves."

The murmurs rose, though Hattie and Mattie fell suddenly silent.

"Cabs at midnight," Jo said, to shut them up.

The girls were gone like leaves.

When they were alone, Lou said, "Don't you want the girls to know you set me up with Tom?"

"No," said Jo. "I don't want them to think I can pull more decent men out of a hat. He's the only man I know."

"Nonsense. We know nothing but men." But Lou frowned. "Jo, I want to be free of this house, but—what will happen to you?"

"Get your dress on," said Jo. "You should look good tonight."

Hattie and Mattie slid into the taxi opposite Jo and Lou. Their matching shoes were clutched to their chests, and two identical pairs of wide eyes gleamed in the dark.

"Who has Father chosen?" Hattie asked.

"Has he told you yet?" Mattie said.

Jo shrugged. "As soon as I know, you'll know."

"But he won't make us marry anyone we don't like, will he?"

Hattie said, "We're not like Doris and Lou. We've never met a man we'd want to have around."

"We want to go on just as we are—"

"—and you can't just let him—"

"Quit it," said Lou. "Like she doesn't have enough to handle without you two squawking at her about things she can't help. Pipe down."

(Lou had never contradicted her in front of the little ones; a general needed a united front.)

Jo wondered what Lou was thinking now, besides that she would soon be out from under their roof forever.

Maybe Lou really thought there was something Jo could do, as if she was just waiting for the full moon to turn them all into swans and throw open the windows.

The twins settled into a tense silence.

Jo looked out the window and counted the streets as the numbers on the buildings dropped, falling closer and closer to zero on the way to the Marquee.

Autumn was coming, and the sidewalk was just cold enough that they all danced on their stocking feet over the pavement and up the stairs, where the burly doorman couldn't help but smile back at the chorus line of grinning faces pressing into the doorway.

When they went in and down the first hallway, she didn't look up the stairs.

Just before the man at the second door opened it, Jo wished Tom wouldn't be there, that he and Lou had already left, so she could stop half-looking for him.

It was better just to know he was gone.

It was dangerous to care for him; there were some rules that never broke.

Never tell a man your name. Never mention where you live, or any place we go. Never let a man take you anywhere; if you take one into the alley to neck, tell one of your sisters, and come back as soon as you can.

Never fall for a man so hard you can't pull your heart back in time.

We'll leave without you if we have to.

Their effect was almost as impressive the second time; though they didn't have much, the Hamilton sisters knew how to wear what they had.

When Tom made his way through the crowd, he smiled at Lou first, but his gaze stuck on Jo, even as he leaned in to accept Lou's kiss on his cheek.

Jo frowned at him.

He blinked, remembered himself, and smiled around at the rest of them as he returned Lou's kiss lightly.

Jo looked at the bandstand. The singer was just finishing a waltz. Araminta would be sorry.

"Let's get you all to the table," he said, and even as they walked the edge of the dance floor the little ones were pressing him with questions and loaded statements about what Lou was like.

(Mattie said, "She's awfully clever," and Hattie said, "Even if she can't waltz worth a penny.")

"Better you than me," said Rebecca, with a doleful look over her glasses.)

Rose and Lily were shaking his hands, assessing him in stereo, and Araminta was peering at him as if looking for flaws in a gem.

Jo hung back a little behind the others.

She didn't want to be close to Tom, and there were eleven girls who had to be counted.

He danced with Lou first, a Baltimore, as the others gathered in little knots to discuss him.

"He seems like a real gentleman," said Araminta.

Rebecca frowned. "He seems like a crook."

"We only know crooks," said Lily, and Rose laughed.

Sophie said absently, "As long as Lou likes him," and smiled out at the floor.

Doris, oddly, didn't have a thing to say.

No one asked Jo what she thought of him. No one had talked to Jo since they reached the door of the Marquee.

Seeing them gathered at their table with their backs all turned to her made her want to crack open the emptiness she carried with her and leave it for them to clean up.

On the other hand, she didn't have much to say about Tom, so tonight it was for the best.

He danced next with Violet, who was visibly the youngest, and Jo wondered if he was trying to work his way up the chain by age.

She wished him luck; in their glad rags and painted faces, it was hard for most men to tell them apart, even if he was a ringer. If he thought he could pinpoint them all based on guesswork, he'd have a night of it.

But that wasn't his game, Jo realized a moment later—he was cleverer than that.

The song he'd asked Violet for was fast enough that it didn't look suspicious for a man of thirty-five to be dancing it with a girl of fourteen.

Jo gave him credit for his strategy.

After Violet he asked Sophie, who had been whispering with Rose until Tom held out his hand to ask. But Sophie accepted at once, apparently thinking him neither too young nor too handsome to dance with.

Poor Tom, Jo thought, and bit back a smile.

By then the girls were scattering. Jo watched as men claimed them all for the waltz—except Lily, who claimed Violet, and Doris, who couldn't be pulled into a waltz with a meat hook.

As soon as the other girls had cleared out, Doris slid into the booth beside Jo.

"Thanks, General," she said, glancing out at the dance floor. "For what you did with Sam, I mean, so I didn't have to talk to Father."

"The fewer of us who have to talk to Father, the better," said Jo.

"Ain't that the truth." Doris pulled a face. "You wonder what he must have been like when Mother met him. I've always hoped he was better back then, but everything I remember of how he froze the life out of Mother just makes me think he was always going to be rotten. When we were kids he scared me, and now . . ." She sighed.

"Now you like boats?"

Doris laughed. "I told Sam about that. He said for the honeymoon we can boat it over to the Continent, so the joke's on Father. I can't wait. Can you believe none of us has ever seen a boat?"

Jo frowned. "Doris, I'm glad you like Sam Lewisohn. I really hope he's as nice as you think. But what if he's not? Father must have picked him for a reason. And he was willing to think of a wife who'd never seen anything of the world. What's to keep him from turning into Father?"

Doris thought it over. "Nothing, I suppose. Though it was his mother who arranged to have Sam at the party, it wasn't his idea, so at least he's not guilty of that. It'll be her I'm up against once we're married, that old dowager."

It sounded like a brush-off, but after a moment Doris sighed, sitting back in the booth, and Jo realized she was still considering the question.

"Don't get me wrong," said Jo, "it's hard to get a worse situation than our house. Run while you can. I just—I don't know how you'll protect yourself if anything happens, once you're on your own."

"I'll manage. I'm not as dumb as I look, Jo."

"That's not what I mean," Jo said. "I only mean some people turn cruel on you when you least expect, and it trips you up, that's all."

Doris shrugged. "From all I remember of Sam, he was a sweet boy. I hope he stays sweet. But I guess you can never tell how a man's going to end up."

"No," Jo said, watching Tom's dark head and Sophie's blond making tight turns in the tide of dancers. "I guess not."

By two in the morning Tom had danced with almost everyone.

Still left to go were Araminta, who had no room on her schedule since the waltzes had filled; Hattie, who hadn't been back to the table since they arrived; and Jo, whom he hadn't asked.

They were all making the most of their last night of freedom. The twins were dancing hardest, their Charlestons looking more like a call to war than a dance. Judging by the glare Jo got whenever Mattie came back to the table to touch up her bloodred lipstick, the twins were none too happy that Jo hadn't extricated them all from the house before it was their turn on the block.

When the band took their break, the girls made their way back to their tables, glittering amid the smoke.

"Oh Lord," Rebecca moaned, "my feet are dead. One more dance and my legs will fall off."

"It's because you don't lift them up," Sophie said. "You have to stay light or your ankles will give before the night's over!"

"Easy for you to say," Mattie chimed in, "you're four inches shorter. Rebecca's practically a tree."

"Oh, shut it," said Rebecca.

"Hey," called Lily to Lou, "you owe me one, before you go off and get married."

"She's too busy getting all her dances in before she's stuck with only one man," said Araminta (pretty shrewdly, thought Jo, for someone who tended to the romantic).

Lou laughed and ran her fingers through her hair, sending the curls wilder. "No harm in that," she said. "He's doing his share of dancing, you know."

"There's someone whose feet really are falling off," said Violet. "Trying to get all of us in one night! He's batty."

"Hasn't danced with me," said Araminta, taking a pull from her glass of champagne.

"And he hasn't danced with the General," Violet said.

"She should take her turn," said Rebecca. "He's good at it. And funny!"

"And he doesn't say anything out of place," Sophie put in. "None of that love stuff."

"No," said Jo, "I don't suppose he would."

There must have been something in her tone, because Lou glanced over at Jo before turning to the twins.

"The bows on my shoes are a big tangle. You've got to help me before the music starts."

It wasn't a moment too soon; the music started while Hattie was fixing Lou's second shoe. Then they grinned and rose and tripped away like a line of chorus girls in a flick, leaving only Araminta and Jo behind.

They sat together often, just the two of them. Araminta wasn't a big talker, but Jo felt a little soft toward her, out of the younger ones—the same way she'd felt about Doris, when it was just the four of them going out.

There was something to be said for countless hours watching the same dance floor, commenting on this dancer or that one.

Jo suspected sometimes that Araminta guessed how much Jo loved dancing and was just too kind to mention it.

Araminta's day would come too, to walk down the stairs and be matched with someone their father thought suitable, after meeting him five minutes in the parlor.

That man would probably be the richest of all, Jo thought, watching her profile as Araminta assessed the floor. Araminta was beautiful and sweet, with large, sad eyes and a serious mouth; a beauty of the old kind, the sort Jo remembered seeing on magazine covers back when she was a child.

It was a beauty their mother must have seen right away, to give her a name so out of fashion, fit only for a princess in a tower.

Of course, princesses in towers got rescued. You never heard of a dragon succeeding before St. George did. You never heard of the prince coming through the briars only to find a pile of bones.

"Jo," said Araminta.

Jo looked up and saw Tom standing in front of her. He had his hand out; he must have asked her to dance.

"Oh," she said. She wrapped one hand around the edge of her chair. "I don't know if that's a good idea. It's getting late."

"Go on," said Araminta. "He's practically family."

That was the problem.

But Jo stood up and brushed her skirt back into place, and said to Araminta, "I'll be back in a minute," as if she was reminding herself.

When she took his hand, he held it too tightly. She pretended not to notice.

On the dance floor Tom slid into the line of dance just behind Sophie and her man. For a moment Jo thought dismally, Now there are two witnesses, but shrugged it off. It wasn't the first time she'd danced with Tom, and besides, he was practically family.

The embrace felt natural as always, but even since last night there was something heavier about it, something resigned and older, so that she could hardly hold up her arm, and her hand in his hand was shaking.

The wail of brass carried over the rest of the music, and when the singer started, she sounded the same melancholy note as the trumpet had.

"I waited all night for this," he said.

She said, "Don't."

"You know," he said quietly, "I thought about going straight after I met you."

She thought about the question she'd asked him in the car on the way over, the look on his face as he nodded.

"I figured you must have liked me all right as I was, to keep dancing with me even after you'd worked things out."

He was giving her more credit than she'd ever given herself.

"But I never stopped thinking about it," he said, "even after I got run out of New York. I knew the best thing I could do was raise myself in the world, and that if I really worked to be worth something, then I'd have something to stand on if I saw you again."

She couldn't answer him; she curled her fingers into a fist on his back.

"And it's a good thing, too," he said, all false cheer, "because look how useful my work has been to you."

"Don't," she said.

The word must have been too raw, because he pulled her closer, his fingertips pressing into her ribs so hard that she could feel the seam of her dress.

(No one could see them in the crowd, no one would know, they were safe for one minute more.)

She felt as if her feet were sticking to the boards, as if at any moment she would sink into the floor.

"I can make myself love Lou," he said after a moment. "She's a sharp girl. I could love her, if that's what you want of me."

The singer had given up singing, and the trumpet was crying the last notes. Jo rested her head on his shoulder, just for a heart-beat, like she had when she was a girl.

Then it was his turn to hold his breath, to squeeze her hand, to almost forget to stop dancing. They swayed for a beat after the song was finished.

At last Jo said, "Don't."

She gave herself a count of three before she tensed and pulled away. Tom watched her as she stepped back, sharp-eyed and hungry.

It made her nervous. "What?"

"Nothing," he said. "If I had known last time how long it would be, I would have gotten a look in, that's all."

"Cut it out," she said, crueler than she meant. "Tomorrow you're taking Lou to Chicago."

"I'll come back when she's settled in," he said. "Where will you be?"

Jo didn't want to think about that.

"Go find Lou," she said, and slipped through a crack in the crowd back to her table.

Araminta was watching her with wide, keen eyes. "How did it go?"

"He holds on too tight," Jo said. "We're leaving."

Araminta looked disappointed, but she was already reaching for her shoes as Jo held up her hand like she was snatching a moth from the air, and the exodus started.

Lou or Doris brought up the rear, making sure no girl got left in the crush.

They'd have to pick another girl to hang back, Jo realized, now that both of them were leaving.

Rebecca could do it. She kept her head on straight. But she was still so *young*. One of the twins, maybe, but at any moment they'd be called downstairs, too.

"Ladies," said Tom at the doorway, with a glance at Jo as she passed. "Thank you for a beautiful evening."

Jo didn't listen for what he said to Lou.

She went on ahead, had her hand out for cabs before she was off the stoop, summoning one and another and another.

The girls poured out the door, the tops of their heads smoking in the cool evening air, leaping into the cabs.

Hattie and Mattie sat pointedly with Ella, and when everything was sorted Jo found herself in the cab with Lou and Violet and Araminta, Araminta's eyes trained on Jo as if expecting a revelation.

"So this will be the last night we're all together," said Violet finally.

It must have been inconceivable to Violet, Jo realized, that things would ever change.

Violet had grown up in this glass world. She'd known about the dancing since she was old enough to keep time; for her, there had been no other life than the cage and the dance. Now everything was falling to pieces, one sister at a time.

Lou sighed, said to Violet, "I wish I could take you with me."

"Write to us in three months," said Jo, "and see if I don't offer to send her wherever you are."

Violet laughed. "General, you're not serious."

"Who knows," said Jo. "I might have the money for a train ticket that day."

Violet sat back and stopped asking questions.

Araminta said, "You should let me fix that dress, Jo. It's an all right color, but so old-fashioned. If I lowered the waist and took up the skirt it would do wonders."

Jo said, "And what use do I have for a sharp new dress?"

"Oh, who knows," said Araminta. "You never know when you'll need something nice."

"There's nothing I need," said Jo, and turned to the window.

Soon Violet and Araminta and Lou were talking about this dancer and that one, laughing at an awful partner Violet had landed with ("You should have seen it, he's a menace, I could have lost a toe!"), comparing the bandstands at the Kingfisher and the Marquee.

"I miss their champagne," Lou said. "The Marquee's is so sweet you get sick."

"The dancing tonight felt so sad, mostly," Violet said. "I liked Tom all right, though."

"I like him all right, too," said Lou.

Jo curled her hand a little tighter in her lap, as if to keep warmth in.

None of them mentioned what would happen to Lou in the morning.

When they got home, they slid through the alley and padded up the stairs, disappearing into the attics like ghosts caught out.

Jo, who came in first, glanced into the kitchen to make sure none of the staff was awake and that all the lamps were out.

All was well, and they climbed the stairs, as quiet as they could be.

Their father's study was one floor above them, and neither light nor noise reached them in the kitchen dark; even if his office light was on, even if his door was open to catch some little sound, there was no telling from the back roads they took. There was no warning.

For all Jo knew, no one else was awake in the house.

eighteen
THERE'LL BE SOME CHANGES MADE

Jo woke to the sound of Lou fastening her trunk.

It wasn't quite sunrise. Jo watched gray creep over the ceiling for a little while before she said, "Good morning."

Lou looked up. "Good morning," she said carefully. "I'll be done in a second, and then you can get some shut-eye. I tried to be quiet, I just couldn't sleep."

She moved back and forth to the dresser, twisting her hands. "I think I took one of your pomades—I'm sorry. I'd try to get it out, but the trunk's so full I might never find it. I didn't realize how much I owned—you'd think we own so little, but it gets so crowded."

Jo watched her.

"I'll pay you back as soon as I have some money, I promise," said Lou, "it's just that it would take me forever to find, and I don't want to be late because I'm repacking everything and then maybe something awful happens and I can't go, so I'll just buy you a new one as soon as I can."

"It's fine," Jo said to the ceiling.

"Jo, why did you give Tom to me?"

The question came fast and sharp, as if Lou had been waiting for Jo to say something, anything, and have out with it already.

Jo didn't look away from the ceiling.

"You don't give people to other people," she said. "Don't be stupid."

"Jo."

Jo looked over. Lou was resting stiff-armed on her trunk, watching Jo, looking as though the words were being ground from her.

"I'm not stupid," Lou said. "I know how you felt about him. You loved him something awful. You were one dance away from running off with him, once."

"That was eight years back," Jo said. "You're easy to fool when you're young. It fades."

"You kept that bag in your closet for ages, though," Lou said.

Jo blinked. She'd never told anyone, certainly never Lou— Lou, who had always been suspicious of Jo wanting to leave them and look for something better.

It couldn't have mattered, what Jo felt.

If she loved him, she could have forgiven him for almost betraying them (she never would); surely she couldn't have given him up.

But she'd gone home from Tom's little room above the Marquee without hesitating, just after he'd agreed to take Lou someplace where her father couldn't get at her.

Tom had looked heartbroken and distant the whole way back home, like he was working to shut her out of something she'd come too close to.

She could have said, "I missed you." She could have said, "Keep driving, just you and me."

She was putting Lou in the car instead.

One sister was safe. That was the bottom line. What Jo felt about it was beside the point.

"You'd better wash up," Jo said, standing. "He'll be here soon. You don't want to keep him waiting."

The sisters said their good-byes in the fourth-floor hall, filing into Jo and Lou's room in pairs, red-eyed. Jo had made them put on day clothes (you never knew, these days, when Father would send for you), but they were bleary from the long night and from crying.

Doris was inconsolable, but refused to leave until at last Ella took pity and walked her back to their room.

"But she's going," Doris said between sobs, and Ella said something comforting that Jo didn't hear.

"You shouldn't have woken them," said Lou, blinking back tears. "This is a circus. Too much sentiment."

"You couldn't have left without seeing them," said Jo, and Lou made a face but didn't argue.

"If you even say good-bye to me I'll kick you."

"Just get downstairs before Father changes his mind."

"Louise," their father called, "Tom is here. Is the trunk ready? We have an appointment at city hall that I believe you don't want to miss?"

"Yes, sir!" Lou called back, turning a little green.

"Well, then come down and say good-bye to your father, and we'll take your trunk to the car."

Lou and Jo dragged the trunk onto the landing, where Walters materialized out of nowhere.

"Mister Hamilton would like to see you downstairs for the send-off, Miss Josephine," he told her.

Jo's stomach sank. She didn't think she could bear waving good-bye to Tom as he drove off with Lou in the passenger seat, headed for city hall and the open road.

"Oh, no," she said. "I—I couldn't."

"He'd like to see you there for the send-off," the butler repeated, as if she hadn't spoken. The last scraping steps faded as he went down the stairs to the front hall and out to the waiting Ford.

"You don't have to go," Lou said.

It was a lie; their father issued orders, not invitations.

"Come on," Jo said. "The quicker you're away from here, the better."

"Your problem is that you're too sentimental," muttered Lou.

On the way down the stairs, Jo grabbed Lou's hand and squeezed it once, too hard.

By the time they were in sight of their father and Tom, Jo had her hands back at her sides.

Tom was still in his car coat and had tucked his hat in his left hand.

"Louise," Tom said, "it's wonderful to see you again. You look lovely."

"And you," Lou said, coming down the last few stairs to meet him. Her eyes were fever-bright as she looked up at Tom, her face pale.

In the morning light from the hallway, with Lou in her sharp dress and cloche hat and Tom in his black suit with the tie done up, they looked like a lobby card advertising the wedding at the end of a movie.

Jo could hardly make it down the last few stairs; her body had turned to stone, somehow.

Their father watched Jo with a strange expression as she descended, and she wondered what he saw. If he even guessed, about Tom—

But when she looked again, it was gone, and his face was implacable as ever.

"Josephine," Tom said. "Nice to see you again, too. It's very kind of you to see us off."

"Don't mention it," said Jo.

The ghost of a smile crossed his face before he turned to Lou and caught her hand in his. Then his smile was just for Lou, and Jo walked to the narrow window beside the door, as far away from them as she could get.

The street was bustling; the street was filled with women Jo's age, walking briskly with purses and attachés, hailing cabs to wherever they wanted to go, without anyone minding where they went.

She couldn't imagine.

"Sir," Tom said to their father, "if you're ready, we should get going—we don't want to miss our chance with the judge."

"Oh, absolutely," their father said. "I'll follow you in the car in just a moment."

"The trunk is ready," Walters said from the doorway. Jo hadn't even noticed him.

She clasped her hands behind her back.

Lou kissed their father on the cheek, and Tom shook his hand, and they walked through the door.

Jo had a glimpse of Lou's red-rimmed eyes, and of Tom's face in the shadow of his hat—someone brushed her hands as they passed, either Lou or Tom; she hadn't felt it at first and she couldn't be sure.

Then they were both in the car and pulling away, and the silhouette of Lou's waving arm was lost to sight as they turned the corner.

"Josephine, please pull yourself together."

Jo hadn't realized she'd been crying.

She ran her hand over her eyes and cleared her throat. "Yes, sir. I'm sorry. You wanted to see me?"

Their father smiled thinly. "No, Josephine, I have everything I need at the moment, thank you. Please go upstairs and try to keep some order. I'll be back as soon as the ceremony is over."

The hair on Jo's neck stood up, but she couldn't figure quite why. He was always most terrible when he was trying to seem kind, and there was no telling what it really meant.

The girls were behind their doors as Jo took the staircase (she had seen more of the front stairs in the last month than in the first twenty-seven years she had spent in the house). It was quiet as night; Jo imagined them crowded into the bedrooms that had a view of the street, peering through the curtains to catch a glimpse of the car as it pulled away with Lou inside, their sister set free and making a straight line for the open road.

When Jo closed the door to their room (her room, now) and closed her eyes, she could almost hear the rumble of the car as it turned through the streets; she could almost hear Louise laughing.

She could feel the restless mourning beneath her, ten wide-eyed birds calling to be let out, their desperation pressing against her feet as if she was the lock on the roof of their cage.

Jo wasn't used to crying. She dug the heels of her hands into her eyes stupidly, like it would stop the tears, but the crying had the best of her.

It frightened her how deep her sobs could reach, as if someone was pulling sorrow from her bones.

Jo had closed the door on them all, and the breakfast tray had come and gone without her even getting up for the knock, but at two o'clock the little raps came in urgent bursts, and Jo recognized at last that it was Rebecca knocking and not the maid.

"General," Rebecca was hissing at the door, "General, we need to know about—oh yipes."

Jo didn't want to think about what she looked like. She hadn't slept in days, had hardly eaten, had been worn out by worry; she probably looked like a cadaver.

"What is it?"

"It's about tonight."

Jo stood and crossed the room. "What about it?"

Rebecca flinched at Jo's tone. "Nothing, General. Just wondering if we were, you know, likely to."

Jo realized with a sinking stomach that she hadn't asked Tom what would happen to the Marquee in his absence. Would it be safe? Who was going to be running operations while he was away?

The Kingfisher was out of the question—it was blind luck to have escaped the cops twice, and it would be unforgivable recklessness to go back now, not when there was any other place in the city where they might go. Poor hunting.

It had been blind luck for Tom, too, though he couldn't have known it then.

Jo hoped Lou would be good for him. It was going to be a long drive to Chicago if they hated each other, but somehow she suspected they'd end up getting along like a house on fire.

(He could love her, he said, if he only tried.)

"No," she said. "Not tonight. I'm not ready to take you out."

Rebecca frowned. "That's unfair."

Jo blinked, looked at Rebecca, and raised her eyebrows. Rebecca took a half step back.

(Jo's fist was clenched. Jesus. She smoothed her hand along her dress.)

"Maybe not," Jo said. "But it's your answer. Make your peace with it however you like."

Then she closed the door.

Even though the bed was neatly made just like every other morning, and the wardrobe door was closed, the room was still achingly empty. Every powdered circle on the dresser screamed that Lou was gone for good.

Lou had been the first person Jo told, in this room, as if she'd known even then that dancing would be the best thing they would ever do.

Since Jo could remember, she had fallen asleep to the sound of Lou's breathing. It had been an intrusion when she was young, this redheaded, unwelcome addition from the nursery, a little alien noise that filled the room at night.

Now it was the silence driving her mad; at any minute, she thought, the empty place where her worries lived was going to swallow her whole.

She went to the library, stared at the atlas until her vision blurred.

In the middle of the afternoon, long after the glass of milk on the tray had stopped sweating and the soup had stopped steaming, the note came from their father.

He had questions about Hattie and Mattie.

She was to come alone.

• • • • • •

On her way downstairs, she knocked at Doris and Ella's door.

"Make sure everyone's still dressed," Jo said. "He wants to know about Hattie and Mattie. He'll probably ask about you, too, and after that I don't know what's to keep him from calling everyone else down."

Doris nodded. She was still dressed from the morning, and some of the others went through the motions. The rest tended to do the bare minimum until they could get dressed for dancing.

That was out of the question. Jo couldn't imagine what would happen if their father caught anyone in sequins.

She went downstairs under a stony silence, feeling as though their doors had been shut to protect them from her, rather than closing them inside.

(Fair enough. She hated jailers, too.

Jo swallowed a pang.)

Their father was sitting at his desk. With one hand he was idly spinning the knob of his cane, as if drilling into the carpet for oil, and with the other he was tapping out a rhythm on his blotter.

He didn't stand to greet her when she knocked and opened the door.

"Sit down, Josephine. I trust the business from this morning has passed?"

It took Jo a moment to realize he meant her crying. "Yes, sir."

"Good." Their father sat back in his chair. "I wanted to talk to you about the future of the girls."

She didn't trust herself to say anything polite, so she nodded. Their father seemed on edge, coiled in on himself, as if he was waiting for something. She didn't want to risk a wrong answer.

"I suppose you've guessed by my rather—efficient agreement with Mr. Marlowe that business is not going as well as I could hope at the moment."

Jo had not guessed. She had assumed the agreement came as a result of some form of congenital greed.

"I see," she said.

"As much as I would like to care for you all as long as you

might need it, there are other factors to consider. Therefore, I am relying on you girls to make good matches, with husbands who have the means to take care of you in the style to which you are accustomed."

Four dollars a month, if they behaved.

"Of course, sir."

He sat a little forward. "The men from good families are looking for wives with beauty, manners, virtue. Unlike your sisters, the gentlemen are in a position to choose. Do you understand?"

"Yes, sir."

"Then why have you been disobeying me?"

Jo blanched.

It was as if someone had socked her in the stomach; it took her a moment to breathe.

He had known, somehow. He had only needed to be sure. She'd been called down this morning because he wanted a good look at her red eyes and purple bags before he showed his cards.

At last she managed, "What?"

"You heard me," their father said, a dark gleam in his eye. "I know you and your sisters go out when your foolish father is asleep. You think I can't ask two questions and determine the answer to a third? You think because you're in your stocking feet, no one hears you sneaking in at dawn, if he is awake and of a mind to?"

She hadn't—she couldn't have seen that he was awake, that he was listening—

Jo couldn't breathe. "Sir—"

He slammed the cane onto the desk with such force that Jo felt a breeze. When she looked at him, his face was as smooth and kind as she had ever seen it, as if he wasn't angry at all, as if someone else was wielding the cane.

It was terrifying.

(She pitied her mother.)

"I have tried to be kind—to take care of you, to protect your reputations, to give you your choice of husbands who would, in their turn, preserve the honor of the family name. But this willful display disgusts me, Josephine. What would possess you to disobey me?"

Jo sat closer to the edge of the chair, thought fast, and tried to sound obliging.

"You gave no order, sir, that we were never to go out. Only that we were not to disturb you."

"Don't presume to answer me with jokes, Josephine!"

"Sir, I'm only trying—"

"I don't want any of your lying! You know my wishes, and I expect you to honor them!"

Wishes? He wanted to sell his daughters and wave his cane and talk about the sanctity of wishes?

Then they would.

She looked him flat in the eye.

Jo said, "Honor which, exactly? I know your wish to hide us because you were ashamed of having no son. I know you wished to keep us locked up until you could marry us off to strangers, so we could be chained to a childbed like Mother was for you."

Her rage was building now, and the words came faster, louder. "And now I know you're even ashamed that your daughters have managed something on their own, and you wish they had died quietly upstairs and saved you the bother of caring for them. If there's some other wish I missed, then by all means explain!"

There was a moment's quiet, except for Jo's breathing. She was standing now; she didn't remember when she'd gotten up.

Their father's face went red, then white, with rage.

Jo was too petrified by her own outburst to move, and too sure of being right to apologize. She watched him as she would watch a tethered bear on a fraying rope.

Slowly, he stood up from behind the desk and withdrew his cane, and with his other hand he rested the tips of his fingers on the blotter, supporting the weight of his indignation.

"I had thought at one time," he said, "to settle this with you rationally, and have a helpmeet. I wanted to marry the rest quietly, at first, after I discovered what loose and lawless girls you had be-come—before news could get out and ruin your prospects."

Jo's limbs felt like coiled springs.

"But," he said, "since marriage is so distasteful to you, I feel I have given you ample lenience until now, and I can address the matter as I should have done from the start. I've asked Dr. Whit-man from the Three Willows Asylum to evaluate my daughters, who are suffering from hysterical alcoholism. I had been thinking of you, at first—if they have disobeyed, it is because of you—but if this same vile temper has spread to all of them, then it will have to be addressed. He's an old associate of mine, and very much in agreement, as it happens; he doesn't approve of the new fashion for loose behavior . . ."

An asylum. A mental hospital. There were stories about what happened behind those walls, stories that worried even the men who went out drinking at night.

Those who went in rarely went out again.

Horror filled Jo's mouth. Across the desk from her, their father was reaching for his newspaper, calmly; the discussion was over.

"He'll view me as a negligent father," he said, as if making party conversation. "Well he should, but it's cheaper to keep a daughter in the hospital than to keep her in style, and at least I'll be spared anyone else knowing about the traitorous women who called themselves my children."

Before he had finished speaking, Jo was bolting out of the study. She prayed they weren't angry enough to ignore her—she prayed they still trusted, that they would not disobey her now.

"Beat it!" she shouted from the foot of the steps, her voice raw. "Get out, get out!"

For one awful, endless second, everything froze.

She couldn't breathe, and she couldn't hear—everything was suspended in water. If her sisters had even heard her, they were too frightened to move, and then it would be too late, and the men from the asylum would come and run up the stairs and find them all just as they were, sitting on the edges of their beds, as still as a photograph.

Her heart was pounding—she could swear, she could swear ten hearts upstairs were pounding in time.

Then Doris shouted, "Damn it! Move!"

The world started up again.

There came an answering chaos of beds scraping and chairs crashing, of quick calls back and forth, of shoes being shoved on, of the first few bodies charging wildly down the back stairs, pausing at the back door as if wondering where to go.

Behind her, their father was approaching.

"He knows!" Jo screamed. "Nothing's safe!"

He grabbed hold of her wrist, and as he spun her he had his hand up to strike—he was holding his walking stick, the blow would be terrible.

But she hadn't spent eight years in dance halls for nothing, and she ducked under his grip and shook herself free in one sharp move as she skidded away from his reach.

There was a thundering from the upper floors as the rest of the girls made a break for it, and he froze for a moment, overwhelmed by the sound.

Then it was silent, and when Jo spoke it gave her words the gravity of a curse.

"They're gone," she said, "and you'll never see them again."

It took him a moment to understand what she meant, and even as it dawned on him he looked around as if there was a jailer handy who could trap them all inside until they could be given to men who would pay for the privilege.

But it was too late—the doctor, if he came, would never find them.

They knew how to disappear.

Jo hoped they would never stop running.

Their father fixed his gaze on her; his face was empty with rage, the mask of a hollowed patriarch.

"You've done this," he said, too calmly. "You drove them away from me. You've been up there for years, planning to ruin me, and now it's come to nothing, and they'll go to the ground."

Jo was ashamed to think how little planning she had really done for them, but she wasn't about to fall for a game like this—she knew what was true.

"You did this yourself, sir, and you know it."

"We'll see," he said.

He swung his cane.

She dodged for the front door and tried to pull it open; her hands were shaking so much the handle slipped out of her grasp halfway. The door was painfully slow—she'd never touched it before, and it weighed twice as much as she expected—and even as she wrenched it open, he struck a blow on her shoulder.

She cried out and swung blindly. Her fist connected, and he howled and staggered backward, just enough to give her a few seconds' time.

Jo didn't slow down—couldn't—her heart was pounding painfully and there was no stopping. She tore through the doorway and staggered halfway down the stairs before she ran into some-one—someone gripped her shoulders, someone was twisting with her impact to bring her behind him.

"Hamilton, what's the meaning of this?"

It was van de Maar.

"She's gone hysterical!" their father said, voice shaking, the picture of a man incensed by the worst form of impudence. "She struck me!"

"He's trying to send us to an asylum," Jo gasped out. "He struck me with the cane." She yanked at the neck of her dress, pulling it to one side to show the red mark blooming on her skin.

(Van de Maar hesitated a moment before he glanced down—he was so used to not looking at her.)

"Asylum?" Van de Maar held her a little farther away from him. "What for?"

"They go out at night," their father said, fighting for control of his voice. "You know what that does to a man's reputation, van de Maar, if he can't even keep hold of his own daughters?"

Van de Maar half-cleared his throat. "Hamilton, perhaps we could discuss this inside."

"No," said Jo, and carefully pulled her arm out of van de Maar's. "I won't go back in that house."

"You see what I mean, van de Maar," their father said. He was already calmer, resting on his cane, trying to pull his breathing together. "She won't listen to reason."

Van de Maar seemed unconvinced, but he turned to Jo. "Josephine, perhaps we had best all go inside and discuss this civilly. I'm sure there's something that can be arranged."

"No, sir," she said, as steadily as she could. She took another step down. "I have no reason to go into the house. None of my family lives there any more."

Every time she spoke, van de Maar looked less certain of things. As if against his will, he held out his arm and caught the cuff of her dress. "But your father said we had business to discuss, about the marriage."

(Jo could feel his fingers as if they were a metal glove, she was so on edge, so ready to run.)

Jo smiled thinly. "I'm sure he did. You'll find when you talk to him that Lou has married, and I'm guessing that Father was going to suggest that if you liked them younger, he had other daughters who were amenable."

Van de Maar had the grace to pull an expression.

She went on. "Or maybe he would say that I was willing, if the doctor wouldn't take me, and if you liked the look of me."

Van de Maar looked up the stairs to the threshold, where their father was standing.

"Be fair, van de Maar," said their father. "I would never suggest you liked the look of her."

Van de Maar glanced at Jo, frowning.

After a moment, without agreeing with her, he let her sleeve go, pulled back his hand.

Jo summoned a smile that felt more frightening than anything so far.

"Thank you very much for stopping by, Mr. van de Maar."

She took the stairs without looking behind her, and, afraid to hesitate, she turned south and kept walking. She kept an eye out for her sisters, but the street was quiet as the grave, and Jo knew that they had scattered as far and as fast as they could.

She wondered where they would go—Tom was gone from the Marquee, and the Kingfisher wasn't safe.

Had they managed to stay together? Would they split and make a run for it?

Would any of them try to get word to her? How could they, if she didn't know where to look?

Had any of them taken a penny?

(She could see her own breath; had she sent them to the streets without even enough to keep them from freezing?)

As she turned the corner, a white police truck drove idly past her, painted on its side with a sketch of a landscape and a trio of willow trees. As it passed her, it slowed.

Her heart jumped into her throat.

The driver winked at her.

Through her sour stomach, she smiled back, blew him a kiss like Lou would have.

After he had turned the corner, she cut across the avenue and walked faster in a new direction.

She walked east until the houses gave way to the shops on Lexington, on Third, that she remembered from her last solitary walk. When Second Avenue seemed too loud, she walked south until the shops gave way to grocers and tenements. She walked long after her feet went numb, aimlessly, letting the city wash over her.

(She was so lost that Union Square startled her when she came upon it, as if the buildings had collapsed just a moment before. She skirted the north edge and headed east.)

At last, she stood in a grassy park in the shadow of the bridge and looked out at the river, which she had never seen during the day.

It was deep blue, pockmarked with gulls and bits of paper. Farther out were a few little boats skidding past on the breeze, and the distant, low silhouette of Brooklyn across the water.

The air was sharp and cold, the late afternoon sun was bright, and Jo was all alone.

nineteen
WHAT'LL I DO

Jo sat on a bench for ten minutes, shivering, before the cop found her.

She had a moment of blank relief (police had a different meaning when she wasn't in a dance hall, as though maybe she was being looked after by someone). Then she realized that her father might well have put the word out on them—a pack of hysterical women who had gotten free and needed rounding up.

"Everything all right, miss?"

She gave him her practiced dance-hall smile. "Yes, Officer. Just had a dustup with my fella. Cooling off for a minute before I head home."

He half-smiled. "In this weather that'll be no trouble. But you'd better get moving before the sun goes down—this is a bad neighborhood after dark."

"Oh," she said, "thank you."

She stood, and looked wistfully out at the water, and smoothed her skirt, until the cop had finally turned and walked out of sight.

Then she walked the other way—slowly, not a care in the world—heading north, back uptown through the shops and the noise of Greenwich Village and the far-off skyscrapers she was getting a good look at for the first time in her life.

(The city was such a stranger in daylight.)

Washington Square Park was still a cram of people, and Jo didn't have the energy to check every face for recognition. After only a few blocks, she turned south and ducked down a side street where there were fewer prying eyes.

It was all the evasion she could manage. She was numbed by everything that had happened since the morning. Even when she thought of her sisters, the panic wasn't real; she worried for them the way you worried when you read in *Photoplay* that a screen siren and her paramour were parting.

And though she couldn't have imagined it as she ran out of her father's house, the list of her troubles was growing.

She hadn't eaten a thing all day, she had no money, night was coming, and she had nowhere to go. What charmed a cop at sunset wouldn't seem so sweet when they were making rounds in the park at three in the morning and she was frozen half to death.

Jo wondered if their father had put the word out for them with the cops as well, or if he was still ashamed enough of himself to keep things quiet until he'd heard from Three Willows about how many of her sisters they'd managed to round up.

Oh God, she thought. Please let them all have gotten out of the danger all right. Please let them be smart enough to avoid places where we might be known.

Even as she thought it, Jo looked up and saw that she was only a block away from the Kingfisher.

The worn-out brick and the chipped cement staircase looked more like home than anywhere Jo had ever seen, but she didn't dare go closer.

(She thought she'd been a careful person before this morning, but you learned something every minute, if you were smart.)

A block past the Kingfisher was a little café with some outdoor seats. Just past that, a pair of men dressed for long exposure stood on the corner, glancing too often down the street toward the Kingfisher's unmarked door.

It could mean a lot of things, none of them good.

Jo kept walking steadily, cut through one more block, then ducked down an alley to the next street.

Their father knew where they had gone, of course. He could afford the man who'd told him; he could afford to hire a man or two to keep an eye on their second home.

(She wished Jake's boss could come to an agreement with the cops like a decent businessman. She needed all the help she could get.)

So, scratch that. She looked down the street in both directions and wondered if there were any boardinghouses here that worked on credit.

She'd need money, and soon, with some forward-thinking employer who didn't mind a little disgrace in their shopgirls.

She'd need a roof and four walls, before dark.

She wondered if there was a restaurant where she could snatch a dinner roll off an empty table and make a run for it. Her hunger had spread to her limbs, and walking was getting a little tricky.

Earlier, she had passed a market, but pride had stopped her from stealing. She was paying for it now.

Jo passed a row of sweetly lit shops: Veronica's Gowns for Ladies, a shoe store, a tailor's storefront.

She froze in front of the tailor's window.

Myrtle had owned a shoe shop. Myrtle, who had a worthless husband.

Myrtle, who had been playing too close to home at the Kingfisher, who got picked up by the cops and bailed out by her husband's girl on the side.

If anyone would understand what it feels like to be in a pinch, Jo thought, she's it.

With the fever of the hungry and desperate, Jo canvassed the neighborhood, up one avenue and down the other, making a Jacob's ladder across the side streets. Time was working against her now, on top of everything else—the air smelled like frost, and soon the shops would be closing for the night, and Jo would lose her chance.

She was too panicked to go about her search some better way, too tired and wary to risk asking anyone else for help.

(Jo hoped desperately that the others hadn't all been forced to split up—that some still had each other.)

Ten minutes later, just as the light was beginning to move from orange to purple, Jo stormed past Finest Imports Shoe Boutique, a tiny shop next to a candy store.

Then she stopped.

The smell slipping under the door of the candy store was sickening on an empty stomach, but after a moment she forced herself to snap out of it and turn back to the windows of Finest Imports.

Lit up in the dusk, it looked almost as sweet as the candy shop, the front window lined with delicate tiers presenting one satin shoe each.

(For a moment she thought, If only Araminta could see these. She'd never looked quite right in the sturdy catalog clompers.)

At the very back of the shop there was a long wooden counter, and behind it stood a woman with a black bob and a velvet band; she was bent to her ledger now, but Jo had just glimpsed her face as she was passing.

It was Myrtle.

Jo brushed off her dress, ran her hands through her hair (already starting to tangle), ran her tongue over her teeth, and stepped inside.

The store was scented with lavender—Sophie's favorite, Jo thought, and had a pang of loss that stopped her in her tracks.

Myrtle glanced up.

There was no recognition on her face, which Jo thought was just as well, but there also wasn't the sneer she'd expected, walking into a fine store, with her shoes dirty and her hair a mess.

"Can I help you?" Myrtle asked. Her tone could have meant anything.

Without thinking, Jo said, "God, I hope so."

Myrtle half-smiled.

Jo felt suddenly very young, even though Myrtle couldn't have been more than a few years older than she was; Myrtle looked like she was indulging a child.

(Maybe Myrtle thought that was fair, Jo thought. In a lot of ways that might be fair, but not about this; not tonight.)

"I need a job," Jo said. "I remember you mentioned having a place here, a little while back. I wanted to see if there was anything that needed doing."

Myrtle blinked as though she couldn't imagine how Jo would have come by this information.

"There are no openings at the moment, I'm afraid. I've just hired someone."

Her husband's mistress, probably.

"Is there anyone you know who might need someone? I'm willing to work nights, or cleaning, or anything."

"Sorry, hon." Myrtle closed the ledger, flicked off the light on the desk. "Nothing doing."

Jo's palms were clammy (hunger or panic), and her mind swam. It was impossible that this was all for nothing, a chance like this. There had to be something she could do, however small.

"Are you going to the Kingfisher?"

Myrtle looked over sharply, narrowed her eyes. "Beg pardon?"

Jo knew how she sounded. She didn't care.

"If you're going back to the Kingfisher, could you bring a note for Jake? I can't go myself. I'll pay you, as soon as I have money."

There was a long silence as Myrtle froze, frowned, and looked Jo over in the dim light.

Finally she said, "What do you think you know about my going out?"

Now was no time to be coy.

"I know your husband has a doll who pays your bail money," she said, "and that maybe you understand what it's like to be out of options."

Myrtle's silhouette tilted its head. A moment later, Jo heard a click, and the lamp flickered back on. Myrtle was still frowning, but a smile was pulling just at the corner of her mouth.

(She looked like Doris, whenever Doris was trying hard not to be impressed.)

Myrtle looked her over—no purse, no coat, old shoes worn down almost to nothing.

"What sort of trouble are you in?" Myrtle asked.

"More than you think."

"Shouldn't you be talking to a cop about all this?"

"They're one of my troubles," Jo said.

Myrtle raised both eyebrows.

Then in a series of practiced movements, she turned off the lamp and plucked a cloche and coat off the rack behind her.

"I need to stop by the chemist," she said. "It's a short walk, so I'd say you have two minutes to give me a good story before I start to get insulted that you hold on to drunk-tank gossip. Hold my hat for a moment, would you?"

Jo hadn't spent much time doing anything as domestic as this; she was a strategist, not a storyteller. She didn't know how to make things sound more exciting than they were, and her story lacked some of the tension and flourish it would have had if Ella had told it.

On the other hand, if there was one thing Jo knew how to do, it was deliver information with conviction.

The walk to the chemist's turned into a sandwich at a coffee shop, almost without Jo's noticing.

But she kept things as short and swift as she could, cutting out real names, pinning only what mattered most. By the time the bill came, Jo was going full sail.

"—and after I'd shouted for them to get going, my father hit me. I got free before the truck came. But now I don't know what my father told them, or what he's told the police, and I don't dare go anywhere we've gone that might be raided. That's why I'm asking for your help."

They were back on the street now, and Myrtle paused in her tracks.

She hadn't said a word since they'd left her shop, except to motion for coffee and sandwiches. Now it took her a moment to manage any.

"What—about your sisters?"

"They all ran for it." Jo crossed her arms despite herself. "There's no knowing for sure, I guess. I warned them nothing was safe, so even if they all made it, I don't think I'd see them around."

"You think they all made it?"

Jo shrugged. "They know how to get out of a tight spot."

"All except you?"

Point taken.

"Can't win them all," Jo said. "Besides, being a jailbird has come in handy since then." And, after a beat, "I hope."

Myrtle blinked. Then a pack of cigarettes materialized in her hand, and she shook out one for each of them.

"The real problem, it sounds like," Myrtle said after her first drag, "is that there's no way of knowing what your father is up to now."

Or ever, Jo thought, recalling an office door that was almost closed but never quite.

"Assume the worst," Jo said. "That's probably about right."

Myrtle didn't argue it. "And you don't have any other friends here?"

I had one, she thought, but I sent him away.

"Jake," Jo said. "He tends bar at the Kingfisher. He helped me once already, when I was desperate. I hope he'd be willing to help again."

"He'd probably be willing to help you with plenty," Myrtle said, with a glance up and down at Jo, "but you should go in and tell him yourself."

"I can't risk it. My father's watching the place, and he won't hesitate to call the cops. If I get pulled in this time, I'll end up in the Willows or back at home."

Myrtle made a face.

After a moment she shook her head. "You know, I always thought my father was cruel because he told me my shoe store would never make it in a city where they had a Macy's."

Jo, softened by the cigarette smoke, only smiled.

Myrtle dropped the butt of hers, ground it decisively into the pavement with the toe of one shoe. Jo admired the deep-green velvet before she remembered that, of course, what else was Myrtle going to wear?

"I feel for you," Myrtle said. "That's a tough story. But I'm not sure what I can do. It's not like I'm a police sergeant, if you get me, and the help you need is more than I can manage. I'm on my own now, and money's tight. I don't have room for charity cases, and I don't have the means to hire you." She fastened and unfastened her purse twice. "I have a friend who might have a place for a shopgirl. I can ask her, maybe."

She looked worried enough that Jo was beginning to believe her.

Myrtle pulled five dollars from her purse. "This should put you up for a night or two at a half-decent place and keep you from starving. I hope the worst will have blown over by then."

The street around them seemed to slow down.

In a way, in some world far away where none of this mattered, it was a fair deal: Myrtle had been helped in a time of need by a half-sympathetic woman with a little money. This would clear the slate.

(It was impossible for Jo to tell her that she had needed the sympathetic ear more than she'd ever needed money, that the hardest thing about facing all of this was having to do it alone.)

The fear of losing Myrtle now because she took five dollars froze Jo cold, but still it took all Jo's pride to keep her hands at her sides. She didn't have a penny, and she knew what five dollars would get you.

"Getting a message to Jake wouldn't cost you a dime," she said finally.

She didn't dare say, That's what a friend would do.

Myrtle startled.

Then she laughed.

"No, I suppose it wouldn't," she said.

After a moment of holding the money, she tucked it back in her handbag with an expression Jo hoped was impressed.

Then Myrtle pulled a little notebook and a pencil from a pocket of her bag and held them out instead.

Jo hesitated only a moment, making some quick guesses and gathering the courage to commit to the plan she was making.

(Things were changing every minute; there was no going back on anything after this.)

By the time Myrtle said, "All right, let's have it," Jo was already writing.

The man at the door of the Marquee knew her face by now, and when she turned to go upstairs rather than into the dance hall, he didn't question her.

Jo had never wanted anything more in her life than to go inside right away and strap her aching feet tighter into her shoes, and Charleston across the floor with someone until she couldn't think any more.

(She would, if she'd ever be able to forgive herself for dancing while her sisters were gone.)

The door was unlocked, and she thanked every saint there was that Tom had been too distracted or angry to cover his tracks as they left.

(That was probably how he'd ended up in trouble in his old line of work, too.)

The little studio still smelled slightly of whatever fourth-rate moonshine had fallen. The effect was vaguely antiseptic.

Jo didn't mind. The last thing she needed was to run into some lingering cologne that would remind her of Tom.

She freshened up as best she could and wished she could get a little sleep. Had it been two days? Three? She could hardly remember. It felt like one long string of panic and sadness between then and now.

Jo was too tired for tears, but she struggled for breath the more she thought about it, slipping back into the hushed silence of the cab that first night; walking into the Salon Renaud with Lou's hand held tight in her hand; the first song they had ever heard live, played as if it had been waiting just for them.

What were the chances all ten of them had gotten out? Were they safe? Would she ever find them all again?

Where were they now?

Beneath her feet the music was playing sharp and bright, like the night of the next-door party, when Jo had been brave for the first time in her life and taken her sisters out dancing.

When Jo passed the second doorman with a nod and entered the Marquee proper, the band was launching into a Charleston, and she watched the dancers laugh and take hands and start with flying feet.

It wasn't home, yet, but it was dancing, and tonight that was close enough.

(*Watch out for any princesses*, she'd written to Jake, in her fit of bravery. *Not safe for them there. Send them to the Marquee. Wish me luck.*)

The bar was nearly empty. Before she could even ask for a drink, Henry (the blond bartender with the staunch jaw, no older than Rebecca) was setting a glass in front of her.

"Are you alone tonight, Princess?" he asked, disbelieving. A second glass had materialized out of nowhere, and he was still holding the bottle, looking over her shoulder for the others.

She ignored the pang, the urge to turn.

"I am," she said.

Henry raised his eyebrows.

She rested her folded arms on the bar and gave him a smile that felt startlingly real.

(Sometimes, once you start being brave, it's easier just to go on that way.)

"Tom Marlowe sent me," she said. "I'm here about the job."

Henry, flummoxed, offered her a half smile back.

"What job?"

Behind them, the music had picked up in earnest, and the room was going wild.

She said, "The one you're going to give me."

twenty
MY REGULAR GAL

Doris would never have become Jo's lieutenant on purpose, not in a hundred years.

Doris remembered when Jo's feet didn't reach the floor if she sat on her bed; she remembered how Jo had sometimes fudged the passages of a dance she didn't know for sure.

She and Ella and Lou understood what "General" meant to the younger ones—there had to be a General if they were ever going to manage—but the three of them knew Jo too well for it to stick.

When they began to take over the second and third cabs, it was only because Jo ran a tight ship, and they knew what they were expected to do.

("It's strange," Doris said to Ella once. "I don't think she was always like this, but really, she must have been. You can't become a General out of nothing."

"Poor Jo," said Ella.)

They hadn't had time to think what might happen to them otherwise.

As Jo went up and down the stairs to speak to their father, and even as Lou departed, they had the vague but comforting sense that Jo would handle everything, somehow, and they need never become like her in the process.

This sense lasted until the moment Jo screamed up the stairs for them to get out.

Then they ran.

• • • • • •

Doris and Ella moved first, and burst from their room at the same moment—the other girls were already piling out of their rooms into the hall, charging for the back stairs.

A few of them were clutching things in their arms; others had nothing but the clothes on their backs, but there was no time to go for anything now.

Ella raced down the fourth-floor corridor with Hattie and Mattie just ahead, Doris and the others thundering on their heels.

Doris fell back until they were all ahead of her—counting sheep.

Their footsteps were enough to drown out any other sound in the place, but because Doris was last, the riot faded just enough for her to hear Jo's voice, nearly buried, call out, "Nothing's safe!"

The girls sprinted past the kitchen—as she brought up the rear, Doris was just in time to see Walters rising as if to come after them, and Mrs. Reardon standing square in his way.

(Doris wished, later, that there had been one moment's respite in the escape, so she could have saluted the old lady on her way out.)

By the time she reached the end of the alley, the others were running in pairs and threes, following Ella's lead, heading across the street and around the corner and out of sight of anyone who might be looking out the windows of the house.

Ella was cutting across the street with Hattie and Mattie close behind. The twins carried matching pairs of silver shoes—no surprise, thought Doris—but Ella was already too far away to see anything but a blond head and a pale green dress.

Lily and Rose were next, charging hand in hand, and Araminta and Rebecca lagged a little behind (Araminta's arms full of the ugly coats Jo had bought them a hundred years ago).

Violet and Sophie were hanging back, glancing over their shoulders as if waiting for Doris, which made her so angry she could've spit.

There was a moment's sharp and unexpected sympathy for Jo.

"Go on," Doris snapped, "pick it up, this ain't the waltz!"

Ella and the twins were a full street away by now, and there was a flutter of panic that Doris tried to ignore. It would be all right—of course they'd stay together—wasn't that what they were best at?

At the corner, Doris heard the hum of an approaching truck, and from around the front of the house carried a rumble of raised voices, two of them men, and one of them unmistakably Jo.

"Damn," Doris breathed, but she didn't dare stop. Jo had told them to go—they had orders.

Ella and the twins were already out of sight. Lily and Rose seemed to have a bead on them, bearing left as they crossed the street, and Araminta and Rebecca had reached the facing curb safely and were turning to glance behind them, and even through her guilt at leaving Jo behind, Doris thought that the rest of them might end up making it after all.

Then the truck rounded the corner.

Doris had heard a rattle like that before—that was a passenger wagon, and the last time she'd heard it the cops were closing in on the Kingfisher to haul Jo to jail.

"Down!" snapped Doris, and Violet and Sophie sank like magic into the nearest alley.

Doris followed, twisting at the last second to try to get a look over her shoulder, but the rattle and thump of the truck suggested it was big and it was empty, and the only thing Doris could think of was Jo being hauled into it and disappearing. She pulled herself as far back into the dark as she could.

She had to keep safe. There were Violet and Sophie to think about now.

She closed her eyes and prayed the others were fast enough to get out of sight.

(They had to be. Eight years of sneaking around wasn't for nothing.)

The truck slowed down. Doris pressed her forehead to the chilly stone, listened for shouting, wondered if she'd be able to run around front in time to punch the driver senseless and get her sisters back if he tried anything.

She might be able to, but Sophie and Violet were waiting in the shadows, and then what would happen?

For a few heartbeats, she felt like she was pulling out of her own skin.

But then the sound of the truck puttered around the corner and was gone.

Doris snuck to the edge of the alley and looked out, but by the knot in her stomach she already knew what she was going to see:

Nothing.

"Doris?" Violet whispered. "Did they make it?"

"I don't know," said Doris. Then, "Come on."

They crossed—"Slow and steady," Doris said under her breath, "the last thing we need now is to look guilty of something."

The traffic went another direction on this street, and they couldn't be followed without fair warning from around the corner. The streets were quiet, but there were still enough kind faces that Doris could hide behind someone if she had to.

They pulled up in a little knot in front of a church—good enough sanctuary in a pinch, Doris thought. It worked for Quasimodo.

She looked up and down the street as far as she could for a sign of other Hamiltons, but she didn't hold out much hope.

They all knew how to disappear.

They hadn't been pulled in, at least. And if they were out in the world, and they weren't alone, then maybe it would be all right.

Violet and Sophie stood flat against the wall. They were out of breath, though Doris figured it was more from panic than the run. She was willing to bet the Hamilton sisters were the fittest group of girls in the city.

And thankfully Jo had trained them well; all three of them were dressed decently, down to their catalog shoes, so that they looked like the junior typing pool leaving the office and not like a sleepover run amok.

It was the first time Doris wanted to really thank Jo for the way she'd marshaled them. Jo had her faults, but lack of foresight wasn't one.

She could do this. They could do this.

"All right," said Doris in a stern voice, falling back on the facts—another borrowed habit of Jo's. "We're together, and we're out of that damn house. So the worst is over, and now we have to decide what we're going to do with ourselves."

The other two visibly relaxed at the idea that after the facts were sorted, they would be all right.

For a moment there was the comfortable quiet of a cab as it pulled up to the curb of the Kingfisher, waiting for the night to begin.

"Did you see where they went?" Violet asked.

Doris shook her head.

"They're smart girls," she said, which was true. After a moment she added, "I'm sure things will work out," which was slightly more uncertain.

"And Jo?" Sophie ventured.

God only knew what had happened to Jo. Doris sighed.

"If any of us is going to make it," she said finally, "it's going to be Jo."

She hoped.

Violet looked up and down the street one last time, then laced her fingers in front of her as if it was an interview.

"So," she said, "what do we do now?"

They looked strange somehow, and all at once Doris realized she had never seen Violet or Sophie outside in daylight.

They seemed odd and out of place among the other girls on the street; they had the flinty confidence of their older sisters from years of going dancing underground, and the prison pallor of two frightened little girls whose world had just flipped over.

But they only waited for her to instruct them; Violet didn't even look around at passing strangers, she was watching Doris so intently for her orders.

It was almost sweet, Doris thought, even as she thought, Thank God these two hadn't ended up on their own. They were so young, and so used to someone else having plans for them.

Not that Doris could talk.

She wished she'd read more novels about desperate young ladies who found sensible, lucrative jobs without any education or references.

Her first instinct was to head for the Kingfisher, but Jo had shouted that nothing was safe, and Jo knew her business. Now wasn't the time to test theories about where the police might be waiting.

Going back to that house was absolutely out of the question.

They had no money to reach someplace outside the city—and even if they did, Doris couldn't imagine leaving until there was some idea where everyone else had gone.

(This city was still home, even after everything; surely they would all stay here and try to find one another. Surely no one would go too far until they knew for sure that everyone else was all right.)

There was really nowhere left to go, unless she took a very long shot.

Finally, Doris shrugged.

"I guess we'll find out if I have any taste in men," she said.

Doris decided on the Ansonia Hotel as the place to make the phone call.

(A long time ago, some man at the Kingfisher had told her that's where he was staying while he was in town. He had described the hotel in vague terms that sounded interesting—"Seals in the fountain," he'd said, and Doris still wasn't sure if he'd been lying.

Then he'd described the bedroom at a level of detail that made Doris nervous.

"Just in case you're looking for a place to spend the night," he said, and gave her hand a squeeze like she was slow on the uptake.

"I live in a convent," she said. "Sorry. Thanks for the dance.")

She figured a hotel lobby—especially this lobby—was public enough not to draw attention, and there were a lot of places to disappear to, just in case.

It looked enough like a castle fortress to make an impression, she'd give it that much. It soared up almost higher than they could see, round turrets and a thousand coils and curlicues, and stamps of copper and green against the sky.

"Oh, that's what it looks like at the top," Sophie said as they got closer, and Doris thought about all the nights when Sophie had rested her head against the glass and watched the rooftops passing.

As they walked through the doors, Doris said, "Try not to look too impressed, all right?"

Violet, wide-eyed, said, "Too late."

Doris turned around, and didn't blame her. It was like Paris had coughed into a lobby on the Upper West Side.

"Then try to be forgettable, at least," she told them. "Let's see if I can sweet-talk somebody at the desk into a grubby phone call."

Violet raised her eyebrows at the idea of Doris sweet-talking anybody into anything, but Sophie only said, "All right," and took Violet to a place within sight of the exit. (They were all learning fast.)

As it turned out, the gentleman at the desk was more than happy to let Miss make a call. He handed off the telephone and smiled indulgently behind her at Violet and Sophie, who looked like a Coca-Cola advertisement as they gazed around the lobby.

Thank goodness, Sam Lewisohn of Lewisohn & Son was an easy man to find.

"Right," Doris said, after she had hung up with the operator and shaken the clerk's hand like they were about to arm wrestle. "We're taking a long walk downtown. Strap your shoes tight."

"Don't you want to call him first?" Sophie frowned. "What if he won't take us in?"

It was likely he wouldn't want anything to do with them—his mother had wanted him to marry a Hamilton because it looked good or because she thought they had money. Now that neither one was going to be true, things were going to change, and quick.

It was likely that the Lewisohns would turn them out on the street.

On the other hand, Doris knew you didn't have to take bad news gracefully. (Once pride was out of the way, a whole host of options opened up.)

Doris wasn't going to make it easy for them to say no. She could filibuster on a doorstep with Mr. Lewisohn Sr. until they had to run from the police, if that's what it took to give Violet and Sophie a chance at protection from their father.

"Then he gets to tell me no in person," Doris said. "Come on."

Lewisohn & Son operated from a building smack in the middle of the Garment District that had a rickety elevator that made you worry whether you'd ever reach the top, and Doris had to knock three times before someone heard her over the sound of machines and came to the door.

The kid couldn't have been any older than twelve, and for a second they regarded each other with equal surprise.

The boy recovered first. "Yes?"

"Doris Hamilton to see Sam Lewisohn, please," Doris said, hoping this was still the thing to do when you came to someone's door on business. Her most recent education in manners was about as old as this kid was. She'd never even knocked on a door that didn't lead to a speakeasy.

He disappeared, leaving the door open just enough that Doris would have felt rude stepping inside. Behind her, Violet and Sophie were fidgeting. She was hyperaware of them now, as if she'd grown an extra pair of limbs.

"Someone to see you," said the boy through the din. "Doris somebody."

There was the sound of a chair scraping the floor, and then footsteps, and then Sam appeared and opened the door halfway, trying not to smile. He wore glasses; they suited him.

"Oh, *that* Doris," he said.

She laughed despite herself, but as he looked past her to her sisters she remembered the situation they were in. That sobered her up, and she took a breath, shoring up for the long argument.

"There's been some trouble at home, Sam."

His face changed as he registered her words, her tone, her expression.

He said, "I see."

Before Doris could explain—before she could even open her mouth to say anything else—he stepped aside and waved them in.

It's odd, Doris thought, how fast you can fall in love with someone.

twenty-one
HOP SKIP

Rebecca and Araminta froze at the sound of the truck.

There wasn't enough time to hide without looking suspicious. Rebecca thought quickly.

By the time the truck had rounded the corner and was passing them, they were walking arm in arm, coats draped over their shoulders, pretending to giggle at some joke and taking no notice of the truck at all.

Rebecca held something in her right hand under the knot of their joined arms, half-hidden by fabric, and prayed it looked like a purse and not like a woolen stocking shoved full of dollars and coins.

(When you'd saved as much as Rebecca had saved, you kept it close at hand, in something easy to carry. When you were Rebecca, you didn't think about the aesthetics of that thing until it was too late.)

Araminta was trembling, but when Rebecca squeezed her hand to remind her of her part, Araminta laughed all at once, light and clean as a bell, and for a moment Rebecca caught hold of the sweet sound and felt bold.

The boldness lasted until the corner, when the fear set back in.

"Let's get out of here," she said, and they let go of each other, shoved their arms into their sleeves, and picked up the pace.

Rebecca's mind was already a mile ahead of them.

They walked for a long time in a comfortable silence, which Rebecca thought was strange—they shared a room but nothing else, and had never been able to do so much as dress without getting on each other's nerves.

("Again?" Araminta had sighed whenever Rebecca pulled out the gold dress.

Rebecca had gotten so used to it that she was almost annoyed if Araminta let it go; what was the point in wearing the same dress every night they went out if it wouldn't put Araminta out of sorts?)

They slowed down several streets later, when the hum of crowded businesses overtook the hush of houses and it was easy to shuffle through strangers without attracting attention.

"We've lost the others," said Araminta, looking dolefully over her shoulder. "We'll have to go back for them."

"No going back," Rebecca said. "We don't know who that truck was for—God forbid we go back and get caught. And Father's probably still murderous, and the rest of them will all have scattered by now."

"They'll be in trouble!"

"We're not," said Rebecca.

Araminta looked around as if that wasn't a comfort.

Rebecca thought it over, trying to stay somewhere between optimistic and realistic.

"If any of them managed to get hold of a little money, they'll probably be all right. If not, they can probably wheedle some off a fella. Or steal it."

Off Araminta's scandalized look, Rebecca said, "They'll need money, and they're quick on their feet. Sometimes you make do. Don't look at me like I'm suggesting they pose naked in the Hudson for pennies, please."

Araminta tried to compose herself. Rebecca appreciated the effort, if not the effect.

(Of all the sisters to be stranded with, she thought, with a certain fondness.)

"We'll have to think about what to do," Rebecca said, "and situate ourselves, and then we can think of a way to reach them."

"The Kingfisher," Araminta said at once.

Rebecca had been thinking the same, but she also thought of Jo's return the morning after she'd been in jail. It was a mistake worth learning from: if you were going to go someplace that could get raided, you'd better have a place to reach someone who would bail you out.

No such luck.

Even if the Kingfisher was all right, Rebecca couldn't quite imagine wandering on the streets all day until it got dark, hoping not to get caught. Even one day was too long to go without a safe place waiting.

Jo had proved that, too.

Rebecca felt a pang, let the idea of the Kingfisher go.

And though she didn't want to hash the idea out with Araminta in the middle of the street, Rebecca suspected that even if they could find all the others again, and their old house was by some miracle left open and empty and ready for them, she and Araminta would still be looking for a place to stay.

Rebecca kept a weather eye out, in the way a middle child does. She suspected that some strange emancipation had just been forced on all of them and that whatever happened now, for once, would be of their own making.

They had dreamed so often of a chance at freedom, and here it was. Awful, and frightening, but freedom.

"We should find a room," Rebecca said.

Araminta glanced around. "A hotel room?"

There was a certain sort of hotel that was safe for young women alone. They probably frowned upon girls who showed up with wool stockings full of money and asked for a weekly room at the minimum rate.

"Maybe boardinghouses would be best," she said. "Less odd looking."

Araminta nodded. "We should buy a newspaper and see which boardinghouses are advertising, and then maybe if there are any places where I can pick up a little work."

Rebecca raised her eyebrows. "Work?"

Araminta smiled. "Well, surely someone in this city could use a girl who can sew?"

Rebecca was surprised by Araminta's ambition, which she knew was a little cruel—of all of them, Rebecca should have known better than to write someone off as dull just for being quiet.

But here they were, and Araminta was smiling in the street despite having been run out of her house, and taking charge of herself, and making plans, even though her hands were laced and shaking from more than the cold.

"Are you all right?" Rebecca asked. It was a dumb question, but she didn't know what else to do.

Ella would have known, but she and the twins would be a mile away by now; Rebecca was sure of that. Ella loved them all, but before she had been made a half-unwilling mother, she had been a dreamer. Rebecca remembered a little what she had been like before all the younger ones started going dancing, with her head full of plays and movies she'd never seen. Ella had spied against the nanny's door so often her ear was practically shaped like a keyhole.

Rebecca suspected that, at the bottom of things, Ella and the twins had only ever wanted a moment's excuse to chase some dreamy foolish notions right out of that attic and disappear.

"I will be fine," said Araminta, squaring her shoulders, "as soon as we find a newspaper." Then, quietly, "And maybe a meal, if we can afford one. I'm hungry."

Rebecca looped one of her arms over the other as they set off, trying her best to hide the lumpy stocking.

"We can," Rebecca said, and Araminta smiled as if they could cross it off the list of their troubles.

Their first meal didn't worry Rebecca. It was everything else that did.

When Rebecca and Araminta turned onto Fifth Avenue again, they had to squeeze through a swell of people, their thin shoes slipping on the pavement as they tried to keep pace, and they held on to each other with white knuckles.

(When they went out dancing, deciding who was cruel had been an academic exercise. Lou and Ella and the twins, and Jo, were a wall that protected you from harm.

But now they were alone, and the world was full of strangers; now they were playing a numbers game.)

Ella and the twins were already across the street by the time they heard the first sound of the truck.

Police, Ella thought wildly, and hissed, "Get down!"

The three of them banked a sharp left and smacked to a halt against the nearest building.

They stood in a knot, trembling, listening to the truck putting closer and closer to the back of the house.

What a coward our father is, Ella thought, that he wouldn't bring his daughters through the front door even for this.

Ella glanced at the twins, who right now looked more like greyhounds than girls, and wondered if they had the patience to wait out the truck (knowing they didn't, knowing that they'd have to act or ruin everything).

"Ella," Mattie said, without enough air to even support the word.

Then Ella whispered, "Go," and they were running.

For a moment, behind them, the truck rolled to a stop with a grind of brakes—Ella imagined the driver watching them, and the horrible quiet of the idling engine, and terror overtook her.

The first time the Kingfisher had been raided, Hattie and Mattie had had to grab her hands and drag her to get her moving into the tunnel.

Strange, what time changes—now she ran so fast she outpaced the twins for a full ten seconds.

(Ella wondered for a moment at the twins' ability to shadow her around a corner almost before she had decided to take it, a mirror double pacing her as she fled, before she remembered that they were all dancers, and the twins were used to following.)

When she finally stopped, the twins pulled up on either side of her, breathing steadily and in time with each other.

Out of habit, Ella waited a moment longer for the others to catch up.

Then, suddenly, it sank in that no other sisters were coming.

They were parted, now, because Ella had been frightened and left them behind.

"Oh God," Ella said. She couldn't breathe. "Oh God, what's happened?"

(I was selfish, she thought; I ran for myself.)

"They'll be all right," Mattie said.

Hattie said, "No one was alone."

That's not true, Ella thought, remembering Jo shouting for them to run.

Ella was already heading back the way they had come before the twins could catch hold of her elbows.

"Father's out for war!" said Hattie. "You're crazy!"

Mattie didn't say anything; she only held on to Ella's arm with one hand, so tight it hurt, as if she was looking for an anchor.

That much from Mattie was strange—the twins needed so little reassurance outside each other—strange enough that Ella actually did stop and turn.

For the first time Ella could remember, Mattie's mask had cracked. Her eyes were serious and scared and the size of dinner plates, and she was looking to Ella, not to Hattie.

Hattie must have seen it, too, because she let go of Ella to stand closer to her twin.

"Stop being such a 'fraidy," Hattie hissed. "You look ridiculous."

Ella knew what it really meant (*Are we twins or not?*), and from Mattie's guilty flinch, she did, too.

"I'm only saying we shouldn't go, that's all," Mattie said, dropping Ella's arm and turning to Hattie at last. Ella could feel the little flicker going out.

"Who should we send to look, then," asked Ella, "the police? I don't think they'd do very much against Father, and we don't even know yet why we had to run. Suppose he's put the cops on us himself, for dancing? Good luck trying to explain that."

"Don't say we can't go dancing," Hattie breathed. "You can't be serious."

Ella couldn't imagine. Dancing was a dangerous game, but it meant that at night, at least, they knew what to do with themselves.

Mattie went pale, but still she shook her head. "We've waited twenty years to get out of that house. Why would we ever go back?"

"Because maybe your sisters are afraid," Ella said. "Maybe they're scared and alone, and looking for us."

"Well, Doris had the little ones in hand," said Hattie, "and Rebecca had a sackful of money. The only thing she's looking for is a bank."

Ella smiled despite herself. "Then she'll do all right, and whichever of the other girls managed to stay close to her will benefit from her prudence and quick thinking."

(She hoped Rebecca had rescued Araminta, and Lily and Rose; the last she'd seen of the younger girls, they were half-falling down the stairs to be free, without a thing in their hands.)

Hattie and Mattie looked momentarily chastised and glanced down at the silver shoes each of them carried in one hand.

"I don't know," said Mattie. "If I had to choose again between a pile of money and a decent pair to dance in—"

"I'd still choose these," Hattie finished.

"Only because you never saved a nickel in your life," said Mattie.

"Because someone keeps making loaded bets with them!"

Their faces were a matched set again, and Ella felt equal parts disappointment and relief.

"Well, I don't have one thing to my name," she said, "and if we're really going to go out dancing somewhere, we'd better make it count the first time. No one likes a mooch who comes back to the table."

"You have your face," Mattie said. "Helen of Troy managed plenty with hers."

Ella gave her a circumspect look. "Just the outcome I'd hope for," she said.

(Though if that's what it came to, she had no trouble picking the path of least repute and shacking up with a fella for money; their father had wanted nothing better for them, and this way, she might choose.)

"We need to pick a real bee's-knees place tonight, then," said Ella. "Somewhere we can be seen."

Mattie pulled a face. "By whom?"

"By the sort of men who enjoy throwing money at pretty girls," said Ella.

Mattie and Hattie froze and looked at each other.

"You can save the dowager faces," Ella said. "We're not in a position to be dainty."

They had started walking, at some point; ahead of them was an enormous lawn ringed with trees, big enough to run out of sight in all directions.

Ella realized it must be Central Park. She'd always wanted to see it.

(Before this, she wasn't sure she'd ever have the chance to explore beyond the walls.)

The twins approached it nervously, looking around, overwhelmed by the open space.

"We'll go to the Swan tonight," Ella said. "They had photographers."

"In this?" Hattie said, at the same time Mattie said, "Ella, you can't be serious."

"If we can convince someone at Bloomingdale's to start us a line of credit for the house," Ella said, "we'll try to get something decent to wear."

A nice fat bill would serve their father right for thirty years of miserly catalogs.

"Then we'll go to the Swan and look pretty like our lives depend on it," she said. "We'll make what we can of it, and pray it's not the Funeral Parlor Supper Club once you get in the doors."

The twins gave her blank looks—of course, she thought; they'd never been to the cramped little club from years ago.

The only other three who would know that joke were scattered through the city somewhere, missing and frightened and maybe alone.

Ella composed herself.

"Are we looking out for anyone, there?" Mattie ventured.

Ourselves, Ella thought, but that was too theatrical a thing to say, even for her.

Looking for the other girls tonight was too soon. They were all smart enough to find their feet, but if their father was as terrifying as he seemed (Jo's screams had curdled Ella's blood for a reason), then doing something too soon might get them in more trouble.

Until then, she couldn't worry about what had happened to Jo, or run through the city in a panic about the others. (Had Lily and Rose even made it out of the shadow of the house?) She had to look out for the two sisters who were with her now, who had the faces of two flappers in a *Cinemascope* and matching silver shoes that weren't yet worn out.

They had to go somewhere for the night—there would be no camping out in this cold. They knew how to look like they belonged to a dance hall, by now.

And inside, there were men who'd pay money for the company of the right girl.

There were girls who needed money enough to be company.

"We look for them tomorrow," she said, fighting to keep her voice from shaking. "Tonight, we're going out."

••••••

Rose and Lily were close enough to Ella and the twins when the truck came rattling past that, if they wanted, they could have followed them.

It would have been the smart thing to do. It would have been second nature; they'd been taught young how to follow well.

They reached the other side of the street in time, and watched Hattie and Mattie and Ella become three little shapes in pale dresses huddled in the shadow of a building, coiled in terror and ready to run. Two brown heads and a blond one were turned in the same direction.

Rose and Lily saw where they were headed, could have joined them before they ran—there was time, still, to catch up with them, and run all together to wherever it was you ran when there was nowhere to go.

Ella would be kind to them, and maybe even the twins would be, and they wouldn't have to worry about being in this wide, snarled city all alone.

But it was the first time they had been outside in the daytime without a nanny keeping watch; it was the first time they had been without orders coming down from Jo and could do as they chose.

They didn't move.

(It was terrifying, but here they were, and they were together.)

It was the first time they had been alone with each other outside their little room, and for the first time they were running hand in hand, like twins.

Without a word they linked their fingers tighter, angled their path away from all the other girls, and ran as if they would never stop.

twenty-two
AFTER YOU'VE GONE

The first night at the Marquee nearly killed Jo.

As much as pulling things into line had been her stock in trade for twelve years, and despite how used she was to proving herself at night to a room of four hundred people, one way or another, Jo realized that the stakes were very different when you were pretending to a throne.

"Funny, I haven't heard much about you, Miss Renaud," Ames the bandleader said warily when she introduced herself that first afternoon.

He was younger than her father, but enough older than Jo that when she folded her arms and raised her eyebrows, unimpressed, he seemed surprised.

"That's too bad, then, I suppose," she said, "because I know you like foxtrot right after Charleston, and that one of your trumpet players goes a little sharp on 'Forgetting You,' and that I'd just as soon keep you, and that you charge more than any other bandstand in the city, and that while Tom's away, I'm the new management."

After a second, his expression changed, and he said, "Did you want to talk about the contract?"

"It would send me over the moon," she said, and at last, his face slid into a smile.

• • • • • •

When the band had left rehearsal for dinner, Jo pulled Henry aside.

"I'll need a dress," she said, trying as hard as she could to sound as if it had just occurred to her. "I simply haven't a thing worth wearing."

Henry knew someone who could carry a message to a shoe store on the Lower East Side, where there was a woman who couldn't risk stopping by a speakeasy in full daylight but who had impeccable taste.

Can't dress myself worth a damn. If you could send help to the address the gentleman mentions, will save me from being a laughingstock. Jo.

Two hours before the Marquee opened, a nervous girl appeared at the front door, carrying a flat dress box.

She couldn't have been older than Sophie; Jo pushed down a pang.

"Oh," said the girl, "I'm—is this—?"

"I'm Miss Renaud, yes."

The girl tried a smile.

This is what it looks like when a girl is new to the vales of the wicked, thought Jo.

She wondered if they'd looked like this, she and Lou and Doris and Ella, the first time they went out dancing.

She took a breath. "Come in, then," she said, and managed a smile. No sense in looking standoffish. She'd need to dress herself, for as long as this lasted, and she had to at least look like she knew what she was doing if anyone was going to buy it.

But the dress Myrtle had chosen was just Jo's size, and the netting beaded gray and gold was finer than anything Jo had ever worn, cut high across the collarbones so that her neck looked almost elegant. Little gold earrings danced just beneath her earlobes, the screws in the back two reassuring points of pain.

"Myrtle said you seemed like the practical type," the girl ventured, setting down a pair of black shoes, "but that if you want anything that's actually stylish, just send word."

They had a sturdy heel, but the T-strap was embroidered in gold, and when Jo put them on they fit like a fairy tale.

Araminta would love them.

The girl peered at her. "Do you—are they all right?"

"What's your name?"

"Elsie," the girl said, with the air of someone who wished she'd thought up something fake.

"Elsie, they're perfect. Thank you. Is there anything I can do for you? Did you want to stay for the dancing? You're my guest."

"Oh, no, not tonight," Elsie said, glancing at the door a little wistfully. "I have to get home. I don't like being out after dark much. My mother would worry."

"Of course," Jo said. "Can't have that."

The Marquee opened for business at ten in the evening.

At nine fifty-five, Jo was ready to have a heart attack. Her new shoes weren't sturdy enough to run in, not like catalog shoes, and her dress made too much noise, and if anyone thought she was a fraud, this would be the last mistake she ever made.

"I don't suppose Tom had some sort of marshaling call ahead of the doors," she said as she took a last tour of the room. The floor was spotless, the chairs aligned on the grid, the bandstand setting up and tuning. "Any wise things he used to say?"

" 'Don't drink with the customers or I'll fire you,' " Henry recited.

"Timeless words."

He raised a bottle. "You want one?"

"Don't tempt me."

The room had its own momentum; it was too late to call it off. The doors were going to open whether she stood here or not.

But she had been terrified the first time she took the others out, and terrified the first time the cops descended, and terrified the first time she realized Tom was never coming back.

Terror didn't matter; only that you stood your ground.

She nodded to Ames, who struck up a gentle waltz, and the bouncer at the door (McGee, Jo remembered) opened the door, and the guests began to trickle in.

If she was fighting not to gnaw off her nails until the room had two hundred people in it; she thought that was only fair for a first-timer.

If she looked at every face in case it was a sister, she tried not to mind it. Either they were smart enough to stay away, or she might get one or two back safe again.

On the third day, someone told their alderman that Tom had disappeared, and a girl was in charge.

When McGee summoned her, she came downstairs and saw the alderman's lieutenant (Parker, McGee had told her) waiting at a table, a bottle of their finest whiskey open in front of him with a couple of rounds already knocked out, and Henry behind the bar, polishing the same glass over and over.

Parker had a broad face and sharp blue eyes and the expression of a man who got his own way.

Still, the stakes here were lower than any time she'd been summoned to her father's office.

She took a seat.

"Strange that Tom never mentioned he was going to skip town," he said by way of introduction.

"That is strange," she said. "That doesn't suggest you're in his confidence much."

"He and I were discussing prices before he left."

"I'll bet."

"The cost of doing business has gone up."

She didn't answer. He frowned.

"I'm here for my money."

Why this seemed familiar, she couldn't say. She'd never had any money worth fighting for, until now.

"Well," she said, "I doubt *you* see much of it. Bosses have a way of walking off with the profits if there are any—have you noticed that? I mean, Tom pays me fair, but I bet sometimes you look at the money you're carrying home and just *wish*."

Parker snarled. "I get paid fine. A damn sight more than you do, I bet."

She changed tactics. "No doubt," she said. "Glad to hear your boss isn't hurting for money, then."

"I'm here for what Tom promised."

"He's not here for the next little while," she said. "You want a deal, you'll have to strike it with me."

"I don't do business with women."

She suddenly recognized what was so familiar about being here.

This was how her father did business.

She could do this. She knew how to herd someone who had to ask you for something. She knew the lure of unknown resources to someone who was desperately guessing.

She folded her arms. "Maybe not with your clothes on, but I'm sure you can adjust."

"You keep giving me lip and I'm going to teach you a lesson," he said.

"You can try it," she said, "and then you can see what contingency plans Tom left me with. He knows the oddest people, in offices you wouldn't expect."

He froze halfway to a word.

She smiled. (She held it until it softened—it was time to back off the challenges and get him on a path out the door.)

"Didn't Tom ever mention that police protection costs the kind of money that eats a man's livelihood?"

"We never—"

"And this is a generous place," she said. "He's been looking out for your alderman every week, and he told me to look out for you, too. Your alderman charges a fair price, he told me. I want to believe that's true. We all try to take care of our own."

She sat forward, arms crossed.

"What, exactly, was your alderman looking for?"

"Three hundred more a week."

She laughed quietly, gave him the look of a man to his fellow soldier in the trenches.

"I can't pay that and our supplier," she said. "I don't want to give up doing either—being safe is less exciting with only second-rate gin—but I just don't have it. I don't have half that."

Parker's face had lost its dangerous edge. "I'm under orders."

"I understand," she said. "Me too."

She paused, like she was thinking it over. "I can give you two hundred more, to start with," she said. "And when Tom hears how fair you've been, I'm sure he'll agree."

She smiled just shy of kindly, as the sidelong warning sank in.

"Of course," he said vaguely.

"Wonderful," she said, letting her smile get bigger, genuine. "Listen, I have to start putting my curl papers in, but I hope you'll come by tonight? I'll keep the rest of this bottle behind the bar, and you can go right to Henry there for anything you need. Have you ever been here at night?"

"No," he said, "never made it."

"Well, if you can get away from the boss, you should. This bandstand is the bee's knees, and it's the least the alderman can do, making you do the rounds before the fun starts. I'll tell McGee. Come by around eleven. We'll be expecting you."

Parker stood up with his hat in his hand, looking slightly concussed, and said with the air of someone who suspects a trap he can't see, "I'll present your offer to the alderman."

That was less than reassuring, but she'd take a respite; a respite meant another round of negotiation—another shot at winning.

"Wonderful," she said again, and gave him a firm handshake on his way out. He looked a little concerned, a little glazed, and too late, Jo wondered if he'd brought a weapon.

The door closed behind him.

Jo rested a hand on the table for balance.

Henry came up beside her, the whiskey bottle in his hand.

"I thought you were bluffing before about Marlowe willing you the gig, but he picked the right man for the job. Those are decent tricks."

"I'm my father's daughter," said Jo.

That night, as the crowd filed in, she felt as though she'd lost something.

She checked inventory, but they were stocked. The bandstand showed up on time. Even Parker showed up close to midnight, in the same suit and a nicer tie.

(She sat him at a table close to the dance floor on the far side of the room from the bar. A man who was dancing all night was a man who wasn't keeping a close eye on volume.)

Four times, she checked in with the boys at the door to see if they'd felt that any of the newcomers were plainclothes constables.

It was near closing when she realized it was Lou she had been looking for.

It was Lou, because for the last twenty years, if Jo had done something, terrible or not, Lou heard it first.

Jo had been trying to tell Lou, all night.

She went into the basement, took heavy breaths in the darkness for three minutes until it felt less like she was going to cave in.

They won't be there when you go back upstairs, she told herself sternly. Get ahold of this. They aren't there, and you have a business to run, and you have to pull yourself together.

(I've failed them all, she thought, and her throat closed tight. I marshaled them because I could, and now they're gone and there's nothing I can do, and that's the reason that when I go back upstairs, everyone is going to be a stranger.

I'm my father's daughter, she thought, and she wanted Lou beside her, to lie and say it wasn't so.)

What really killed Jo about the Marquee was watching the crowd dancing every night.

What killed her was her old, unbreakable habit of looking for sisters who weren't there.

She was relieved, most of the time, once she'd thought it over calmly.

(She needed to think about it calmly once or twice a night, whenever the band struck up "Charleston Baby of Mine," and she was flooded with the memory of them scrambling for the dance floor, Hattie and Mattie skipping at the front of the line with their arms already over their heads, and Jo had to blink carefully for a second until her eyes were clear.)

It was for the best that they had scattered. If any of them ever showed up at the Marquee, it would be because they had run into trouble everywhere else and were willing to seek sanctuary in a place they'd been to only twice.

As long as they were elsewhere in the world, then Jo could imagine that all ten of them had made it out all right and were enjoying their freedom in daylight hours, at long last.

She hoped it was true. She liked to imagine them as a flock that made their way through the city and came to roost at sundown, together and happy.

(Dance had only ever been meant as a way for them to pass the time, until the worst was over and they could surface. Jo hadn't known, back then, how long the worst would last.)

But even as she tried to believe they had all landed on their feet—they were clever, and the world couldn't be any worse on them than their father had been—there was always the chance that something had gone wrong.

There was always the gnawing fear that none of them would ever come here again, because one way or another, their father had gotten hold of them.

That's what killed Jo.

twenty-three
SOME OF THESE DAYS

Jo called Three Willows one afternoon, asking if it was possible to speak to "Miss Hamilton."

It was not. Staff were not permitted to discuss patients of the institution.

"I'm Mr. Hamilton's secretary," she tried, but whether he had warned the staff about it or their policies simply forbade it, it got her nothing, except a request to come in and make the request in person, if she was willing.

(She was not.)

"Henry," she asked one afternoon as they were setting up, "if you had a sister and she had to run away, where would you want her to hole up?"

"Back home," Henry said.

"Not helpful."

He shrugged. "It's a big city. You can hide anywhere. A hotel, I suppose, if she had the money. Maybe boardinghouses, though they don't give out names to strangers."

"How long would it take to go to them all?"

Henry laughed like she'd been joking, and after a second, she smiled as if she really had been.

• • • • • •

At the end of her first week, a representative of the New York Police Department stopped by the Marquee to inspect operations and pick up the milk money.

Jo had worried that she wouldn't recognize an off-duty cop in this crowd—so many men looked edgy when they were underground.

But when he appeared, Jo looked up and saw him and took the stairs smiling.

"Officer Carson!"

"Sergeant."

"Congratulations, then," Jo said. "I remember when you were still manning the drunk tank and being kind to young ladies who had no one to call. You've moved up in the world."

Recognition dawned on his face, and he smiled.

"So have you," he said. He frowned, then said a moment later, "I mean, I hope."

Jo laughed, took his arm, and escorted him to the bar.

She had no desire to discuss the past or the present with a cop (any cop, just in case), but it was good to cultivate kind people— you never knew when your alderman was going to turn sour and you would need a friend on the inside to let you know before the worst happened.

But the milk money was behind the bar anyway, and it was just good business to make sure no valuable associate left still thirsty.

She never moved out of the empty studio above the Marquee where she'd spent her only night with Tom.

That one she tried not to think about; you can't worry about everything, and she'd manage if it meant free room and board.

Not that she was sleeping much. As things turned out, it was impossible to sleep well when you were used to eleven sisters around you, the floorboards and bed frames and rustling blankets making a little symphony that let you know you weren't alone.

• • • • • •

Luckily, she was used to getting by on little sleep (who would have guessed her attic life had prepared her so well for employment of ill repute?).

She was also used to spotting trouble just before it started, and putting out fires in short order.

Once she saw a man who was getting too fresh for her liking, and she'd crossed the floor before she'd thought about it.

"Who made you chaperone?" a guy asked, when she tapped him on the shoulder and told him to get his hands off the lady and get out.

"She did," Jo said. "Leave before I make you."

The girl was Elsie.

Jo didn't realize at first. Then she looked twice.

She must have been staring; when Elsie said "Thanks," she looked as nervous as she had with the handsy fella.

Jo started to ask if her mother knew she was out on the town. But she wasn't anyone's general any more, and people had reasons for coming out nights.

She only said, "Grab a drink at the bar. Tell him it's on me."

She wiped her palms on her dress (left two wet spots near her hips), tried to shake it off.

On her way to her office, Mr. Parker stopped her.

"Didn't realize you were running a boardinghouse," he said.

She half-smiled. "Sure thing," she said. "I'm going out for a cig. If anyone else gets handsy, you just tell them to leave room for the Holy Spirit until I get back."

He watched her go.

Outside, she looked up at the sky through the halo of the streetlights out in front.

It was calm, and cooler here than inside with the press of bodies, and it was easier to sort things through.

There was no harm in what she'd done. She had a business

to run and couldn't go getting sentimental, but all the same, no woman in this dance hall would get less than she'd given her sisters.

Maybe someone was doing the same for Rebecca, somewhere, for the sake of this girl that she looked like.

Jo stopped drinking.

She started standing at the corner of Thirty-Eighth after the workshops let out, to scan faces.

She started wearing black gloves at night.

"I wish you'd tell me what the matter is," Henry said, once. It was afternoon, and in the daylight he looked even younger, as blond and guileless as a prince in a play.

"If wishes were horses," she told him.

He raised an eyebrow, said, "We're low on champagne." A little hesitation after it, some word he didn't fill.

(One of her sisters must have talked to Henry about her; whenever he was impatient with her, he called her General.)

After dark, it felt like some magic kept the worst of the world at bay, and she was able to forget everything except the flow of the music, and the flow of the dance floor, and the flow of booze, and she presided over a room full of strangers every night.

She saw girls who looked like her sisters. Every time a baby vamp came in with a dark bob and bright red lips and a string of fake pearls down her front, Jo checked twice, just to make sure it wasn't one of the twins.

Every time it wasn't, she had to take a breath.

Be clever, she thought, all the time, like the words flew out the door and into the streets. Be cleverer than I was.

• • • • • •

A few days later, Jo went to the post office near her old home (it was already her old home — it was somewhere she had lived a lifetime ago) and, as Mr. Hamilton's private secretary, asked to see if there was any word from Lou.

The man at the teller's window looked at Jo a moment too long, asked too sweetly if Jo would wait just a moment before he disappeared.

Jo knew by now what it sounded like when someone was going to turn you in.

She vanished.

It was her father's best move yet, that he'd thought to warn even the post office against any stray women asking for letters. That little revenge cut her more than she'd thought he even could.

(They had been at war, and she hadn't realized; they'd been at war, and he was winning.)

More than the idea that her sisters had run off in little knots and were working together to stay well, more than the idea that she was alone, it kept her awake at night to think that Lou might be trying to send some word or to beg for help and would never be answered.

Three pairs of shoes were lined along an empty wall.

After two weeks, Jo was wrapped up enough in her work that she could sometimes ignore the familiar knot in her stomach as long as the dance floor was moving smoothly and no one stood out more than the rest, as if the rise and fall of each bandstand set was a metronome she could time her worries to.

(The waltz didn't bother her much. Every Charleston, she ached.)

Sophie's white knight from the Kingfisher, Mr. Walton, made an appearance that week.

Jo must have been more of a cipher than she'd thought, because she greeted him and guided him all the way to a table, and it was only when she asked what he was drinking that he recognized her.

"You're without your retinue," he commented, after a hopeful glance around the room. "We've been missing them since the Kingfisher. Do they come here often?"

She had a face she could hold up for things like this now, polite and still.

(She wasn't sure how fond Sophie was of Mr. Walton—she always seemed vaguely fond of everyone—and Mr. Walton seemed a little overfond of Sophie.)

"Not for weeks," Jo said, and tried to smile, "though I hope for them any day now."

That night, it hurt just to look over the dance floor.

Jo got used to dressing in an empty room, putting on makeup in the little mirror in the bath, so quiet that she could hear the beads on her dress as she moved.

(Myrtle was making good use of her commission; Jo had a dozen dresses now, all her own, and three pairs of fine shoes, and earrings that clinked in the silent room when she lifted them up from a tray.)

But there were eleven ghosts that she always half-expected whenever she passed a window or a mirror or opened her closet too quickly and saw twelve dresses hanging, and that little heartbreak never faded.

For weeks, she lived on champagne, and bread and cheese and fruit from the grocer down the street, and the thrill of working well in a place she'd never expected to see again, and the terror of not knowing what had happened to her sisters.

(The terror fed her more than anything. She had taken to walking through the tenements downtown whenever she was out, peering up at girls on the fire escapes that looked too much like

Sophie or Rebecca, ducking into every shop she passed just in case there was a familiar face behind the counter.

She was wearing out shoes faster than she ever had when she was dancing.)

But the Marquee opened every night, and the police hadn't raided them, and the alderman hadn't burned them out. Yet.

If Jo felt like she was going to lose her mind from worry, she just had to make sure it wasn't during business hours.

It would be all right, she thought, if she could just keep from crumbling.

Then Jake came to see her.

Jo was developing a sixth sense for who was walking through the door—a benefit of a staircase that presented every entrant.

It took away some of the romance of Tom coming to meet her the three nights she'd come here (watchfulness, nothing else) but made it easier to see when an old friend came to visit.

He had the disadvantage, peering over the crowd as he took the stairs, but his sharp profile and slick dark hair stood out against the plaster walls, and she saw him all the way from the bandstand.

She avoided the dance floor and took the stairs through the mezzanine, past tables scattered with gloves and hats and glasses (past the corner booth that always sat empty), and was at the bottom of the stairs before he reached them.

Just seeing someone she knew robbed her, for a moment, of courage.

His face was grim—he might be bringing bad news. He might be angry at her for being competition; he might be here to tell her the police were right behind him.

As he caught sight of Jo, she moved forward to greet him like a businessman would.

(It was the same way she'd met Carson, smiling and one hand out to shake, when you were still sizing each other up and deciding on your options.)

But he came down the last two stairs in a rush and caught her up in a hug that surprised her so much that when he let her go again and stepped back, she still had her hand out to shake.

"Hiya," she managed.

He smiled, but something behind it was too worried for it to stick. "God," he said, "it's good to see you doing all right."

(I've seen you look at Lou, she thought, this sort of nonsense will get you nowhere. But she couldn't bring herself to say so—he looked, in this light, a little like Tom, and maybe it wasn't fair to make fun of where someone's heart was.)

She said, "You, too. What's happened?"

"What makes you think something's happened?"

"It's been a month," she said. "Either something wonderful has happened that couldn't wait, or you're bringing me news you'd rather not."

Jake said, "Maybe it's tricky to explain to your boss you want a night off to visit the competition, so you have to wait until everyone's happy and the cops are off your case before you go sneaking around. Especially in a neighborhood that's not always welcoming."

Jo made a face. "Point taken."

The staircase filled up for a moment as a little waterfall of people descended; Jo absently greeted two regulars, and realized she didn't want to hear Jake's news right here on the stairs.

"Well," she said when the others had passed, "as long as you're risking it all, you should find out what the competition's drinking. Bar's this way."

He glanced down at her grip on his arm as she pulled them toward the back and then across the crowd to the bar, which was doing brisk business in between songs.

"So this is how you run your place, manhandling your guests and getting them blotto?" He raised an eyebrow. "I approve."

"Not as much as you will," she said, and flagged down Henry for two glasses of the good whiskey. It was expensive as hell but a step up from Canadian Club, and she kept it behind the bar just in case cops or old friends came calling.

When she passed him his glass, he looked at her a moment too long. His eyes were dark and steady.

"What's your name?" he asked.

A lot of things were changing, these days.

"Josephine. Jo."

He nodded. "Nice to meet you."

"This way, smart aleck."

In the back office, she pulled up her chair, set down her glass, planted her hands, and waited.

Jake tasted the whiskey, made an impressed face, and peered at the glass in the dim ceiling bulb.

"Top-shelf stuff. Let me know if you ever need a bartender."

"For you, always."

He grinned. "Either I'm a fantastic bartender, or you've learned how to flatter people since you left the Kingfisher."

She didn't answer. Too much had happened since she'd left the Kingfisher, and she'd played host as much as her nerves would let her. Now she needed the news.

In this light, he sure looked like the bearer of bad tidings; he looked as if he'd aged ten years since she'd seen him that morning in the police station and he'd saved her hide.

(It felt like ten years, to her.)

"Jake," she said finally, when he seemed lost in his own thoughts. "Be a pal."

He sobered and set down his glass.

"Someone came to see me," he said.

Oh, God, oh God, the girls were in trouble.

Her heart turned over, and her breath caught, and she pressed her hands into the desk so hard her fingertips hurt.

When she trusted her voice she said, "Go on."

"I haven't seen any of them," he said at once, meeting her eye. "I'm coming to see you now because I couldn't be sure this news was the right stuff. I tried to find out more, but I know so little about—" He stopped and frowned, as if surprised at his own frustration. "I just didn't know what to do about any of it, and it was driving me batty not being able to find out."

Jo remembered the night he'd led a handful of them to safety, the look he'd given Lou when he thought no one could see.

He went on. "I was only able to find out that Tom left town and there was some woman running his shop. The rest of it seemed so under the table I didn't know what to do, until I could come see you myself."

There had, apparently, been no doubt that she was the woman running the place.

"It's still nothing much to go on."

She didn't blame Jake for thinking this might all be something untoward—for fearing the worst, as his grim face gave way.

Something terrible had happened. Oh God.

"Tell me," she said.

twenty-four
LUCKY DAY

"Some man was asking for you," Jake said.

Jo couldn't breathe. "What?"

Jake said, "You, or any news of you. I didn't know your name—well, yet—but I could guess who he meant. Not many people answer your description, not the way he gave it."

She could imagine.

"He called you Jo."

She knew Jake was watching her, and she shouldn't give anything away, but she felt hope creeping in, all the same.

"I wasn't about to tell anything to some stranger," he said, "but it struck me how sure he was that I would have heard from you already. I don't know what to make of it. Said his name was Sam."

Jo had to wrap her hands around the edge of the seat to keep from screaming.

Sam Lewisohn. Sam Lewisohn had been to see her.

She didn't even bother to change clothes. If what Jake had told her was true—if even half of it was true—what she was wearing wouldn't matter.

As soon as the floor was swept and the locks thrown, Jo was in a cab headed for the Lewisohns.

Even though the streets were nearly empty this early in the

morning, it felt as though the cab was crawling, and Jo pressed an open hand to the door as if to speed it forward.

Every second was too long now.

She didn't know whether Doris was even with him any more, if she'd ever been with him, or if he'd seen any of the rest—he hadn't said anything about the sisters to Jake.

(She'd told Jake some of the facts—if he was going to be her friend in earnest, she owed him a little of the truth.

"Sisters?" he'd repeated, and frowned, as if trying to reconcile the picture of twelve strange and disparate and near-magic girls swanning over the dance floor with the dull notion of sisters being brought one at a time into the fold. "You've had your hands full, then."

"Until a few weeks ago," Jo agreed, and told him the bare bones of what had happened with their father.

It had gratified her that Jake hadn't laughed it off as an adventure, or suggested anything to her as though it would be simple enough for her to force her father's hand if only she would speak to him sharply.

Instead he'd said, "Then I hope he ends up taking a long walk off a short pier," and Jo had smiled and said, "Me too."

Then she'd told him about Lou and Tom; that had been harder.)

Jo tried not to hope. There was still every chance that her sisters were scattered and lost.

But if Sam Lewisohn was looking for her, Doris had sent him.

She would find one of her sisters today, at least, or she'd know the reason why.

· · · · · ·

Sam Lewisohn's house was a narrow, tidy town home on the Lower East Side, and even though the taxi ride felt like ages, it must have been less than ten minutes before Jo was charging up the stairs.

She took them so quickly that the beading on her dress jangled and knocked against her knees as she ran, and her stockings slipped an inch down her calves from the exertion.

She didn't care—the Lewisohns could take her as they found her.

She knocked harder than was polite, five sharp raps with a shaking fist, and braced herself for whatever would happen.

Sam Lewisohn opened the door.

Her heart sank at the look on his face—surprised and wary—and she braced herself for the bad news (and to stick a foot in his door if she had to, until she knew whatever he did).

But that dark expression only lasted a moment; then he was glancing behind her at the street, and then he was opening the door for her.

"In the garden," he said.

She was already running.

She'd thank him later. This couldn't wait.

Doris was in the center, a book open on her lap. Next to her was Sophie, who was quietly bent over some sewing, and a little farther away at the edge of the garden, Violet was practicing the Baltimore, stepping gingerly over the stones when it was time for shines.

The relief was like a punch to the stomach, and it took Jo a moment to make sure she was still breathing.

Doris glanced up just before Jo shouted her name.

Over the surprised bleats Sophie and Violet made, Jo trampled down the stairs so quickly she missed one and staggered the last step into Doris's arms.

Something was pinching her between two of her ribs, but by then Sophie and Violet had reached her, and she was trying to encompass all three of them at once, and for a moment it was a tangle of limbs and Violet and Sophie welcoming her back and telling Doris not to cry and Jo was holding them too hard, and Jo knew she was probably making a fool of herself.

When she had herself under control, she pulled back and held them at arm's length, until she could rub the tears from her eyes and focus on them all properly.

"Tell me what happened," she said.

Doris laughed. "There's the General we missed."

She wiped her eyes with her cuffs, then frowned at them.

"I have to stop things like that," said Doris. "Mr. Lewisohn Sr. gets in a fit when he sees you mistreating clothes, and I'm in enough hot water with him."

Jo looked down at Doris's left hand, which had a thin gold band on one finger.

After the first shock faded, she said, "When? Why? Where is he?"

"Well, don't hit him or anything," said Doris.

"That depends—now tell me."

"He's been the bee's knees," Doris admitted. "He was the first place I went after we ran—"

"Did you all get out?"

For a moment, Doris went pale and gripped Jo's hands. "Oh my God, Jo, you really had no idea what happened to us, did you? Not for a month—oh, Jo, I'm so sorry."

"So you all made it?"

"Yes," Doris said. "Everyone."

Jo's legs turned suddenly to jelly, and she concentrated for a moment on standing up. She locked her knees.

"All right," she said. Her mind was racing, she couldn't focus—she wanted to know everything at once. "All right, tell me what happened to you."

Doris grinned. "Well, I went to see him, with these two in tow, no less, and I was prepared to make a scene like you can't imagine, but I never had to. He took us in lickety-split, and we were settled here before sundown."

"Romantic. Is that why you just couldn't wait another minute to get married?"

Doris blushed. "Not exactly. Father got in contact with Sam the next day, to warn him that we'd all gone off the rails and were hysterical and roaming the streets. Father said that if we ever contacted Sam, he should let Father know and he'd take care of it all."

The hair on the back of Jo's neck stood up.

"But Sam's not simple," Doris said, "and he knows a threat when he hears it. So he and I decided to get married by a justice of the peace, sooner rather than later, so that Father couldn't make a case to drag me back."

Jo raised an eyebrow. "Just like that?"

Doris pulled a face. "Mr. Lewisohn Sr. wasn't thrilled," she said. "But Sam pointed out that if I was good enough for him when he was sent to court me, then I was good enough for him now."

Jo wondered if Doris knew she was blushing.

"A week ago we filed adoption papers with the court for Violet. It's going to get ugly, I'm pretty sure, but Mr. Lewisohn Sr. hates Father so much for giving him the trouble of a daughter-in-law with none of the cachet that she promised, I think he's looking forward to a little fight. When things come through, she's going to school. Sophie's too old to get protection for, but she's safe with us until something else happens. We're hoping Mr. Lewisohn Sr. can find her some work for evening gowns."

Jo glanced at the embroidery Sophie was holding.

"Sophie's stitches are so even that she's almost made up for the awkward, poor, sudden daughter-in-law," Doris said solemnly.

Jo saw that Doris's book (it was the edge of it that had pinched her) was called A Tailor's Companion.

She couldn't help laughing. "Doris, of all people," she said. "I hope he's worth it."

Doris's blush spread. "It's not perfect, but as problems go I'll take these over the ones we had before. And he's been a prince."

"He has, truly," put in Violet.

"We all like him," Sophie said.

Jo still stumbled over who "we all" might be, but then she heard a noise on the stairs and saw that Sam Lewisohn was just appearing in the doorway. He had loitered a little, then, to give them time.

"Come down, then," she said. "I'd like to shake hands with my brother."

Sam grinned and came down the stairs into the garden, though as it happened, he preferred to hug his sister rather than just shake hands.

"You had us worried," he said. "We couldn't find hide nor hair of you."

"We even tried the paper," Sophie said, "in case you'd left a message."

"Of course we'd already thought about the Kingfisher, but we didn't know if Father knew about it," Violet added. "So Sam offered to go."

"The man I spoke to froze me out but good," Sam said. "I couldn't tell if he even knew you."

"And that was two weeks ago," said Doris. "We were trying jails by then, but if you were under a false name we'd never know, and of course you would have been."

Jo smiled. "I was last time."

"You see, I knew it," said Doris.

Jo watched some silent conversation between Doris and Sam, and a moment later Sam was going down the stairs into the kitchen—calling for breakfast, then.

(She'd have to learn not to worry about those things; just because Jo was in the habit of pulling people aside for news for the last month didn't mean every private moment was a dangerous one.)

"All of us were stumped after that," Violet said. "We worried Father had gotten his hands on you."

"*Some* of us did," said Doris. "I always figured that if he had you, you'd have cut the phone line so he couldn't call around scaring people."

"Some of *who* did?" Jo said. "Who else have you seen? Is everyone all right?"

"Rebecca and Araminta are still in the city," Sophie said. "Araminta already has work at Bloomingdale's. She's a seamstress there, does alterations in Ladies' Gowns." There was a note of wistful envy in the words.

"And Rebecca's gone to school for stenography," Doris said. "She had so much money stashed away that she could afford school three times over, but she'll end up somewhere that does her good."

Jo frowned. "So why aren't they here with you?"

Doris cocked her head. "Why would they be? They found a place on a quiet street not too far north, and they have some money to live on."

"But—" Jo faltered. "But wouldn't you want—?"

"They like it," Violet said. "Sam even offered, but they didn't want to."

"Because they didn't want to impose on Sam," Jo said, "but I'm sure if I found us a place to be all together again we could—"

"Jo," Doris said. Her eyes were dark and serious. "They're happy where they are."

For a moment, Jo's mind failed her, and she could only think in terms of things missing, as though she'd left something behind—something she couldn't name—and it was already too late to ever find it again.

(They hadn't failed, even though she'd failed them. It hadn't come to her worst fears. She should be happier than this.)

When she looked around, she and Doris were alone in the garden, and Doris had led her to the garden bench and was looking at her a little strangely.

"Jo, I can't imagine what you've been through, all on your own. I can't even think—I had Sophie and Violet with me and I knew the others had gotten away all right, but I still didn't sleep for a week, not until I'd heard from Ella."

Ella. "Where is she? How did you find her?"

"She found me, actually," Doris said. "She guessed where I would go, and that Sam would be brave enough when it counted. She called him up—she was prepared to shout him out of town, I think, if he had let us go—but the next thing I knew he was handing me the phone."

That made Ella a sharper judge of character than Jo had been.

"And Sophie found Araminta," Doris said. "They both answered an advertisement for a position in alterations at Bloomingdale's—they found each other in line on hiring day. You could have knocked me over with a feather. When Sophie came home with Araminta and Rebecca in hand I thought I would faint, I really did. I ruined two cuffs, I was crying so hard."

It felt like Doris was laying stones on Jo's chest.

"When—when did that happen?"

Doris said, "Just over two weeks ago. That was the night I asked Sam to go to the Kingfisher and ask about you, because I thought if we had one miracle in a day we might as well have two."

"I wish you'd gone over yourself," Jo said. "Jake thought it was a trap—I had warned him that nothing was to be trusted—and it's why he waited to tell me."

Doris sighed. "Well, that's what happens when you let twelve suspicious girls loose on the streets, I suppose. Can't be helped."

Her skin prickled—she needed to see them all again, as many as possible and as soon as possible (sheep-counting was a habit that was hard to break).

"Boy," Doris said, "do I wish Ella and the twins had gone a little later."

Ella was with Hattie and Mattie, then. All three of them had gotten out all right. Jo made fists, released them.

"Where did they go?"

Doris wrinkled her nose and braced herself a little, as if she was still fourteen and waiting to be told whether or not they could go out dancing.

"Hollywood."

Jo laughed.

It was a little loud and a little too long, but the morning's emotions had been piled on too fast and too heavy for her to believe everything now; she'd have to laugh now, think later.

Doris barged on. "They went to the Swan the first night—to pick up men, I guess, from what the twins told me, though Ella won't say anything now about what she'd really planned. I suppose picking up men is as good a way to make money as anything else, in a pinch. A producer saw Hattie and Mattie dancing. When he saw them going back to sit with Ella . . ."

Here Doris only shrugged. It was no question what would happen if a Hollywood man laid eyes on Ella.

"They did a screen test," Sophie said from the window.

Violet said, peevish, "We didn't get to go."

Jo smiled at her, wondered if she would ever be able to look at her and not see a girl in a nursery.

"And they're already on a train?" she asked Doris.

"They left on Thursday," Doris said. "They wanted to wait to see if you would find us again, but the scout said this was going to be their only fare-paid invitation, and I told them to take it."

Jo raised her eyebrows.

"Don't look at me that way, Jo, please. You know that she and the twins are going to be the toast of the town, and they'll get better work there than here. They had two appearances lined up before they even got on the train. Ella's going to send me a postcard when they're settled, to let me know their new names—they have to talk to the studio about it first, apparently. No one wants them using the old name."

The old name. Ella and the twins would leave it behind; Doris already had; Violet might soon. No one had called Jo by her last name since she'd left the steps of her father's house.

The Hamilton legacy was doomed in earnest.

Jo thought that served her father right.

"And what about Rose and Lily?"

Doris shook her head. "No word. They left together. We're hoping they're all right."

Poor twins, Jo thought with a twisting stomach.

She recalled every time she'd ever overlooked them, all at once; she felt what she should have felt, then, and a rush of awful imaginings of what could have happened—images of them trapped in some factory, in some train car, in some alley frozen dead. They were still missing, and they'd had no one to look out for them, no one who even knew them well enough to guess where to start searching.

Jo was beginning to realize how little she'd known about them, when it mattered.

She was beginning to realize how little they needed her now.

(Why did she feel so tangled?)

"Jo," Doris said. "You look pale—what's wrong?"

She shook her head. It was too embarrassing to say aloud. She had to pull herself together.

"And where have *you* been?" Doris shook Jo's sleeve once to punctuate. "At least we knew the twins had gotten out—when we ran you were still shouting at Father like to raise the dead."

Jo could only imagine what it had sounded like from the outside. "He threatened me with the mental hospital," she said.

Doris went pale. "What?"

"For all of us," Jo said, "if we insisted on defying him."

Off Doris's horrified frown, she explained, "Father found out that we went dancing at night. He wanted us put away for it."

"Oh my God." Doris pulled her hands back and pressed one open palm to her chest. "Jo, tell me that's not where you've been. Please, no."

Jo shook her head. "I got stalled by van de Maar, but he faltered and I made it out of there before anyone could reach me."

"So where have you been? What are you doing now? Have you seen anyone?"

"Here," Jo said. "I've been here the whole time, and I've seen everyone in the world but the people I wanted to see. I host the Marquee."

There was a beat of silence. Then it was Doris's turn to laugh until she cried.

"We've all been *dying* for a dance," she said, "but we were too afraid to go out anywhere until we knew what had happened. We didn't know what to do, and Ella went to that new place and never went back because it wasn't the same. You're awful for keeping it a secret, Jo—don't think I'll ever forgive you because I won't."

Doris stood up, said, "Wait until I tell them all we get to go dancing tonight!"

Then she ran into the house, her little gold ring catching the light.

Still, Jo couldn't shake, just for a moment, the image of Doris at eight years old, learning new steps, grinning like her face would split the first time she got them right all the way through.

And now Jo sat in Doris's husband's garden, where most of her sisters had already been and gone, and wondered if any of them would ever need her again the way she must have needed them.

(Lou. Lou had loved her in earnest; but that didn't bear thinking about.)

After Jo had told Jake about Lou and Tom, there was a long and measured silence.

"Married," he said finally.

"A month ago. They were on the road to Chicago, last I knew."

Jake frowned, shook his head like he was clearing water out of his ears. "Are they in love?"

"I don't know," Jo had said, around a lump in her throat. "She needed to get out, and he was willing to take her. I wouldn't know what happened after that."

Maybe nothing had happened between them. Maybe they were sniping back and forth to cover an awkward silence every time they crossed paths.

Maybe they were in love by now. (She tried not to imagine what that would look like—a dance floor, maybe, a tawny head and a bright one, two wide smiles.)

Jo knew that even Lou, sooner or later, would have to love somebody, and Tom could make himself easy to love.

"I never took Tom for the scoundrel type," he said.

"He isn't," said Jo, because at least that much she was sure of. "He did it as a favor."

She stopped herself there, and she had said it so plainly that it might have sounded like nothing but the facts, but still Jake looked up at her for a long time, as he ran his finger around the rim of his empty glass.

After a while he said, "You have a real knack for getting people to do you favors."

"Only with the ones who care about us," she said.

She didn't want to pin Jake down on his longing for Lou just now—it was cruel to make too fine a point—but she would if she had to.

He must have seen she was willing to do it; he didn't answer.

"I don't know how to reach them," he said instead.

She dropped her head into the frame of her hands for a moment, fingertips framing her temples and chin.

But he was thinking things over.

A moment later he said, "I never knew his associates in Chicago—not in the loop out there. But I have a few old friends there—they might know where to find someone who doesn't mind being found. So if he's in business or Lou really is at a decent place, I could send someone to look. It's better than nothing."

It was more than Jo had hoped for. She'd take it.

Jake looked a little steely across the desk—maybe worried about what Tom and Jo had gotten Lou into—but he was still willing, and it would do.

"What do you want to say?"

Jo said, " 'Come home.' "

twenty-five
IT'LL GET YOU

Doris and company showed up in force at the stairs of the Marquee.

It was good to see them. It was so good to see them that Jo could almost forget the ache of Rose and Lily (still ghosts) as soon as she fixed eyes on Rebecca and Araminta again.

The band was in the middle of a Charleston, and even as Jo made her way to them from the other end of the dimly lit club, she could see Doris's eyes shining and Rebecca tapping her toes.

Rebecca was in a different gold dress, and Araminta had another long strand of beads wrapped around her neck, and Jo couldn't help laughing. It was comforting to think that even if some things had changed so much, some things never would.

When Doris saw Jo, she grinned and led the others down the stairs.

(Doris seemed to have gotten pretty good at taking the lead since they'd all run away, Jo thought, trying not to be jealous and almost getting there.)

Rebecca and Araminta threw themselves into Jo's arms. Jo inhaled the familiar scent of soap and primroses and felt the same unraveling knot as when she'd seen Doris and Sophie and Violet and known that those sisters, at least, were safe.

Araminta pulled back sniffling and wiping her eyes, but Rebecca was only squeezing Jo's arm and beaming and looking around at the room.

"I can't believe you run all this," she said.

Rebecca was still candid, then.

Jo said, "Nah, I'm only the host—you know it's the bartenders who actually run the place. I like the new dress."

Araminta groaned. "Can you believe it? I nearly threw it out the window when she showed me. All the dresses in the world and this is the one she picks."

"It's not the dress that counts," said Rebecca, "it's the dancer. And"—turning to Jo—"Araminta should be happy anyway—at least I bought these."

She and Araminta each held out one foot, and Jo had the satisfaction of finally seeing her sisters in dancing shoes that fit. Araminta's were apple green, and Rebecca's were red, and somehow Jo couldn't stop smiling.

(They were such a little thing, but they weren't—they were the freedom that came after the prison.)

"We put them on in the apartment before we came down," Rebecca said, and Jo heard what Rebecca was really trying to say (we're happy, we're safe).

Araminta glanced down and saw Jo's shoes—black velvet—and smiled. "Not bad," she said, "even if your dress is still a little old-fashioned."

"Not all of us work at Bloomingdale's," Jo said. "Now get on the dance floor before Rebecca has a fit."

Rebecca laughed, but she was disappearing into the crowd, already looking for a partner. Sophie wasn't far behind her, and Violet slid by a moment later, stopping just long enough to peck Jo on the cheek and say "Hi, Jo" on her way past.

(It sounded like the first time Violet had ever called Jo by her name. Jo couldn't remember if it was.)

Jo realized Sam had come with them, a beat too late to be polite about it—she wasn't used to looking for men who weren't Tom or Jake—and when she grasped his hand in greeting he was grinning slyly.

"You'll get used to me," he said.

"He keeps saying that," said Doris, "but I'm still waiting. Where should we sit?"

Jo had set aside their table, and by the beginning of the next song, Doris and Sam were already on the dance floor, and Araminta was getting settled for the long wait before the waltz.

The champagne came right on time (Jo made a note to thank Henry for keeping a sharp eye), and the room seemed to be tending itself well enough that Jo could risk sitting beside Araminta.

Araminta smiled and rested her head for a moment on Jo's shoulder.

"I didn't realize how good it was to see everyone," she said. "When we were all crammed together all you ever wanted was enough room to breathe somewhere quiet for a minute, but when I saw Sophie in that hiring line, I'd never been so happy to see someone in my life; I could hardly stand."

Jo knew the feeling.

"I cried when Ella said she was leaving," Araminta said. "Don't tell Rebecca—she was so happy for them. She said she'd known this day was coming since the first time Ella saw a movie poster, and if Rebecca says it it's probably true. But it was so close after we found them again, I couldn't help it."

"I won't tell."

Araminta smiled. "Doris said you were running this place all by yourself. Is it exciting?"

"It is," said Jo. "And so long as I keep the cops happy, it's exciting in a good way and not a way that ends with me in prison."

Araminta raised her eyebrows. "Did you run out of the frying pan and into the fire?"

"Not yet," said Jo. "If the cops got me tomorrow, I could at least make a phone call. It would have been impossible if Father had still had hold of any of you. Sometimes I think there was no way out of that house but the one that happened."

"Maybe not," said Araminta. "But still, now look at us."

Jo glanced at the crowd, picking out her sisters without thinking.

It had been a long time, and they were different women now than they had been, but she could still single them out of the hundreds; she knew just how they held their shoulders, how their fingers behaved in their partners' hands.

(She'd been in practice, all this time.)

It was nice that she could still look out for them, even if they weren't hers any more.

There was a little empty space, near the center of the floor, where strangers were dancing where Rose and Lily should have been.

"Maybe if I had tried to be your mother instead," Jo said, "this would be easier."

The words surprised her so much she actually looked at Araminta as if she had spoken them instead, but Araminta was looking at her with heartbroken understanding.

Jo wished she could pull the words back.

But Araminta only said, "Things will work out, General," and smiled, and looked out at the dance floor. "Who should I pick for the waltz?"

"Henry," Jo said. "One of the bartenders. The blond one, there. He's not a bad dancer, and he'd gnaw off a finger for one dance with you."

"Don't be mean," said Araminta. "I'd love to."

Jo smiled and stood. "And don't be too hard on him," she said. "A good bartender's hard to replace."

Araminta's admonishing face followed Jo all the way around the dance floor. It was enough like old times that Jo smiled the whole way.

She visited the Kingfisher early the next afternoon, a few hours before it opened to the public. It was her first time there since she'd come back to the Marquee; the bright press of the daytime streets still made her nervous, and she wondered briefly if the damage had been done, and she'd only ever feel comfortable at night.

There were some professional courtesies she was experiencing for the first time these past few weeks; elite entrances were one of her favorites. (The others—late hours, free drinks—she had been living for too long to think much of, even now.)

Without the crowds and the smoke and the music, she felt a little like a ghost in her old home.

Jake was in the cellar, kneeling beside a flat of wine and marking inventory on a sheaf of paper. When she knocked on the nearest barrel he looked up, grinned, and sat back on his heels.

"No free drinks for the competition," he said.

"You're all manners."

He handed her the inventory, and for a while they worked together quietly, Jo ticking off the bottle names that he called out. Jo decided to start doing this with Henry as well; it was a handy way to keep inventory and keep company at the same time.

She was still trying to discover how people related to each other, and how you met the world when you weren't trying to hide something from someone. It was a lesson slow in coming.

After a little quiet she asked, "How did you fall into this line of work?"

"Recruitment brochure, same as you." Then he paused and glanced over his shoulder at her. "My mom did piecework with some other Irish girls, couldn't have me underfoot. My dad worked in a hotel—easier to bring me. I learned it young. I didn't want to work under my father, but it's hard to tend bar out there in dry establishments." He gave her a wry smile. "This seemed like the smarter gig."

"And so calming," she said.

He laughed. "I'm missing a bottle of the French here. Remind me to box somebody's ears."

She made a note.

"Your information led me to the right place," she said finally. "I have some of them back."

He smiled. "Glad to hear it."

"You should stop by, sometime when you can get away. They'd like to see you. We're on the prowl for honorary family at this point."

"What about the others?"

Jo shook her head and shrugged. "We're at a dead end on the young twins. At this point I'm almost worried enough to put an ad in the paper and let my father find me if he dares. I have to keep looking until I know they're all going to be all right."

He stood up, brushing sawdust off his clothes with the flats of his hands, and took back his inventory.

"You know," he said, flipping through the pages and pointedly not looking at her, "I wonder what it must have been like to see you coming through the door the first night you ever went dancing."

"We were four kids. We looked like easy targets, that was all."

He glanced up. "But what were you thinking, standing there?"

Nothing, she thought. She had been beyond thinking—she just remembered terror, and anger, and pinching shoes, and the sense that she'd come across the first good idea of her life.

"I was thinking we'd be lucky if half a dozen of the men could dance," she said.

He grinned and shook his head, and she watched him stop just short of saying "Liar," and by the time she left she had his promise to stop by.

She wanted Jake to do more than just stop by, someday, but she didn't think now was the time to broach the topic, even if he had already mentioned it himself.

It was probably rude to poach bartenders from right under their employers' noses.

The next two weeks passed quietly.

Doris and the others came to the Marquee nearly every night, and Jo's heart jumped every time she saw them.

If there was something missing—if she wished for Ella's blond head and the twins' matching glares and Rose and Lily trying nervously not to be seen—that was all right, for now.

She would get used to it. She'd gotten used to a lot of things recently.

And it was enough, in the meantime, to look up at the stairs and see her family.

At the end of the next week, Jo placed a small advertisement in the back of the *Times*, using a post office box as a return address.

She was more nervous these days about leaving any trail by which their father could find her than she had been in those first desperate weeks of being alone.

She had too much to lose again.

The ad said only: PRINCESSES SEEK SISTERS, FOR GOOD TIMES AT HOME.

Please, she thought as she handed it over, Rose and Lily, please see this. Please be looking for us still. Please recognize that I'm calling for you.

Doris got a postcard from California.

Ella already had a small part as the younger sister of the leading lady. The girls were getting feature work in dance scenes.

"We'll have to arrange some outings to the movies soon," Sam said. "I've always wanted to know some movie stars."

Doris patted his hand absently, and Violet grinned over at him with a hopeless puppy love that Jo could already see coming.

Jo would need to find Violet a fella sooner rather than later, which would be fine, except that she was running out of bartenders.

(Araminta hadn't seemed bowled over by Henry, but Henry didn't mind, so long as he could dance with her once or twice a week and pine the rest of the time.

"Better men than you have tried," Jo warned him, but there was no talking to someone when he was in love with Araminta. It would burn out sooner or later. She'd let it be.)

Ella had also written about their new names: on the silver screen, Ella would be "Olivia Bryant," and the twins were "Flo and Jo Banner."

Mattie tried to talk them out of Jo as a name, Ella had written, *but there was nothing doing. Please apologize to Jo, when you find her—I hope by the time this card reaches you that you're all together again. Please write and tell me everything. Much love always, Ella.*

We're not all together, Jo thought, and as long as you're a country away, we never will be.

But that was a cruel thought when they sounded so happy, and so she only said, "There go three more Hamiltons."

"And Father was so worried about the family line," Doris said as Sam took her hand for the quickstep. "That'll teach him."

"I like boats," said Jo as they passed, and Doris laughed all the way to the dance floor.

Finally, Jake stopped by.

The girls had come out that night, and Jo was glad; even before he'd gotten his coat off, he had the satisfaction of rushed thank-yous and kisses on the cheek, and to see some of them collected happily again.

"Jake, dance with me," Doris said, "I've never seen you dancing."

"You'll soon see why," he said, and then paused and frowned. "Sorry, what's your name?"

Jo laughed and made some introductions that were eight years overdue.

He wasn't going to light the town on fire, Jo decided after watching his quickstep with Violet, but he was far from awful.

Still, after he'd brought Violet back to the table, Jo saw Violet give Sophie a so-so face.

That suited Jo, too; it was good to stay a little cold these days, even with those you thought were your friends. People had a tendency to surprise you, otherwise, and she'd had quite enough surprises recently.

"Jo?" Jake was asking, his hand out for hers.

She glanced at Doris, who nodded encouragement.

New lives for everyone. There was no reason, any more, for Jo to turn down dances.

There was nothing left to be afraid of.

"Sure thing," she said.

It was a waltz, and for a minute or two she and Jake danced companionably. He was a smooth dancer, and his hand was warm, his thumb just brushing the tops of her fingers.

Then he said softly, "I heard back from my man in Chicago."

He was a brave man to break that one out in the middle of a dance floor, she thought, but she couldn't quite make herself say it.

Instead she breathed, "Tell me."

"He couldn't find them," Jake said, "either one. They came into town, that's for sure, but there's no reaching them now. Some people said Lou went underground and Tom got picked up, some people said they left town again." After a second, he added, "Together."

Missing, then. No traces.

Either Lou and Tom had decided to start a new married life in some other city, or Lou was alone, and in so much trouble that Jo would never find her.

Either way, if Lou wrote home to tell her, Jo would never get the letter.

Lou was gone now, truly gone.

"Guess I'll cancel my full-page ad in the *Tribune*," she said, but it was the joke she'd had ready—the last reflex before the news really set in—and her voice cracked on the last word. Her fingertips went cold under his, and the knot in her stomach tightened so hard she feared, for a moment, that it would pull her entire body down around it.

He must have known how the news would go over. She

appreciated his kindness, now, in drawing her away from the others so she could find out alone.

He didn't seem surprised when her open hand tightened against his back, or when she didn't give him any other answer, or when they stayed in the embrace until the next song began.

It was a foxtrot, and Jo thought that was fitting.

When she closed her eyes and turned her forehead to his cheek, he only hesitated a moment before he held her closer.

"Jo," he said, "how can I help?"

She said, "You can't," quietly, her voice so hard and final that he shivered.

She was sorry but didn't dare be kinder. Sometimes it was best to stay a little cold, even with people you knew were friends.

Four nights later, Doris managed to maneuver everyone out onto the dance floor during the waltz.

Jo was watching Sophie dancing with Mr. Walton (that was going somewhere, and Jo was debating whether to let it), and she didn't realize until she saw Violet and Sam dancing together that Doris had done it all to get Jo alone with her.

"All right," Doris said. "What happened with Jake the other night, General?"

Jo smiled at the nickname but faltered.

"He was trying to find Lou," Jo said. "But no luck. His friend in Chicago thinks she went underground, or disappeared out of town, but there's no way to know anything, and no sign of her now."

Doris looked a little ill. "God. What if she's not all right?"

"Yes, thank you," Jo snapped, "I've got the worrying all covered, Doris."

Doris flinched. "Sorry."

She sighed. "I just—I never thought that it would be a mistake to get Lou out of that house. If I had just waited, she'd be all right by now, but I was so anxious to manage it all."

"You did everything you could," Doris said, leaning closer. "And when it went sideways, you warned us. But we all did all right for ourselves, I think—Lou got her shot, and here we all are. We did all right. I'm sure the others have, too."

Free, Jo thought, as I always wanted, and now we're all starting again.

"I've been the General for a long time," Jo said.

Doris said, "You've been our sister longer."

That was a comfort—a strange thought, but a comfort—and Jo was still smiling when Doris said, "Watch out, or Jake's going to fall for you."

"I don't think so," Jo said. "I think both our hearts' desires took the road to Chicago a little while back."

Doris didn't say anything to that (Jo was grateful), but when the song was over and everyone came back, she and Sam had one of their silent conversations, and then Sam was asking Jo for the Charleston.

"Not this time," Jo said. "I'm shirking work sitting here. Tomorrow night, sure thing."

Sam smiled. "All yours," he said, and swiveled to face Rebecca, who laughed and said, "Second-string, I see how it is," but took his hand anyway.

Doris watched them go with the kind of smile Jo had always hoped to see on them, on any of them—a smile that was open and untroubled.

Jo would have to work to be happy with what she could have. It was no good turning useless over pasts and small things.

She went to the bar to glad-hand a pair of city councilmen she recognized. Half the reason she read the paper these days was to catch up with the clientele.

Then it was checking in with Henry ("Not mixing tears with the champagne, I hope?" "No, General") and greeting a few of the most finely dressed ladies.

The Charleston was almost over when she saw Myrtle standing on the stairs.

"At last," she was saying as she moved through the crowd, her voice pitched to carry, "I was wondering when you'd take me up on my invitation."

Myrtle was turning to look behind her, ushering a young couple to stand beside her—

But it wasn't a young couple, Jo knew even as she thought it.

It was a young girl in a dancing dress, and another with her hair slicked back and wearing trousers, and Jo recognized them at once, out of long habit and long wishing.

She was too happy for dignity—she waved with both hands overhead, like a drowning swimmer, and when Rose and Lily saw her waving they nudged each other and leaned in to say something to each other out of the corners of their mouths.

They had become twins, Jo thought, though it seemed a strange thing to realize only now, when they couldn't have been more differently dressed, and when the truth was so obvious. They'd always been twins. Jo was getting imaginative in her old age, that was all.

By the time Jo reached them, Doris had seen them, too, and Jo only had a moment to pull them into her arms before the others descended (Myrtle stepping back to give way), and it was a flurry of crushing hugs and kisses on the cheek.

Lily had adopted bright red lipstick to go with her new black slacks, and her kisses happened in the air, to preserve the color.

"You look scandalous," Jo said, but it was a compliment and Lily only beamed.

"The men don't know what to make of it," she said, "but for some reason the women go wild!"

"*Some* women," said Rose, and she and Lily shared a fleeting smile.

Doris was crowding Jo from behind, gasping, "Lily, *what* are you wearing?" as Rose laughed, and it gave Jo a moment to cup Rose's chin and get a good look at her.

She was thinner—they both were—and there was something

flinty behind the eyes that hadn't been there before, and Jo's stomach sank to think of anything awful happening to them.

"Where have you been?" she asked, every word a plea.

Rose shook off Jo's fingers, looking embarrassed. "Nowhere, General."

Jo tried not to look too stung. "I'm not asking as a general," she said. "I'm asking as someone who was worried about you."

That got a flush. "We're all right," Rose said. "Don't worry about us."

Lily appeared at Rose's elbow. "We got your message in the paper," Lily said, "but we thought for sure it was a trap, at first."

Rose said, "There are plenty of people in this town who don't mind setting traps."

Jo glanced down at their hands—Rose's fingertips were red and callused, and even though Lily's hands were in her pockets, Jo could guess that these twins hadn't gotten so close to each other by keeping separate jobs.

They had been factory girls after all, at least for a while, and from the looks of things it had been rough going.

She didn't push them. General Jo would have, but some things were too fragile; reunions were one of them.

"Come and dance," she said. "We're at our regular table. Catch the ring on Doris's finger, and see what Rebecca's wearing, still."

"I can't believe she married him," said Lily. "She hardly knew him! What a way to go about it."

"He's a nice fellow," Jo promised, "and he came through in a pinch. Even I like him. Now, stay and have a decent drink. You don't know how long we've all been waiting to see your faces."

Rose and Lily linked hands without looking (Lily smiled at Jo, Rose not quite), and moved past Jo toward the sisters' table.

"Thank you," Jo said to Myrtle when the twins were out of hearing.

"Not my idea," Myrtle said, around the cigarette holder clamped in her teeth. "The cat dragged them in. Jake pointed them out to me as two of yours, and I thought I might as well bring them over—they seemed so lost that I pitied them, that's all."

Jo let it pass. If Myrtle wanted to do a good deed, Jo wasn't going to stop her, and if Myrtle didn't want to be thanked twice, Jo was happy not to thank her.

"There's a nice whiskey at the bar," Jo said instead. "Even Jake thinks it's top-shelf. Come and have a taste of some quality, as long as you're here."

That offer Myrtle was happier to accept, with a wink at Henry, who was already smiling ear to ear at the sight of two more Princesses who had come home.

Then Myrtle was happy to accept a dance, and another dance, and finally a dance from Lily.

(Lily had gotten better at leading, Jo noticed. Whatever they'd been doing when they were out of sight, they'd been dancing.

Though it must have been a strange time, all the same. Lily wore her trousers like armor, and Jo had no doubt it was a habit of necessity as much as whim.

Poor girls, Jo thought. Where have you been?)

Jo kept busy and let the others crowd around and fight to tell stories and disappear for dances. She didn't want to push them—she didn't dare lose them.

When Rose was left alone for a moment, Jo took a seat at the edge of the booth.

Jo said, "What have you been up to, with those hands?"

She'd tried to make it sound as kind as she could, but Rose still pulled her hands under the table.

"The Palmolive factory," she said finally. "Over in Hell's Kitchen."

Jo pulled a face before she could help it. "Oh, Rose, how did you ever end up there?"

Rose shrugged and shook her head without conviction. "We ran until we couldn't any more, and that's where we were. We didn't want to be caught, and we knew he'd never look for us there. Once you get used to a place, it's amazing what happens.

There's a dead dog outside our boardinghouse, and I didn't notice for three days. Everything just smells like soap by now."

Jo knew that whatever she said next was important, but she also guessed that it was pride as much as anything that had kept them away from their sisters until Jo had gone begging, and she'd have to be careful.

"Well," she said, "if you're happy there, then stay, but I can help you find something if you ever feel like a change. Let me know."

It hurt—every inch of her wanted to tell them to move out of wherever was starving and overworking them before the sun was up, to just stay here and leave behind whatever was left where they were living now, and let her take care of things.

But those days were over.

And after so long a pause that Jo feared the worst, Rose looked up and said, "I'll talk to Lily."

Jo nudged her shoulder before she slid back out into the crush of people, all the way behind the bar.

There was a bottle she wanted to set aside for Jake. A little decent drink was the least you could do when someone sent you two of your sisters back.

The twins had replied to the ad, gloriously and in person, and so it was more than a week before Jo returned to the post office.

She'd intended to close out the box (she had already closed out the advertisement at the newspaper office).

It surprised her, then, when she asked if anything had been delivered and the gentleman at the post office counter handed her a letter from an attorney.

Oh God, she thought for a terrible moment, please don't let anyone have found me at the Marquee. I don't want to have to run from home again.

It was from van de Maar, she saw when she opened it; it was

sent from his address, and the header named him as estate executor to a Joseph Hamilton.

She skipped the pleasantries—her father always had—and caught the first sentence that mattered.

Your father is taken ill, the letter read. *He wishes very much to see you on an urgent matter.*

He must have been combing with a pretty fine tooth, she thought, her skin crawling, to contact her here from one small reference in the paper, with no names or places to give them away.

(It helped a little to know that the three weeks she had suffered with no word to anyone had been a necessary precaution. God only knew what would have happened.)

Jo would have stopped reading and thrown it in the trash with a "Good riddance," but she caught something that gave her pause.

It would never have occurred to her that the letter could be anything but a trap, but underneath the official typed letter was a handwritten note that she suspected her father had never seen.

And so she hesitated, and stood beside the trash can, crushing the side of the paper from the pressure of her fingers, reading the note over and over.

I worry for his health, and recommend you come as soon as you can. You seem a reasonable young woman, and I know you will understand the obligations of family.

He is asking you to come home.

twenty-six

SHOW ME THE WAY TO GO HOME

Jo stood on the front steps of her old home for the second time in her life.

It had been two months since she'd been chased out the front door by a man brandishing a weapon at her—a man who had now summoned his oldest daughter back to his side.

But the woman standing on the steps was different from the one who had staggered down them, nearly blind with panic and unable to do anything but run for her life before the truck came to carry her away.

"Should I come in with you?" asked the man at her side.

She looked at him and smiled. "That won't be necessary, I'm sure, Sergeant Carson. But thank you. I'll be down in no time."

Van de Maar was waiting for her at the threshold, looking remarkably like Walters.

"Miss Hamilton," he said.

"Mr. van de Maar. I trust this won't take long? I don't want to leave my associate waiting."

"Not at all," said van de Maar, with a glance at Carson's uniform.

"Shout if you need me, Miss Hamilton," said Carson, fixing van de Maar with a level look. "I'll have my ear out."

Then Jo smiled in earnest.

"Sergeant, if I need you, you'll hear it for miles."

• • • • • •

"You look well, Miss Hamilton," said van de Maar when he'd closed the door and it was just the two of them in the foyer of the house.

"Thank you," she said, and tugged the cuffs of the mustard-colored dress out from under her coat. She refused to be in anything that looked like mourning—not today.

"You've been all right, then?"

If this was his way of drawing her out, he didn't know how to do it very well.

She said, "No doubt it's just the benefit of sunlight and some clothes that can be bought in person."

He didn't have an answer for that, and before the silence got strained, she went on. "I'm glad to see you again. I've wanted to thank you for the help you gave a while back."

"Please," he said, looking uncomfortable. "It was nothing."

"Not to me," she said.

"Don't mention it," he said. He glanced at the door.

It took her a moment to realize why he was uncomfortable; he didn't want her father to think he'd had a hand in her escape.

She spared him. Sometimes a good deed done out of bewilderment and disbelief was still a good deed, and there was no need to force the other party to agree.

"You said my father wanted to see me," she said. "What about?"

"Well, he'd like to speak with you himself, of course," said van de Maar, taking a step toward the stairs and offering his arm.

"And he may," she said. "As soon as you've told me what this is about. You didn't specify when we spoke on the phone what exactly he wants to discuss, and my father has not earned any trust from his daughters."

"Well, your father—"

"Mr. van de Maar, the days of me walking blindly into my father's offices are over."

Van de Maar looked truly taken aback, and she wondered what her father had told him to expect, that a daughter who disliked him could be such an unpleasant surprise.

"Your father is dying, Miss Hamilton," he said at last. "He wishes to speak with you."

He said it with all the gravity he could possibly want the words to carry, as if the statement would shatter her composure.

Instead she thought, I wonder if this is an illness that came on slowly, or if he had a heart attack after he tried to beat me.

She asked, "Is he alone?"

"A nurse is with him," said van de Maar. "I'm happy to accompany you, if you'd like."

"Do you already know what he's going to tell me?"

After a pause, he nodded.

"Then there's no need," she said. "I'll see him myself, thank you."

She took the stairs, and paused on the landing for a moment before she heard rustling from one of the doors, halfway down the hall on the right-hand side.

It was the bedroom directly under Rose and Lily's, and Jo was grateful those girls were so quiet. It might have gone wrong for them sooner, if it had been Rebecca and Araminta bickering over his head.

(It was across the hall from the clean, quiet room that Jo had entered only once, long ago, to look for their mother.)

She knocked at the closed door. A moment later, a nurse answered.

"Miss Hamilton?"

"Yes."

The nurse beamed. "He's been expecting you all morning," she said. "Please come in."

Jo stepped inside and froze in the doorway as her eyes adjusted. The curtains were drawn tight, and her father was just a shadow under the covers of his dark-wood bed.

"I'll leave you two alone," the nurse said.

"No," Jo said, too loud. "Stay. Thank you."

The nurse hesitated in the doorway, and Jo took one step closer, then another, until she could see her father's face.

He looked sweltering under the blankets, his face strained. It was the first time she'd ever seen him less than able, and it made her uncomfortable, as if she was spying.

His arms were folded on top of the coverlet, and his limp fingers under thin skin seemed a good twenty years older than the hands that had curled around his cane as he moved to attack her.

It was unfair that he would call her back now, when she would be tempted to pity him.

"Father," she said, "you asked to see me."

He opened his eyes, and she saw that no matter what else had happened to him, his mind was still as sharp as ever.

"Where are your sisters? What is this? Did you come alone?"

"I've brought a police sergeant with me," she said. "He's waiting downstairs. None of my sisters have come, or will."

Behind them, the nurse sucked in a quiet breath. Jo could almost see the thought forming in the nurse's mind: What an ungrateful daughter.

But her father hadn't forgotten the promise she'd made about his never laying eyes on any of her sisters again, and he grimaced.

"I suppose you didn't tell them," he said. "You didn't even have the decency to tell your sisters that their father is dying and asking to see his children again—"

"They know."

He faltered, but even now that wasn't nearly enough to throw him.

"Well. I suppose I should expect that. I can't imagine what terrible things you've told them about me, during all those years."

The years they were upstairs, he meant. The years he'd held on to them. Jo waited with clammy hands for him to say it, to admit it at last.

But he had stopped for breath, and she realized he was going to go no farther.

"No," said Jo, her voice steady, "you can't imagine."

He flinched.

"Josephine," he said, "I thought you would be ready to put all this behind us."

She raised her eyebrows. "Then I hope that this isn't the only reason you asked me here, or you've wasted our time."

Behind them, the nurse shifted her weight.

He let that sink in for a moment.

Then he said, "I would never have believed, before this moment, that any of my children could be so poisonous."

Jo knew better than to listen—the word was meant to cut her, and she couldn't let it—but part of her was sorry, very sorry, that this was how her father had chosen to make his case, at the last twilight of his life, for her loyalty.

(He seemed like a stranger, just for a heartbeat; it was a comfort.)

"Sir," she said, "why did you ask me to come?"

He huffed a laugh that rattled into a cough, and the nurse took a step forward, thought better of it, and hesitated.

Jo waited him out.

When he recovered, he took a deep breath. "I wanted to talk to you about my will," he said.

He turned his head to better fix his eyes on her, as if waiting for her to change her tune.

She thought about all the money her father must have made in those years. The girls could make use of that sort of money—of any sort of money. If he was trying to apologize to family with his pocketbook, he wouldn't be the first man to have tried and succeeded.

But then she thought about all the money he had doled out to them one begrudging dollar at a time, and the money he'd been willing to take as payment for his daughters' hands in marriage, and the money he had been willing to part with to lock them all in an institution, just for defying him.

"I see," she said.

Her voice was sharp. It snapped on the "S."

He shook his head. "I didn't want it to come to this, Jo. I don't understand how you can stand there so cold, knowing what's happened between us."

The nurse let out a breath.

"I know what's happened," Jo said. "So do you. It's why there's a policeman downstairs. If you're trying to get an apology out of me in exchange for my name in your will, then I'm only sorry you called for me at all."

Her father pulled his lips back from his teeth. "Josephine. What's happened to you, that you speak this way to me?"

Jo was trembling so hard she had to set her jaw against her rattling teeth.

"Eight years of dancing at night," she said, and tried to smile. "It does wonders for the constitution. Once you're free to take it into the streets, there's no telling what happens."

He blinked.

"Eight years," he breathed. "Eight years, you were defying me."

"I hope I was," she said.

It was too close to an admission. She breathed in and out, slowly; her throat was tight.

There was a long silence. Jo refused to do so much as shift her weight until he spoke again. She had been too well trained to stand in her father's presence to break those habits now.

Her father closed his eyes.

"And have you—are they all right? How is Ella, have you seen her?"

Oh God, she thought, this was even worse. She could have hated him cleanly if he hadn't been worrying over them; now it was all awful.

"They're well. Thriving. Now."

His expression hardened.

"Well, I'm leaving my share of the business and my personal interests to van de Maar," he said. "The full estate will go to him. I've signed the will already, it's all sorted. What do you think of that?"

And there it was.

A will already signed, a decision already made, and this whole conversation with this news lying in wait, whenever he needed it to sting.

She smiled thinly.

"I think you must have been agonizing over whether or not I would come here so you could tell me that."

She passed the stricken nurse and made it to the door before she heard, "What will you do now?"

His voice was softer now, and brittle, the voice of a man whose pride was slipping.

Jo missed, suddenly, a father she'd never had. She wrenched the idea apart from the man as fast as she could, but still she ached.

"We'll be happy," she said. Her voice came out steadier than she felt. "Good-bye, sir. I hope you feel better soon."

She turned and went into the hall before he could answer; suddenly, she was feeling weak enough to return to him if he called.

Then, almost out of habit, Jo went upstairs.

It was eerie to be there when no one else was. She'd never been near these floors when they were empty—they lived together, they left together, always.

She moved in and out of their old rooms like a ghost. The dust had hardly settled, which surprised her. It felt as though she'd been away for ages.

In each of the rooms there was a small thing that felt most as if it had been left behind. She picked them up, until there were more things than she could carry, and her arms were laden with ratted-out ribbons from dead pairs of shoes and empty tins of rouge and a music box that had long ago gone out of tune.

On her still-made bed with its layer of dust, she rolled all the trinkets into the black dress she had worn a lifetime ago and tied the package closed with one of Sophie's blue ribbons.

There was nothing for Lou. Lou had left nothing to take. The room was as if she'd never lived in it.

She stood still for a moment, until the grief passed and she could move.

Van de Maar was waiting at the door to the study when she came down the stairs again; a document was unfolded on the desk behind him.

"Have you reconciled?" he asked, half-hopeful.

"No, sir," she said. "He said the estate would go to you, and I understand."

He looked pleased enough that she thought about one last advantage, and added as though it was an order from her father, "I should take nothing but these mementos from our old rooms, and the letters from my sister."

He nodded, unsurprised, and a moment later he was returning from inside the study with three letters. One of them had never even been opened.

Jo held her breath as he handed them over; when she took them, she forced a smile.

"Thank you again for all you've done," she said. "I'll never forget it."

Her footsteps echoed in the foyer as if she was comfortable there, as if it had always been her home. Strange how things sounded, sometimes.

Sergeant Carson was waiting for her on the front stairs and fell into step beside her as they walked out to the waiting car; he cast one dark look back at the door, as if wanting to make sure he had at least done something threatening, since he had come all this way.

Jo felt the press of the package between her ribs and the crook of her elbow. Two dollars' worth of cast-offs, folded so small that she carried it under one arm, weightless.

As inheritances went, she thought, this was enough.

• • • • • •

At home in the little studio above the Marquee, Jo opened the letters from Lou as if they would crumble.

The first one had obviously been written for their father's benefit, in case he felt like reading something out loud for the amusement of the others—the language didn't even sound like hers. "Beautiful sunsets." "The sweetest hotel, with fresh lemonade."

It was a treacly travelogue of the first stage of their journey to Chicago that could have been written by anyone, except Lou.

(She had an image of Lou sitting at the writing desk in some lovely hotel room, taking laughing dictation from Tom, pacing slowly behind her and rattling off a letter that sounded like it came from a brochure.)

The second letter, after another long and effusive ode to pleasantries, eventually sounded a little more like Lou: quick sketches of the people she was meeting in the neighborhood, with just enough to tell Jo some of what she really needed.

Jo knew to read "meeting" as "working with" and could already pick out the alderman who would be giving Lou the most trouble, based on Lou's mention of his twice dropping by for tea.

As landlords go, wrote Lou, you could ask for nicer, but I'm determined to stay on good terms, and I've already been bringing my own touches to the place.

Jo couldn't imagine, unless it was bullet holes in the plaster.

At the end there was a little bit of sighing and missing them all, some general scolding of the girls, and a little singing of Tom's praises.

It stung, but still she read that section twice, looking for any evidence of love. She couldn't tell. Lou had a way of putting things that could mean whatever you most hoped or feared, just to draw you out.

He's very clever, Lou wrote, and shows every sign of being a loyal partner.

The last letter, the one her father hadn't bothered to open, was the most honest. Lou had gambled, rightly, that by then their father wouldn't bother going through his daughters' mail.

And on the third page, this letter had a few sentences tucked into the middle of an extremely long paragraph about shopping for dresses that their father would never have been able to force himself through.

Chicago isn't the town for us—too many deliverymen, not enough dancing. You haven't written me. It's not like you. I don't know what to think, I can't sit still here from wondering what's going on. Tom and I are going to hit the road soon, I don't know where to, we keep changing our minds—if you get this, please, please hurry and let me know you're all right.

I am, I promise; Tom takes good care of me, for your sake.

Something Jo had noticed—no matter how tired you were, some things could still keep you up all night.

twenty-seven
THE SONG IS ENDED
(BUT THE MELODY LINGERS ON)

Jo's gifts were a second Christmas.

Each girl exclaimed over the thing chosen for her—"Exactly what I would have taken, this stupid thing," Rebecca said, carefully winding the music box—and didn't ask too many questions about Jo's visit there. (That was good; that had been half the point of bringing them back in the first place.)

The sisters were so impressed with the getaway that Doris insisted on mailing Ella's paste-gem earrings and Hattie and Mattie's matching peacock-feather headbands all the way out to their apartment in Hollywood.

"They deserve their trophies from that lion's den," said Doris, and nobody argued.

It was as if the mention of it jogged their memories, because a moment later Rebecca asked, "How did he seem, when you spoke to him?"

"Ill," Jo said. Just because the worst was over didn't mean the facts were less important.

"Did he ask about us?" Violet's eyes were the size of saucers.

"He did. He seemed happy that we're all well."

Violet smiled, and Jo remembered that she was still young enough to hope that he would wake up one morning and become a father.

Rose took her tango-postcard souvenir to the bar, to show her new friend Martha. Jo was beginning to suspect that Martha held some appeal for Rose besides someone to talk to between sets.

She must have been getting more in the habit of letting things happen on their own, because Jo's only real worry about Martha was that Lily wouldn't like her, if it came to that.

For her part, Lily seemed supremely unconcerned by it. She slung her souvenir pearls around the neck of her shirt and slipped into the arms of a young man for a Charleston. (The way she dressed was still a scandal, but a little scandal was good for business.)

When they were alone, Doris turned to Jo. "How was seeing him, really? How is he?"

"Not good. He's very ill. It will be the last time I see him." It was half regret and half relief to say it out loud.

Doris nodded, her brow furrowed. "I know I shouldn't be sorry, but I guess you can't help it when it's your own blood. I cried when I found out about Mother, too, and I only saw her four times in my life. I don't know what I would have done if I'd seen him."

"You'd have tried to understand him," Jo said, "and there's nothing doing."

Doris seemed content, but Jo's skin was crawling, and when Sam came back she asked him for a dance just to be moving for a little while, just to feel the floor under her feet and know she was there.

A week later, Jake showed up at the Marquee.

It was early enough in the afternoon that the man at the door called her from the studio to meet him, and Jo came down bare-faced and with her short hair still in tangles.

"I've been thinking of a change," Jake said. "Is there any chance you're hiring?"

"You might have to go ten rounds with Henry," Jo said, smiling, and folded her arms.

Jake shrugged. "If that's how it's done, I can adjust to new methods."

She laughed and motioned for him to follow her. "I'll show you the cellar," she said, "and when Henry comes, he'll find a place for you."

"I promise not to fall in love with Araminta, if that helps my case."

Jo cast a look over her shoulder. "Those who live in glass houses shouldn't throw stones," she said.

It was half a joke, but he looked at her a moment too long before he said, "You're right."

She showed him the cellar. He whistled low as soon as she opened the door, and again when he saw some of the wines she held in reserve, and as he peered at labels they discussed salary, hours, and availability.

"I'm able to start this minute, actually," said Jake.

That was a surprise. "What happened at the Kingfisher?"

"Change of management," said Jake, in a tone that indicated it wasn't worth being safe from the police under whoever had bought out the Kingfisher.

So when Henry came in to set up, Jo introduced them, and had the satisfaction of seeing that Henry wasn't the type to pull rank, and Jake didn't seem inclined to make him.

When she came down a little later, with red lips and her hair properly pomaded, it gave her a startlingly pleasant feeling to see Jake behind the bar, stacking glasses and wiping off bottles.

She decided she must have been so pleased because she was trying to build something she could really live in at the Marquee, and every little bit helped.

If he smiled at her when he saw her, she didn't dwell on it. There was no future there.

Jake was just looking for someone to love, and another broken heart was the last thing she needed.

• • • • • •

When the others appeared on the stairs that night, Jo's happiness seemed almost complete.

The place was packed, and Ames could hardly contain the energy on the bandstand. Parker had been and gone (which was just how she liked Parker), and Carson had stopped by for a drink and never left; he was eyeing the dancers now as if deciding whether or not to risk it.

After every song, the applause resounded. Success, Jo thought as she took the stairs to meet her sisters.

Doris was urging Sophie and Violet over to one side of the stairs, and Rebecca and Araminta were helping each other off with their winter coats and bickering about something, and Rose and Lily stood holding hands and silently daring anyone to think ill of them.

It had been nearly four months since their escape, and they had changed so much that it always took a moment of worrying that things were wrong before she remembered everything was fine, and then happiness rose and warmed the tips of her fingers.

I can live with this, Jo thought, if this is as good as it gets.

Sam smiled and kissed her cheek and headed for the bar to pick up the first round. The younger ones barely waved as they ran straight for their table to fasten their shoes and get to dancing.

(Most of them had adjusted well to their new situations—Sophie, who floated through life, seemed to have forgotten the house completely—but Rebecca and Araminta and Violet had fallen back into the habit of carrying their shoes in one hand until they were safe inside and ready to dance.

"It's to preserve the shoes," Rebecca said when she caught Jo looking.

But Violet only said, "I don't feel right unless I carry them," and there was nothing Jo could do about that but understand her.)

Doris always lingered a moment longer than the others, standing beside Jo and looking out at the room as if admiring Jo's work.

Jo was grateful above everything else that Doris had sent Sam one night to look for a serious woman with dark brown hair, just in case Jo was somewhere in the city and looking for them, too.

"I got a letter from Ella," said Doris.

(Only Ella ever wrote; Hattie and Mattie were too busy doing what they had been made to do.)

The letters got thicker every week; Ella was finding work left and right.

The pack of them had already been to see her as the sweet young sister in *A Summer Affair,* and the camera loved her even more than her dancing partners had.

At home, Jo tore out magazine pages that mentioned what Olivia Bryant was filming or had a snap of her standing outside the Brown Derby in a satin dress, throwing the camera a look. It was silly to collect clippings, like something Violet would do in secret, but it didn't stop Jo from collecting stacks of *Photoplay* knee-deep.

" 'I'm up for a bigger part next,' " Doris read. " 'Cross your fingers I get Jane Bennet!' "

The twins were in even more places than Ella, because they danced so often and so well—they had been in *Cinescope* and *Flapper,* and *Featuring* THE BRILLIANT BANNER SISTERS could sometimes be seen crawling in tiny letters on a movie poster at the cinema down the street.

Doris read, " 'The studio wants them to have some real roles soon, but only Mattie seems to want to—Hattie is happy to dance and have it over with.' "

"Imagine my surprise," said Jo, and Doris laughed.

Then Sam was coming back, and Doris was tucking the letter carefully into her evening bag and joining him for the Charleston.

(Jo had expected a change of habit in Doris, but no amount of romance had succeeded at getting her on the dance floor for anything slow.

"Lord no!" Doris said when Jo asked if she ever felt the need for a nice, sweet waltz with Sam. "I'm married, not dull.")

Jo gave Henry one waltz with Araminta. It surprised her as much as it surprised him that Araminta was willing to dance with him (Araminta wasn't fond of men being too in love with her), but his blond head and her dark moved so smoothly and close around the floor that Jo wondered if Araminta was doing Jo a favor, or if Henry really had made the cut.

On the dance floor, Lily was dancing with Martha, as Rose looked on from the bar, grinning fit to burst.

When Jo gave Jake the chance to dance, he handed her a whiskey and said, "With you?"

"Best not," she said. "You deliver bad news just so that I'll swoon."

He laughed, but there was a flicker of something sadder behind his eyes. It shouldn't have struck her (you had to make people sad to move on sometimes, that much she knew by now), but it did, a small jolt of surprise right between her shoulders.

It was enough that when he asked, "Are you sure?" she somehow said, "Well, I wouldn't mind."

It was a Baltimore, just right for them—not too romantic—and even though she and her sisters had been dancing for years by the time the Baltimore got popular, still it made Jo feel as if it was the first four of them sneaking out, the first time Jake had ever called her Princess.

"Lou was really ace at this," she said when the song was over, before she could stop herself.

But he only smiled and said, "I remember."

She squeezed his hand, just for a moment, before she let go.

Sometimes it was a relief to have old friends.

With so many of her sisters clustered at the table or scattering over the floor, with Jake beside Henry at the bar and Sam's laughing face bobbing along in the crowd as he danced with one of her sisters, Jo felt as if she had managed, at last, to find a home worth living in.

She had even been able to think of Ella and Hattie and Mattie without worrying how far away they were. They were happy, and they were themselves, and Jo was learning not to ask for anything more.

The next morning, Jo opened the paper and saw that Joseph Hamilton had passed away.

If this had been the old days, she would have marshaled her sisters into her room and issued the announcement. She would have listened to some of the others debating the merits of staying or going. She might, if she was feeling generous, have taken a vote.

By the end of it, she would at least have known what each of them wanted, and which sisters would be standing firm on one side of the question or the other.

But those days were gone, and she sat in her little studio and sighed, and only hoped that none of them would choose something that would make them unhappy later.

There was nothing else she could do for them now, except give them a place to dance.

Doris called the Marquee to invite Jo to a makeshift wake, and by the time Jo caught a cab to the Lewisohns', Rose and Lily and Rebecca and Araminta had already gathered.

There was lots of coffee, and lots of food, and a few tears (from Violet, sadder for what she had missed than for who was really gone), and Jo watched it all and was surprised how little need she felt to interfere.

She still wasn't a mothering type (it was Araminta and Sophie comforting Violet when she cried) but when Rose said, "Lily and I want to go to the funeral," Jo felt the urge to lay down the law and forbid it. She let it fade before she spoke.

Jo only said, "Watch out for yourselves. We don't know who will be there and you might not want to get in front of any cameras." Then she asked Sam if he would mind pouring her another cup of coffee.

It was an alien feeling to watch them making choices on their own, choices that might be wrong (were wrong—he didn't deserve one damn daughter wishing him a fond farewell), but she was trying hard to be a sister now, and not a General.

Some things you never stopped missing.

Rose and Lily had apparently been speaking for the others; the night of the funeral, Rebecca came out dancing alone.

Jo met her at the table, afraid to say anything one way or the other. Rebecca looked up, her jaw set tight.

"I remember him watching us on the stairs that night he called us down," Rebecca said, all edges. "That was the first time I'd ever seen him. I'm not too sad to go dancing."

Jo nodded. "I know what you mean."

"You did us some good," Rebecca said. "Even and all."

For Rebecca, that was a rousing toast.

They sat for a moment in the quiet understanding of two soldiers, before a young man gathered his courage and asked Rebecca for the foxtrot.

Every night that week, more sisters appeared at the door, and by Saturday night even Doris must have finished what she thought was their father's fair share of mourning, and the Lewisohn-house contingent showed up early and restless, skittering onto the dance floor as if they'd been waiting for weeks.

Doris hung back and looked ready to explain if Jo pressed her, but Jo said only, "It's good to see you—what's your poison?" and Doris smiled gratefully and answered, "Champagne."

Jake brought over the first tray of drinks himself, and kissed Sophie's hand, which made her blush—Jake was too handsome for her to be comfortable with. Jo would have to explain to him, if he asked Sophie to dance and she turned him down.

Then Henry was calling her to deal with a sharp-looking customer who didn't feel Jake had the right to ask a banker for payment (he did, Jo assured him, and he'd get it or the doorman would escort the gentleman out and be instructed to remember his face), and Ames approached her about a raise for the musicians (bad timing, since she'd just upped her payments to Mr. Parker on imaginary approval from Tom, but she was happy to discuss it in the morning—their music was worth the money, and the Marquee had a reputation to protect).

Then there were decisions to be made about what to pull from the cellar (a little of the top-shelf; it was Saturday), and her sisters were small points of happiness on the dance floor, and Jo was so content in all the bustle of usefulness that when she turned around and saw the front stairs, what she saw pained her as if she had forgotten and strained an old wound.

She didn't believe it for one full breath, one endless inhale where she struggled to reconcile the bright red hair and the drawn, worried face of the woman who stood all alone on the stairs—Jo had never seen her that way.

Then came the exhale, and with it a shout that felt halfway between an accident and a curse.

"Lou!"

The bandstand was raging and the trumpets were going to town, and the call was lost in the noise, but Lou was her sister, and heard it.

There wasn't time to go around the dance floor, suddenly—Jo drove into the center, avoiding the shining couples, dodging the line of dance, shaving seconds off how long it would take—

Then Lou had met her halfway, and when the music ended and the couples stopped Lou and Jo were stranded on the dance floor, embracing so tightly that the spangles on Jo's dress dug into her skin.

She didn't care—nothing mattered but Lou, and her new,

strange perfume, and the press of her forehead on Jo's shoulder, and the hot, painful feeling that Jo was going to burst out of her own skin from joy.

"We came back," Lou was gasping, "we tried to stay, but I knew something was wrong and we had to come home again—Tom felt it too, neither one of us could sleep, we were so worried—and then we got here and saw that Father had died and the house was empty, and the Kingfisher is so different we didn't know what to do—we thought you had all vanished, and I got so desperate and Tom said we should come here just in case—God, Jo!"

Jo laughed through a few treacherous tears and held on to her harder, her knuckles getting scraped on the beads of Lou's bronze dress.

She said into Lou's hair, "Took you long enough."

Then Lou was laughing, a sharp, low laugh that hurt Jo all over again (God, how badly she had been missed!).

"I'll tell my old man you said that," said Lou, and it was only then that Jo put two pennies together and remembered that if Lou was here, so was Tom.

She pulled back enough to look Lou in the eye.

It was a Charleston already; the conversations had been drowned out by the bright blare of music, and the couples were swinging past to avoid the pair of addled girls who were embracing at the edge of the floor with no regard for the line of dance.

At the edge of Jo's vision, she saw that the others had gathered to welcome Lou but were waiting for the word. (Old habits died hard.)

She stared at Lou a moment more, still as terrified as when she thought Lou was alone in the world, unable to bring herself to ask any questions with answers she might not like.

"Stop it," said Lou, and it might as well have been *There was no funny business, you dope.* "Go say hello."

When Jo looked up, Tom was standing on the stairs, hat in hand, watching the reunion.

He had a ghost of a smile that got brighter when he caught her eye, and even brighter when she disentangled herself from Lou and slid through the edge of the crowd toward the stairs.

His eyes never moved from her face, and when he saw her coming toward him, he took the stairs down, slowly, to meet her halfway.

Lou must have been good company. He looked a little younger, or night made him younger, or Jo was always going to be young when she met him again. It was hard to tell.

Her heart was a drum by the time she was close enough to touch him.

He didn't waste time with handshakes; he caught one arm around her waist and embraced her, and for once it felt like a beginning and not like an end.

When they pulled back, he was grinning, and now, now, he looked like the young man she'd met eight years ago.

"What in God's name have you been doing with this place?" he asked.

"Running it right," she said with a raised eyebrow, and when he laughed she could feel his shoulders trembling against hers.

(Across the room, Jake was hovering at the edge of the bar, looking at Lou like she was the moon.)

Jo wrapped one arm around Tom and drew him closer, her fist fitting between his shoulders, his eyes bright, smiling like his face would split.

She knew the feeling—her happiness was so sharp it stung— but she was still unsettled, still looking for Lou on the packed dance floor. (Lou hadn't come so far to get lost in this crowd, not while Jo was watching.)

His hand on her waist tightened for a moment, and she looked over at their table, where Lou was hugging the others one at a time and watching Jo over the heads of the younger girls, her smile a lamp that could light the whole room.

"Save me a foxtrot," Tom said, and let go.

She grinned at him and gripped his shoulder like it was an answer.

(There were a lot of things she couldn't yet say, but maybe now, at last, they would have time.)

She took the last few stairs down to the dance floor and up again to the mezzanine, sliding through the crowd to embrace the last of her sisters to come home again.

Then Lou was holding her close enough to hurt, and the others were kissing Jo's cheek as they passed by, as if they were all home at last, and underneath them the music was shaking the boards as the sisters, one by one, took to the floor to dance.

ACKNOWLEDGMENTS

Thanks are due, as always, to many people who gave of themselves to make this book happen.

To my family, for their support (particularly Tally and my grandparents, whose encouragement means more than I can say). To Elizabeth, Veronica, Delia, Stephanie, Kelly, Lisa, Jeanine, and everyone who read it and shaped it; to my agent, Joe, who wanted it to see the world. To Daniel, who championed it all the way there, and all those at Atria, who have been amazing in their support. I would like to thank every amateur historian, professional association, national institution, and all others who make documents, photos, music, and ephemera available on the Web, allowing the hours at which research can be conducted to be Whenever O'clock.

And finally, though this story has been a long time coming, I'd like to thank Anna for making me realize it was time to write this particular book, when she asked if I was ever going to write something in which not everybody died.